NIGHTCAPS

PATRICK THOMAS

PADWOLF PUBLISHING INC.

WWW.PADWOLF.COM

WWW.MURPHYS-LORE.COM

Padwolf Publishing & logo are registered trademarks of Padwolf Publishing Inc.

MURPHY'S LORE AFTER HOURS™: NIGHTCAPS

© 2007 Patrick Thomas

COVER ART BY PATRICK THOMAS AND ROY MAURITSEN

BOOK EDITED BY IAN RANDAL STROCK

SOUL SEDUCTION ORIGINALLY PUBLISHED IN CTHULHU SEX VOL. 3 ISSUE #13

EQUAL RITES ORIGINALLY PUBLISHED IN BLOOD MOON RISING #31

EBB AND FLOW ORIGINALLY PUBLISHED IN DREAMS OF DECADENCE #14 IN 2001

BY THE HORN ORIGINALLY SOLD TO UNICORN 8 EDITED BY MARK-WAYNE HARRIS

Special thanks to Bob Granito for his creative input on *Cute As A Button*.

ISBN-10: 1890096350 ISBN-13: 978-1890096359

Printed in USA

Second Printing

FOR CHRISTIAN

EXCEPT
HAIR TODAY, BALD TOMORROW-
THAT ONE IS FOR
KATHY AND HER DAUGHTER LILLY.
(It's not tickets to see Barry at the Garden, but what is?)

CONTENTS

MURPHY'S LORE:
SOUL SEDUCTION

The War raged, or at least stumbled, along. The Host and the Horde had been at it so long that it was hard to keep the fires of fury and righteousness burning. To maintain the necessary level of strife over the eons would take fanatics. Fortunately for the war effort, fanatics were something neither side had a shortage of.

Ryth didn't fall into that category. She may have been a soldier on the front lines, but it wasn't because she believed in Hell's cause. She did it because it was what a succubus was born to. And she was good at it.

Ryth didn't take any pleasure in her work. Her job was to give it, not to get it. The Apocalypse was coming, or at least breathing heavily. There was not much time left to seduce souls, but the impending climax of doom was still far enough off to justify sending Ryth off to Earth this night at sunfall.

Hovering outside the apartment, the beautiful demon stared wistfully at the scene inside. A family was playing. The daddy was pretending to be a monster, chasing three children and his pregnant wife around the small two-bedroom. The kids giggled, the mother laughed and smiled as the father roared.

Paul, the father, had one half of a pair of boy twins racing around a packed suitcase near the door. They scurried one way, then circled back in the other, over and over, until the father changed the rules and went over the top of the luggage. Paul scooped up his son in a tickle attack that caused the little boy to laugh so hard he could barely catch his breath. The other twin and the little girl circled behind him. Paul pretended not to see them, but even a deaf man would have heard them. As they moved to grab him, he put down the boy he was holding. Moving to run, Paul found his path blocked by his wife. He turned back, only to be engulfed by the tickle attack of his children, collapsing to the floor in a fit of laughter which was only slightly exaggerated.

The wife smiled and looked on, a twinkle in her eyes. With only the greatest reluctance, she broke up the scene and told the children to say goodbye to their father. Paul embraced and kissed each of his offspring, saving his wife for last. His first kiss went to her lips, his second to her ample belly.

Ryth watched it all, troubled by the feelings that swirled inside her. They were new, and the succubus was more aware than anyone what damage she would endure should any of the higher Horde learn of them. In her home, monsters gave chase, too, but they didn't tickle when they caught you. Ryth had never questioned the ways of Hell or her place in it, until recently. The demoness could pinpoint exactly when they began—the first time he crossed her path. Self-consciously, she let her eyes wander away from the apartment. They ended up staring up and behind her, hoping to catch a glimpse of her enemy. He caused even stranger stirrings in her. Disappointed and relieved by the lack of an opponent with beating white wings, she looked on as Paul's family left him for a weekend with his in-laws.

Paul wanted to go with them. He was the type of man who would sooner take a bout with stomach flu than be away from those he loved, but Paul still had bills to pay. There was work for the office that had to be done by Monday, and that wouldn't happen at his wife's parents' house.

That was the basis for Hell's offensive. Paul and his wife had not had sex in nearly six months, not since the conception of their latest pending bundle of joy. The couple was stressed from taking care of three young children, working, and barely keeping a half-step ahead of the bills. When all was said and done, there was little time left for romance, or even a quick romp under the covers. Forget about even the illusion of privacy. Sue had gotten pregnant on their anniversary, when his brother had given them a night of babysitting as a gift. One time was all it took, which of course got Paul to brag about the potency of his super sperm.

Paul was a good man who never dreamed of cheating on his wife, but he was still a man, one with needs—in this case, carnal needs—which weren't being met. He was more than willing to put aside his urges for the sake of his love, vows, and family, but even a good man can be tempted to do something bad. Especially if that temptation was Ryth.

Even among the most succulent of the succubi, Ryth was something special. True, she was beautiful, but that wasn't enough to send her to the top of the class. There was no such thing as an ugly succubus, at least on the outside. The only part of their inside most men were interested in wasn't something they needed to look at. Ryth was sex on high heels, but succubi were chosen for their sensuality. What set her apart wasn't something easily defined, except by the fact that men, down to the last one, wanted it. Desired it. Had to have it and didn't care how, the cost be damned. Which, of course, was the entire point.

Adultery was viewed by a large part of society as a bad thing, unless there were extenuating circumstances. I was drunk. I was careful. It's only cheating if you get caught. She was so hot, I just couldn't turn her down. People see adultery everywhere they look. Celebrities. Politicians. On TV and in the movies. They've grown accustomed to it. Accepted it as a necessary evil. As far as Hell was concerned, evil was the key word, right after accepted.

It wasn't that the sin was sex; that was just the vehicle. The evil was in the betrayal, in totally disregarding the person that one vowed to cherish above all others. That one act could be enough to start someone on the road paved with good intentions. It didn't matter that everyone else seemed to be doing it. To butcher a cliché, if everyone jumped off a bridge, they would all get wet. And some were going to drown. Or in this case, burn.

Ryth had the evening mapped out. She had managed to bump into Paul several times downstairs at the mailboxes. They had spoken, even flirted. Paul assumed Ryth lived in the building, and she wasn't about to dissuade him. In her hand, she held a piece of Paul's mail. The succubus would bring it to his apartment claiming that it had accidentally gotten into her mailbox. She would invite herself in and work her magic.

By the end of the night, Paul would have cheated on his wife. Several times. He would be racked with guilt, but probably not tell his wife, fearful that she would leave him and take his kids. Instead, he would lie by omission, letting the guilt eat at him day after day. It would weaken his moral resolve, and in short order, Hell would have him right where they wanted him.

Until recently, Ryth had not understood why guilt worked on humans, but as she again looked over her shoulder, she felt its power.

Flapping her crimson wings, the loveliest of demons descended toward the sidewalk, but found herself staring in yet another window. This scene was the antithesis of the earlier one. A man was beating his wife with his belt and punching her in her kidneys. She was crying and sobbing almost silently, fearful that her cries of pain would only increase the beatings. As blood began to pour out of the welts on her bra-covered back, she begged him to stop. Pleaded with him to have mercy, but he had none to offer her.

What she saw angered Ryth. She knew the man's type. Her home in the Pit was littered with their souls. Still, it wasn't her place to avenge mortal ills; that would be taken care of much later. She resolved to go, but the sight of the woman's tears kept her floating there like an angry cloud on a windless day.

That's when she felt Mathew arrive. One moment, the sky behind her was empty, the next, the angel hovered there.

Their meetings had been many and confusing. Sometimes they argued and fought, others they simply spoke. Always they warred over the tasks they had been assigned. Whatever the time or the reason, Ryth had begun to enjoy their battles, to long for when they would fight again, just so she could see him again.

This time, something was different. The angel didn't place himself between her and her target. He didn't try to persuade her to stop. He didn't say anything. He simply looked deep into her eyes, then briefly toward Paul's window. Beyond that, he did nothing.

Ryth realized that Mathew didn't have permission to interfere. There was nothing he could do to stop her from completing her mission. She smiled, but the angel didn't smile back. Instead, he lowered his eyes.

Ryth couldn't believe it. The angel was actually trying to divert her from her mission using guilt as his sword. Maybe she had been feeling the barest twinges of that emotion, but that certainly wasn't enough to stop her from screwing up Paul's life in more ways than one.

Furious that the angel would even think for an instant that such a cheap trick would have any effect on her, she dropped to the pavement and became corporeal, appearing as nothing more than a mortal woman storming into the building. The elevator was broken, so she took to the stairs, mail in hand. As she came to the landing below Paul's, she heard the beaten woman's resolve break for the tiniest instant as she screamed under her husband's onslaught. Their apartment was next to the stairwell.

Moving on up, she stopped after only four steps, listening to the rhythmic lashings of the man's leather belt on his cowering wife. Ryth went up to the midway landing, then walked back down. Ryth repeated the process several times, before finally throwing open the lower level's stairwell door.

The demoness easily had the strength to tear the apartment door to kindling, but she didn't. Instead, she knocked, hard enough that the force of her blows rattled the dishes in the cupboards.

The man threw open the door yelling, "What the Hell do you want?" As soon as he saw the vision in his hallway, his tone changed from angry to practically submissive. All thoughts of anger and his wife vanished, and he started scheming for a way to make this beauty his. To touch, kiss, and more, even if just for an instant.

"You. May I come in?" Ryth asked, tilting her head to the side and inhaling deeply, making sure two of her best attributes couldn't be missed. Although in the tight black dress she had manifested, it would have been nearly impossible anyway.

"Sure," he stammered, stepping aside, and closing the door behind her. His mind was already racing with possibilities that seemed to spring up, along with a certain body part that seemed to have the same reaction in all males whenever the succubus was around.

Ryth walked over to where the wife lay, cowering in a corner, near the couch.

"What's this?" Ryth demanded.

"I... I mean she... well, she kinda..." he stuttered, realizing he knew nothing about this woman, other than the fact that she was hotter than the fires of Hell. She could be a cop or social worker or something. He could go to jail.

Ryth turned her smile on, and the already stammering man turned to jelly. "A little S&M action, huh?"

"Yeah, exactly." He nodded enthusiastically as he realized he wasn't in any trouble for his transgressions. Then again, he would have admitted to being behind the Lindbergh baby kidnapping, the disappearance of Jimmy Hoffa, and the tragedies of 9/11, to keep the succubus smiling in his direction. In that grin lay promises of pleasure and pain and all sorts of things he knew he didn't have the ability to imagine on his own.

"She didn't have a safe word?" asked Ryth.

"A what?" said the man, unsure of what the beauty meant. In truth, his attention was focused due south of her mouth.

"Good, I don't believe in safe words either, and I can make a Dominatrix weep and beg for mercy. Now, off with your clothes," ordered Ryth.

"What? You want me to... Here? Now?"

"Did I stammer? No, wait, that was you," said Ryth.

"But what about..." With a crane of his neck, he indicated his wife.

"This isn't a multiple choice test. I told you to do something and you haven't done it. Do you want me to leave, little man?" Ryth strutted toward the door, and the wife-beater sprinted to get ahead of her. He blocked her exit with his body, his arm splayed across the narrow hallway.

"No, please don't go. I'm not used to a woman who's so forceful. And so beautiful. You caught me off-guard," he said, trying to undo his shirt, but his hands were trembling too much with anticipation to let his fingers succeed. He ended up simply tearing the front apart, letting the plastic buttons fly everywhere. "See? I'll do whatever you say, as long as you stay."

Ryth looked at him. "You still haven't finished what I told you already."

The man hustled and stripped himself of shoes, socks, pants, and underwear. He was a briefs man, and they were white, torn, and stained. The wife-beater assumed that, since he was naked, he shouldn't be the only one, so he reached out and laid his hand on Ryth's shoulder. The demoness slapped it away.

"Did I tell you that you could touch me?" she demanded.

"Well, no, but I kinda assumed—"

"Don't let either happen again. Hand me your belt," Ryth demanded and he obliged. The succubus looped it around his neck and led him back into the living room like a dog on a leash, while the battered wife watched. To her, Ryth said, "Do you have any duct tape?"

She nodded. "It's in the kitchen."

"Would you be a dear and get it for me, then meet me in the bedroom?" Ryth asked. The woman nodded numbly before standing and complying.

The wife-beater let out a yelp of joy, thinking he was going to get a two-fer.

Ryth yanked on the belt. "Did I tell you to make a noise?"

"No, but—" His words were cut short by another yank on the belt.

Ryth raised her eyebrows dangerously high, and even the dim-witted man who left welts as a hobby caught on.

He simply shook his head.

Ryth lead him to the bedroom, and his wife followed.

"Get on the bed," Ryth ordered. Once he complied, Ryth told the wife to use the tape to secure his wrists to the headboard and his feet to the footboard. The demoness checked to make sure he was securely fastened and totally immobilized.

"You enjoy hurting women?" Ryth asked.

"Sure," he answered, assuming he was allowed and that she wanted the truth. Too much blood was swelling one organ to allow the logic or fear centers of his brain to send out a warning.

"Well, let's see what we can do to change that, shall we?" Ryth handed the belt to the battered wife, who just stared at the piece of leather in her hand. "Don't just stand there. Hit him with it. Go on."

The wife lifted it up, but her husband cut her off. "Don't you dare, or I'll—"

The wife-beater never got a chance to finish, because Ryth's strong fingers gripped his face, just shy of hard enough to shatter bone. "Quiet. You've had your chance with her. Now it's her turn. Hit him."

Hesitantly at first, she whipped the belt on his chest.

"Not bad, but you can do better. Think of all the times he's done it to you," encouraged Ryth, and the wife did. At first it was a slow, steady beating, but as years of anger and humiliation bubbled up from an emotional spring, the blows came faster and harder, each one leaving a newer, bigger welt on her abuser's skin. The beating continued until the wife was exhausted, both physically and emotionally, and collapsed onto a nearby chair. The husband didn't have his wife's ability to control his volume, so he hadn't stopped screaming or crying like a baby since the beating began.

"Feel better?" asked Ryth.

"Yes," said the woman with a smile, her tone strong for the first time in a very long time.

"When I get out of here, I'll make you feel better, Sue. I'll make both of you feel better," threatened the man.

Ryth moved to discipline him, but the wife beat her to it, smacking him across the face with his own belt.

"Don't you ever talk to me like that again, Wally," she demanded.

"You think you're going to be able to do this when I ain't tied down here? Dream on. I'm going to hurt you like you've never been hurt before. Both of you."

Ryth crawled catlike onto the bed, until her head was over a spot halfway between his hips. "You aren't going to hurt either of us, because if you do, I'll know, and I'll come back for you. And next time, you won't get off so easily, Wally."

Pain and humiliation had made Ryth appear much less attractive in his eyes. Wally mustered up his courage and said, "What are you going to do about it?"

"I'm glad you asked that question, Wally." Ryth's entire head transformed to that of a hideous demon with huge jaws. Ryth bent over and put certain parts—one might say the most precious parts—of Wally's anatomy into her maw, her tremendous glistening fangs closed around them. Still, somehow, she was able to speak, but fear had made Wally shrivel, so her mouth wasn't exactly full. "If I have to come back, I'll bite it all off and make a necklace for myself."

Wally was shrieking and blubbering, begging and pleading for the safety of his manhood.

Ryth opened her mouth, moved back, and transformed back so her face was again beautiful. "So if you think you'd enjoy life as a eunuch, go ahead and hit your wife again. Say nasty things to her. Insult her to your heart's content, but I'll be back to finish what I started. Do we have an understanding?"

"Yes, yes, oh God, yes," Wally said.

Ryth thought about correcting his choice of whom he was invoking, but didn't. Instead, she walked out of the bedroom. Sue followed her.

"When should I let him go?" she asked.

"Entirely up to you," said Ryth, opening the door to leave.

"Wait," said Sue.

Ryth turned and snapped, "What?!" She wasn't looking to build up a weak woman's esteem or be followed around by an awestruck human behaving like a lost puppy.

"I just wanted to say thank you. That was the nicest thing anyone's ever done for me."

Ryth had heard the words many, many times before, but this time it was in an entirely different context. Her mood softened and changed.

"You're welcome," the succubus said, resting her hand on the woman's cheek. "Never let anyone ever do that to you again, understand?"

The woman nodded, but Ryth had her doubts about how long that would last. She almost found herself praying for the woman, but fortunately caught herself in time. After that, she'd never be able to return home, and would forever be on the run from the forces of Hell. Ryth couldn't think of anything that would be worth doing that for. The succubus left, shutting the door behind her.

Ryth's climb up the stairs to the next floor was especially slow. Each step down the hall to Paul and his apartment seemed to take an eternity.

Ryth stood outside the apartment door and took the bit of mail out of her manifested purse. The succubus stood there staring at the knocker. It would be so simple, something she had done so many times before, only the picture of Paul playing with his family wouldn't stop replaying itself in her mind.

Ryth made her decision. The succubus bent down, slid the envelope under the door, and walked away. There would be Hell to pay, but her superior was a male, and she could spin the night's events somehow.

Halfway down the hall, she felt the angel's presence return. Instead of popping up behind her, Mathew appeared in front of her, and he was smiling. No, he was grinning ear to ear. Then he did something she had never seen an angel do—he bowed to one of the fallen. Ryth was taken aback. When Mathew straightened back up, Ryth was unable to control herself. She flashed the angel a smile of her own, only this wasn't any of the kinds she used in her trade. It was the genuine article.

The pair stood there, staring silently at each other for a while. Neither one wanted to end the moment. It was Ryth who finally broke down and moved first. She could fly away, but she chose instead to walk, putting every ounce of effort into making sure this was one sight the angel would never forget.

This time, she didn't need to look back to know the angel was watching.

SPECIAL DELIVERY
a Murphy's Lore tale

"What do you mean I'm difficult when I'm pregnant?" snarled Ryth. The succubus had jumped to her feet and raised her voice. I took a step back, even though I had a bar between her and me. Ryth was on the run from the Hordes of Hell because of who she had married. If they caught up with her today, I think I'd pity them.

Her husband Mathew, an angel in many senses of the word, didn't even flinch. "Ryth, darling, I think you are proving my point for me."

"You have no idea how hard it is to have something growing inside you, fully dependant on you, throwing your body off in every way imaginable," said Ryth.

"I'm trying." Mathew, the ever-brave husband, stepped forward and wrapped his arms around his wife, not an easy task. It wasn't just because of her pregnant belly. That was only half the difficulty. The other half was Mathew's matching abdomen. It wasn't some weird sympathetic angel physiological response to impending fatherhood; it was just Mathew being Mathew. The angel had agreed to put on one of those faux pregnant bellies for fathers-to-be. Ryth had been complaining so much that he not only volunteered to wear it, he suggested the whole thing.

Ryth had knocked over her purse when she jumped up, and it still lay on the floor. There were plenty of gentlemen nearby, plus Coyote, but none brave enough to get close enough to retrieve it for her. Ryth looked down at it and gave an exasperated sigh. "I can't even pick up my purse without looking like a beached whale."

"You've never looked more beautiful," Mathew said.

"All men say that, but you know how many cheat on pregnant wives?" asked Ryth.

Mathew put his hand gently under her chin and lifted her face up so they gazed into each other's eyes. "I can't speak for anyone other than myself, but I mean it. And I would never cheat."

Ryth smiled and her entire face lit up. The succubus kissed her husband. "I know, but I want you to know what I'm going through. You're wearing the belly, so I want you to pick up my purse the same way I would."

"Are you sure about that?" said Mathew, smiling.

"Absolutely," said Ryth.

"Okay. Murphy, if I'm going to play Ryth, would you mind playing me?" asked Mathew.

"Sure," I said, walking out from behind the bar.

"I don't see any bending," said Ryth, her arms crossed over her chest and her foot taping impatiently.

"Remember, you said to do like you would do it, honey," said Mathew. Ryth's eyes narrowed dangerously.

I wasn't sure what Mathew wanted, but I stood there waiting.

The angel spoke in a falsetto voice. "Honey, would you pick that up for me?"

"Sure, dear," I said, picking it up and handing it to Mathew, who in turn turned to his wife, bowed, and handed her the purse.

She proceeded to smack him once over the head with it, but she was grinning. "Pookie wings, I think you've been hanging around with Murphy too much."

"You say that like it's a bad thing," I said.

"As long as I didn't misspeak," said Ryth, giving me a wink some men would kill for. Even a week before her due date, Ryth was still one of the most beautiful women I have ever seen. Mathew wasn't lying. However, the hormones were driving her crazy. "I'm going to go home and put my feet up."

"Wait, honey, I have some food I made for you so you don't have to cook, since your husband has to work," said Demeter. Mathew was the dishwasher here at Bulfinche's Pub. Seemed an odd job for a fugitive angel—Heaven's Host didn't approve of the marriage either—but he truly enjoyed working with his hands. Demeter rushed into the kitchen and came out with a huge tray, wrapped in foil. She even put a linen table cloth and napkins on top. "You shouldn't have to carry this in your condition. One of these men can help you."

In the bar were a lot of menfolk, some very powerful. Demigods like Hercules and Dionysus. Legendary gods like Hermes, Vulcan, Coyote, and even Pluto—who was visiting his wife, Persephone, who in turn was visiting her mother, Demeter. There was even the satyr Fred who works as our busboy and part-time bartender. Lastly, there was my boss Paddy Moran, a leprechaun who had bought this place using his pot of gold. Not a one of them stepped up. In fact, Dion, who was tending bar, and Herc, who was bouncing at the door, both took a step back like they were in an old army movie.

"I'll do it," said Mathew, seeing that nobody else was going to volunteer.

I took a deep breath and spoke up. "No, my shift is almost over. I'll go."

"You sure, Murphy?" asked Mathew.

"Yes," I replied, rubbing his fake belly. "You shouldn't be lifting in your condition, either. You look even farther along than Dion."

"Funny," said the god of wine and orgies, patting his ample wine belly.

There was a chorus of comments complimenting me on my bravery from the peanut gallery.

"Why is everyone acting like they're sacred of me?" demanded Ryth.

"Because they are," I said.

"And you aren't?" she asked.

"I've seen scarier things," I said.

"Like what?" she asked.

"The porta-john the morning after Demeter thought it would be a good idea to serve bean burritos." We keep the porta-john that we use for Rebecca and Father Mike's program to help the homeless in the garage. A few toilet goddesses and a god had suped it up to make it entirely self cleaning, but Paddy won't usually let us use that feature. That day, the boss made an exception. "Shall we go?" I asked, picking up the tray.

"Sure," said Ryth. Once we got out the door, she turned and looked back in. She got a devious expression that would have been more at home on Coyote or Hermes. "Wait a second." She looked both ways up and down the street. Next she rapped on the huge picture window that says Bulfinche's Pub and has our shot o' gold logo on it. When the men turned, she transformed her features and hands into a very disturbing looking demonic aspect, and made faces at the men.

The men looked around uneasily. Mathew was smiling, unperturbed. "Love you, dear. See you later," he mouthed through the window.

"Love you too, pookie wings." A second later, she was back in beautiful woman mode, and we were walking down the street. "I figured that, as long as they're going to act frightened, I might as well give them a reason."

"Works for me," I said as we turned the corner.

"It didn't scare you in the least," said Ryth.

"Startled, sure. Scared, no. I've since you in demon mode before." When she snuck me into Hell to look for my late wife, Elsie. "Besides, I know you'd never hurt me."

"Don't be so sure," she said softly.

"My jokes getting to you that much?" I asked.

"No more than usual. Murphy, you have to remember, I am a demoness from the Pit. My nature is not a pleasant one. There was a time I would have considered flaying a man a fun diversion, and thought nothing of it."

"I'll admit, I only had the barest idea of what you were, but you changed yourself. You left Hell for something better," I said.

"I still get some very dark urges. It's gotten worse while I'm pregnant. I have to fight becoming what I was, which is why we are having Hermes induce me in the back room at Bulfinche's next week, so my demon side and powers won't come into play." No magic, curses, or the like, work in the pub without Paddy's say-so. "Inside, the delivery will be the same as for a mortal woman. If I give birth outside, I could kill a mortal doctor without meaning to. Or worse."

"Worse?" I said.

"You're better off not knowing," she said. "But trust me, there are fates worse than death."

Having definite knowledge that there is existence after death, I agreed with her. But before she started her adult phone service business, Ryth worked as a waitress with us. She risked being captured by the Horde to help me with a very slight chance of finding Elsie. "Ryth, I know you. There is something else going on here besides hormones. What is it?"

Ryth looked at me like she was seeing me for the first time. "Murphy, sometimes I forget you are much more than a clown."

"You've got me mixed up with Rumbles and Roy," I said.

Ryth stopped in the middle of the sidewalk. "Shut up."

"Sorry."

"I'm scared about being a mother. I was raised in a place where the reward for a task well done was getting to torture someone else, and the price of failure was to be the one tortured. I don't know anything about raising a child. I have a temper. I can be violent. I'm strong enough to crush a baby's skull between my fingers. What if I make a mistake and hurt my little one?" They wanted to be surprised about their child's gender, so they referred to the baby as little one. "I don't think I could live with myself. Mathew would hate me and leave me. That would be worse than any torture I've ever endured."

"Ryth, first off, Mathew loves you as much as any man has ever loved a woman, regardless of your heritages. You would have to stop being you for him to not love you with all his heart, and maybe he wouldn't even then. Second, I may not be a parent, but I would have loved to have been. Elsie and I never had any kids. We tried before she got sick. She even got pregnant once, but she miscarried."

"Murphy, I'm sorry. I didn't know."

"It's not something I talk about much. It still hurts, even more after Elsie died. Our child was a girl. I still dream of what it would be like to be a dad. If we had little Elsie, even though my Elsie would still be gone, part of her would still live on in our daughter. It might even have been enough to counter my influence," I joked.

"Murphy, you're a good man," Ryth said.

"I like to think so, but through her entire pregnancy, I worried if I would be a good father," I said.

"Murphy, I've seen you with kids. You would have been a great father," said Ryth.

"I'll probably never know, but I do know that one of the most important things after love is wanting to be a good parent, and turning that desire into the work necessary to do the job. Like you said, you are a demon, but through force of will you left Hell and made a life on Earth. You started a business that has made you rich. You love your husband every bit as much as he loves you, and you already love your child. I can literally say that you won't let Heaven or Hell stand in the way of doing what's right. What more does a child need, except two parents who will do anything for them?"

"Maybe a wise-cracking Uncle Murphy," said Ryth.

"Don't know if your little one will need one, but he or she will have it. And your little one will have one great mom," I said. "And you know Paddy would let you move back if you were that worried about your demon side. Although he might soundproof your room." The couple's lovemaking was thunderous on a slow day. It was why they were asked to move out.

Ryth pushed the tray into my left arm so she could hug me. I even got a kiss on the cheek.

"People will talk," I said.

"Let them," she said.

Ryth took my arm, and we continued walking. When we turned the next corner, the sidewalk suddenly lit up blood red as we stepped on it. A fiery red circle appeared around us.

"What is that?" I said as we stopped short. I reached out, but Ryth pulled my arm back. "Don't. Spell circles can hurt if you touch the invisible walls. I know. I've been summoned in the past." Ryth fingered the gold amulet she wore around her neck.

Demeter made it for her. It had Bulfinche's shot o' gold logo on it, and tapped into the bar's power. Mathew had a matching one. It kept them off the mystic radar. "Demeter made sure I couldn't be summoned as long as I wore this. I guess Hell had to lay a trap for me instead. I'm sorry, Murphy, that they had to catch you, too."

I was already dialing my cell phone, but the spell circle was blocking any reception. Worse, a metal garage door had opened on the side of the building we were in front of, and the sidewalk square we were standing on was sliding inside. There was a homeless man sleeping on the sidewalk between us and the building. I knew him from my mornings working early shift in the garage, where we fed the homeless breakfast. Like many of the people who came to us for a place to stay or a meal, he had some mental health issues, but he was a nice guy. Liked to sing to himself, and had a weird thing for rats. The cement square we were on was about to crush him.

"Hank, get up and get out of the way! Quick!" I shouted.

He stumbled to his feet, blinking as he lunged out of the way and watched us glide past him into the building. "Murphy?"

Another square was moving to replace the one we were on. The door rolled down behind us, and we stood in darkness.

I had to think fast. We needed major magical help, and one person popped to mind. "Mister Hex, Mister Hex, Mister Hex." Hex had set up a spell that let him be summoned if his name was said three times and he allowed it. At the very least, I figured he'd know what was happening and come to get us out of here. I remembered Bubba Sue had duty this week to watch over Loki and keep the venom off him. Loki was trapped, tied to stones that made up his place of torment, but he could view the mortal world if his name was mentioned. "Loki, Loki, Loki." I figured he'd tell the gremlin, and Bubba Sue would tell the boss, who would mount up a rescue party.

A spotlight flared to life, focused on Ryth.

"Calling for help just won't work from in there," said a male voice. I turned, expecting a demon, but saw just a man. Then again, demons could disguise themselves. It wasn't like Bulfinche's Pub, where their eyes turned red so they were easy to spot.

"Who are you?" I asked.

"Ask Ryth," he answered.

I turned to the pregnant succubus who shrugged. "I have no idea."

The man smiled. "You don't have to pretend any more, my love. Nobody will ever be able to tear us apart again."

"Who are you, and what do you want with us?" asked Ryth.

The man looked taken aback, a look of doubt moving across his face. He tried to stop it short with a forced smile. "Ryth, my darling, I told you to stop pretending. This is not funny anymore. It's me, Sebastian."

"I'm not pretending. I have no idea who you are," said Ryth.

"Lying temptress!" shouted Sebastian in a sudden fury. The anger seemed to take him by surprise, and he worked to control it, blinking several times and taking three deep breaths. "Sorry, I didn't mean to shout. It's just that I've been waiting so long for this. After that night of pleasure we spent together, I know you could never forget me, my love. I know memories of that night have haunted me ever since. I've tried for the last decade to find a way to reclaim that magic. I've had sex with hundreds of women, sometimes with as many as five at a time, but nothing has ever even held a candle to the nova of our passion."

"That doesn't really narrow things down much. I've had sex with thousands of men just in the last century," said Ryth.

"Wow, you got around," I said.

"I am a succubus," she said.

"But with us it was different. It had to be. I know you felt what I felt. There was no way you couldn't. At first, I accepted that you could never belong to just one man, although I did fall in love with you the first time I saw you. To have you for a night, all I had to do was kill a friend I wasn't really that found of."

"So you didn't sell your soul?" I said.

"I'm not that stupid," said Sebastian.

"No, he's even stupider. For a night of sex, he murdered a friend. They didn't have to buy his soul. He simply gave it to them. No contract to try and weasel out of that way, just a one-way ticket to Hell," said Ryth.

"We didn't just have sex. We made love," said Sebastian.

"I've only made love to one person, and you're not him," said Ryth.

"Our passion lit up the night," he boasted.

"You aren't even a blip in my memory," said Ryth.

"You've been brainwashed, but we'll fix that. Even though I've tried to recreate with others what we had, I had accepted that I could never have you again. The demon that brought you to me stopped taking my calls."

"Calls? There is phone service in Hell?" I said.

"It takes skill, a brain, and work to summon a demon. Hot lines to the Pit are much easier for the mindless masses," said Ryth. "After they secured his soul, there was no reason to bother with him until he died and they had to collect it."

Sebastian wasn't even paying attention to us. He just kept talking. "But then, purely by accident, I saw you on a busy street. At first, I assumed my mind was just showing me what I had been longing to see. But I followed you. I kept following you for weeks, months. I saw you with the man you were pretending was me, day after day, and I realized that you could indeed stay with one man for a lifetime. You just had to realize you were with the wrong man. So I set this up to snare your love once again." Sebastian looked at me like I was a leper who had just rolled in his ice cream. "I just wasn't expecting him to be with you. It complicates matters, but not for long. He's mortal. He'll die of starvation before too long, and you can eat his body for nourishment or something."

"Ryth, if I die, let me make one thing perfectly clear. I don't want you to eat me," I said.

"Luckily for you, Demeter packed us a snack," said Ryth.

"What were you planning to do about the baby?" I asked.

"As it's from her false love, I figured she could just eat it, too," said Sebastian, twirling an artist's paintbrush. "Or I could just kill it."

At that moment, I heard the metal door rattle, but before I could look to see what made it move, I was knocked to the floor. Ryth had charged the end of the spell circle, barely stopping before she touched it. She was transformed again into her demon form, but she was more monstrous than when she had to fight her way out of Hell. This time, I was frightened. Ryth was nine feet tall, with crimson skin, and claws on her hands and feet, each as long as my forearm. Leathery wings sprouted out of her back, and her tail moved like an angry, barbed snake. Her mouth was the most frightening aspect. Her teeth were as long as beer mugs, and her jaw opened wide enough to bite a man in half.

"You do anything to my child I will do things to you that will make you long for death so you can go to the tortures of the Pit," growled Ryth.

"Oh, I want you to do things to me that'll make me long for something, all right, but it ain't the fires of Hell. It's the fires of love," said Sebastian, wiggling his eyebrows like some kid hinting at a dirty story.

I stood up, careful to move slowly. Ryth was ready to attack, and I didn't want to be her target. "These hundreds of women you claim to have slept with, how much did you have to pay them? Cause with pick up lines like that, nobody ever went home with you willingly."

"Women love me," bragged Sebastian.

"I can say I'm the funniest guy on the planet. Doesn't mean I am," I said. "Although I'm probably in the top ten. I'm just not feeling you, which means there is no way Ryth is."

"Of course she is," Sebastian said.

I shook my head. "No, she isn't. Look at her. She's not impressed. Ryth here is beauty personified." I looked up at her monster demon form. "Well, normally, anyway. No offense."

"None taken," she growled, but the way her huge jaws moved as she spoke made me shiver and turn back to the psycho who had kidnapped us.

"She's been with more men than you or I will ever even meet. She's been with demons and angels. The cream of the crop. If you see a beautiful woman in a bar, do you think you'll win her heart by knocking her over the head, tying her to a chair, and reciting lame lines?"

"I guess not," admitted Sebastian.

"Ryth is so much more than any mortal woman, so why would you think it would work on her?" I said.

"I don't know. I figured a show of strength would be enough," he said.

"It's a good start, but that's all it is. Where are you going from here? Women like romance. Where's the flowers? The music? The poetry written from the heart?"

Ryth said, "I hate poetry." I hit her in the leg, hurting my hand in the process, but she got the message and kept quiet.

"You need gifts to show your generosity—diamonds, jewels, expensive chocolates. Did you bring any of that stuff?"

"No." Sebastian was starting to look embarrassed.

"C'mon, man. I'm obviously not in your league…" A little false flattery wasn't going to hurt anything at this point. "But even I know that. But I figured out what happened. The prospect of getting back with your true love consumed you so much that you couldn't think of anything else. But you have her now. Woo her, Sebastian. Win her heart. You can do it."

"I can just force her to do whatever I want," he said. "Or I will destroy her. And you, too."

I tried to ignore the part about him killing us and went on. "Sure, you could force her, but you're a man of the world." Actually, he came across as rather sad and geeky, in a psychotic kind of way, but I doubt that was the self image he held of himself. "You know what happens when you force a woman to do anything she doesn't want to. She just goes through the motions with the bare minimum amount of effort. When you reunite with her in the physical sense…" Ryth was growling again. I stomped on her foot to quiet her down. "Do you want her to just be going through the motions to light a tiny candle, or do you want her wanting you so much that you ignite that supernova again." I turned and whispered, "Get human and act sexy." The succubus glared at me, and I shivered uncontrollably. I opened my eyes wide and made a face urging her to listen. The demon disappeared and the woman returned. Her dress was torn by the shape changing, so now it showed cleavage that was even more impressive than usual, due to her pregnancy.

"Can you imagine that? Ryth on that first night, night after night? Maybe even seducing you. Can you see her doing a striptease to get you in the mood? Rubbing up against your naked body with hers?" Apparently he could, because his pants became rather bulgy. Ryth picked up on that, and gave him a pouty face that almost knocked him to his knees, then crossed her arms in front of her, to bring even more attention to breasts that would never need a push-up bra. Sebastian moaned and ran out of the room, slamming the door behind him.

"Murphy, what are you doing? You know I'd never do anything of the sort," said Ryth.

"You know it and I know it, but he believes otherwise. Logic won't do a thing to convince crazy. I'm buying time. I think he was telling the truth, or Hex would have been here already. I figure the same thing happened with Loki. When I don't come back, Paddy will call your apartment to make sure everything is all right. They'll start looking, and we're only a few blocks away. Maybe Mosie isn't so drunk today and his psychic powers already picked up what's happened and he's on his way to tell Paddy where we are. Hank saw us. Maybe he'll tell someone. The bottom line is, sooner or later, we will be found. We just have to keep him from doing anything that we'll regret until then. If that means leading him on…"

Ryth nodded, but under her anger, she was frightened. "He can't hurt my baby, Murph. He can't. Not my little one." The succubus was rubbing her belly.

I put my hands on her shoulders and looked her in the eyes. "I won't let him."

"How will you stop him?" she asked.

"I have no idea." But I'd think of something. I had to. "Tell me everything you know about spell circles before he comes back."

There was a lot. A spell circle was a way to concentrate magical energy, usually to create a barrier or prison. There were many kinds. This was a simple circle, as opposed to a pentacle. Symbols were typically used to focus the power. This one didn't have any we could see. Breaking the lines could break the circle, but that option was usually only available to someone on the outside. Ryth thought it was a blood circle, because anyone could make one, regardless of magical ability. The symbols were probably written in blood on dried blood, so nobody could make out which symbols were used. It was dangerous because the person making the circle couldn't be sure the symbols were correct. The magic used could backfire on them, but it was more effective because it would be harder to break. While informative, it didn't give me any brilliant ideas about how to get out.

Sebastian returned with a satisfied look on his face and his fly unzipped. Sad little man.

He stood directly in front of Ryth. "Would this romance crap really work on you?"

The succubus got a sly grin. "I guess you'll have to try in order to find out."

"Go for it. Do it right, but take your time. After all, we're not going anywhere," I said.

"True, but the whole pregnant thing is kinda creeping me out, so first I'll take care of that problem," said Sebastian, taking his small tipped paintbrush out of his pocket. The end had dry, dark flakes that looked like they might once have been the color of blood. He stuck the tip into the invisible wall of the circle, and it started to glow crimson. A red ray shot out straight for Ryth's belly. The succubus screamed, but the beam never reached her, because some bartender jumped in front of it and took the blow.

As I fell to the floor, I heard Ryth yelling my name. Then I felt her cradle me.

Sebastian was trying to repeat the trick, but the brush wouldn't glow. "Damn thing must need to recharge. We'll do this when I get back."

And then my world went black.

"Pity about your planet," said Vulcan, laughing. Pluto and Ares, aka Mars, have been teasing him for years over the fact that they had real planets named after them, but he had none outside of the realm of fiction. The recent change in status of the former ninth planet was enough to have Vulcan make a special trip to New York when he heard Pluto would be visiting Persephone, and he was loving the payback. "I mean asteroid number 134340."

"A lot of astronomers are protesting that. There's a petition on the internet," countered Pluto.

"I guess I'll have to consider signing it," said Vulcan.

"I don't need this," complained Pluto.

Persephone came over behind him, wrapped her arms around his chest, and kissed his cheek. "As far as I'm concerned, it's still a planet."

"Thanks, dear," said Pluto, hugging her arms to him.

"Having one asteroid named after you isn't so bad," said Demeter, in an unusual show of sympathy for her son-in-law. Of course it couldn't last. "Of course, I have two: 1108 Demeter and Ceres. So does my daughter: 399 Persephone and 26 Proserpina. And I know what it is to have a planet named after you, too, only to have it taken away. It was back in the seventeenth century that some astronomers called Earth Ceres. They called the moon Proserpina then. Of course, Earth is a bit more important than some hunk of rock on the edge of the solar system."

"Mother, stop it," ordered Persephone. Demeter started to open up her mouth. "I mean it."

"Hey, at least you still have that cartoon dog," teased Vulcan, knowing full well how much it bothered the lord of the Hades that a cartoon was better known than he was in the modern world.

"I need a drink," said Pluto.

Vulcan laughed and slapped the lord of Hades on the back. "It's on me."

Pluto looked for the punch line, but none came. "Thanks. I'll have a sex on the beach."

Vulcan opened his mouth, but kept silent after seeing Persephone's glare.

Outside, Hank was running, frantically trying to find Rebecca.

The Mother of the Streets seems to sometimes show up just when she's needed, but other times she's nearly impossible to find. Hank didn't have time for an all-out search, so he ran straight to Bulfinche's Pub.

In some bars, if a homeless guy runs in the door acting crazy, they throw him out. It's where the term "bum's rush" came from. Bulfinche's didn't work that way. When Hank came in the door, Paddy offered him food and drink.

"No time. Need Rebecca," he said, huffing and puffing.

The Mother of the Streets was at a table drinking tea, for which she brought her own tea bag. Rebecca stood when she recognized one of her own. "Hank, what's wrong?"

"The sidewalk took your friend Murphy and the pregnant lady who used to be a waitress here," said Hank.

Mathew was stacking dishes and glasses behind the bar and turned around. "Something happened to Ryth?"

Hank nodded his head vigorously. "The sidewalk took them."

"Sidewalks don't just take people," said Hercules who, while not quite condescending, wasn't quite respectful either.

"This one did, right past me. Then the metal door closed, but there was a small crack. I looked in and listened. I heard the man say he didn't like the idea of the baby, and he was going to cut it out or make the lady eat it," said Hank. Mathew threw plates across the room, smashing them into the wall. "Killing babies is wrong. Rebecca, you have to help them."

The Mother of the Streets put her hand on Hank's shoulder. "I will."

"We all will," said Paddy.

"Damn right we will," growled Mathew.

"You did good, Hank. Take us to where the sidewalk took them," said Rebecca.

Mathew was the first one out the door, but by no means the last. Paddy left Dion in charge. Hermes, Fred, Herc, and Coyote followed. Pluto got up to join them.

"Pluto, we got this," said Paddy.

"Paddy, there is a child involved," said Pluto.

"So, what do you care? It's not like you even like children, or I'd have grandchildren by now," grumbled Demeter in her age-old complaint.

Pluto lost it. "Shut up, old woman." Demeter's face started to ice over with fury, partially because of his tone, but also because she didn't like being called old by someone basically the same age as herself. Persphone's face went white, because it looked like the fight she had been forestalling for centuries was about to start. "I've put up with your bitching because your daughter loves you. But she also loves me, and because of that, she has never told you that we have been trying to have children for ages, but I can't. I've been too long in the underworld to spawn life. I want to have children with my wife more than anything, and having you constantly throwing my shortcomings in my face is unbearable, but out of respect for the love your daughter has for you, I have borne it. You dare to say I do not care about children? I have a special place in my realm set aside for all the children who died too early. I make sure they are very happy and treated like children should be. I will not bear this insult. Now shut your trap and get out of my way."

Pluto stormed out the door, Paddy following in his wake. Inspired by the speech, Vulcan followed.

Demeter stood speechless. She turned toward her daughter, her expression distraught. "I didn't know."

Daughter embraced mother.

Outside, Hermes lifted Hank in one arm and Rebecca in the other. He flew much slower than he normally would, so Hank could see where they were going. The rest ran after them.

Hermes landed in front of the building with the kidnapping sidewalk.

Inside, I was having my chest pounded on. Apparently the blast stopped my heart, and Ryth was doing CPR. Not that I could recall any of it. The first thing I remember was seeing Elsie's face and thinking I must have died. Then she put her lips to mine and kissed me. I kissed her back, and woke to see Ryth pulling away from me, giving me a strange look.

"Ryth?" I said confused.

"Who were you expecting?" she said, upset at the kiss. She didn't think I was the type to take advantage of the situation. I wasn't.

"Elsie. That's whose face I saw when…"

The succubus' face softened. "Say no more."

I tried to sit up, but vomited instead. My entire body felt like it was on fire. "That hurt."

"You're lucky he set the blast for a baby. You are so much bigger that it wasn't enough to kill you. If it had been meant for you, we wouldn't be talking," said Ryth.

I tried to sit again, and only fell over this time. "Yeah, lucky me.

"Murphy, what you did…"

"I said I wouldn't let him hurt the baby."

Ryth touched my face with her hand. "Thank you."

"You resuscitated me. We're even," I said.

"We'll never be even. I'm beginning to understand why Nancy has been doting on us so." Mathew had been instrumental in saving the life of Nancy's son, Danny, and she has done anything she could for the couple.

The door on the far side started to open. "I think he's back."

"Let's hope he lost the paint brush," I said.

Sebastian came in carrying so many boxes he could barely see over the top of them.

"I bear gifts my love," he said.

I was about to say "Beware of geeks baring gifts," but had a coughing fit instead. Probably both better and safer that way. The noise got me noticed, though.

"Are you still alive? I'll have to fix that later, so Ryth and I can spend some quality alone time."

"I could just take a nap in the corner. I'll close my eyes and everything. You won't even know I'm here," I said, but he wasn't listening again. Sebastian was too busy opening boxes.

"I thought you might want to wear this," he said, holding up some white lingerie and tossing it at Ryth. It came through and she caught it.

"How?" I said.

"Spell circles can be set to allow inanimate objects to come in at the creator's discretion. Usually nothing can go out," said Ryth.

"Put it on," Sebastian ordered.

"I'll think about it," said Ryth.

Sebastian pulled out his paint brush. "Dress up pretty for me, or this time I'll turn your friend into dust."

Ryth eyes narrowed, but she managed a smile. "Okay."

"I'll turn around," I said.

"Murphy, I'm not shy, and you've seen me naked." Again, it was when we were in Hell.

"He turns. Nobody but me ever gets to see you naked again," Sebastian ranted.

The metal door we had been whisked through started to shake. Locks and chains snapped as the door was ripped off its hinges by Hercules, dressed in his lion-skin trench coat. Mathew came through the door first, flying, his white wings extended. He dove for his wife. He was a seraphim, which allowed him to pass almost anywhere in the universe, including some spell circles. The blood circle flared, not only keeping him out, but hurting him doing it.

I heard Sebastian scream, and turned, expecting to see Hermes holding him upside-down. Instead, Pluto gripped him around his throat and held him so his feet didn't touch the ground.

"You would kill a child? Never again," Pluto said.

"Pluto…" came Paddy's voice of reason.

"Don't worry, Moran, I won't kill him. I may make him wish I did, but first he needs to open the spell circle and let Ryth and Murphy out."

"No," gasped Sebastian.

"You'd best rethink that position," said Pluto.

"Not that I won't. I don't know how," said Sebastian.

Mathew took the man out of the death god's grip. His wings were glowing, and his hair had turned to pure light. It hurt to look at him. Ryth covered my eyes. "Don't watch."

"I've seen people fight before," I said.

"Anything more than a glance will age you." Rebecca and Hank hadn't made it in the door yet, so I was the only one besides our kidnapper who was at risk. No one told him to cover his eyes.

From what I was told, Sebastian's hair started to turn grey immediately.

"Get my wife out of there, now," ordered Mathew.

"Let's not forget Murphy," I said. My eyes may have been covered, but I could hear just fine.

"I don't know how. They never told me how to open it. Only how to put stuff in or go in and out myself," said Sebastian.

Mathew flared up to the point where I could actually feel his light pulsing against my skin.

"Mathew, tone it down. Ye may be putting out even more than Demeter's amulet can handle. We don't need the Host or the Horde here right now," said Paddy.

Ryth took her hands off my eyes, which I rightly assumed meant it was all right to look. Mathew dropped the man, who tried to crawl away. Pluto's boot on his spine changed his mind quickly.

Vulcan looked it over. "We should be able to use his blood to break the circle."

Rebecca moved quicker than a woman her age should be able to, and had her knife pressed against Sebastian's throat. "Why my blood?"

"That's what you used to cast, the circle isn't it?" asked Vulcan.

"No," he answered.

"Why the blazes not?" demanded Vulcan.

"I was told not to," he replied.

"Do you know how dangerous it is to not use your own blood? The moment the magic flared, the entire thing could have blown up in your face, taking out the entire block," said Vulcan.

Coyote sniffed at the circle. "The blood is from a two-legger. Young from the smell. Maybe more than one." The trickster moved and sniffed Sebastian's armpit. "It isn't his."

"Whose blood did you use?" asked Fred.

"I was told to use the blood of three fetuses. I stole a medical waste bag from an abortion clinic," said Sebastian.

"What did you do with the rest of the remains?" said Hermes.

"I was told to burn them," he answered.

"Ye keep saying ye were told this and that. Who did the telling?" demanded Paddy.

Sebastian hesitated, but Rebecca's knife bit in, and Pluto's foot pushed hard, popping things in his back. "Once I had found Ryth, Hell started taking my calls again."

"Who, specifically? What's the name?" demanded Paddy.

After some more not-so-mild encouragement, Sebastian squealed. "His name is Ramos."

Paddy cursed. We all had a history with that demon. He had attacked us in the bar in an attempt to claim our waitress Toni's baby BG before she had even been born. Things got bloody and Father Mike exorcised him back to Hell, theoretically never to return again. I guess he could still do damage from the Pit.

"First thing's first. We need to get them out. Any of ye have any ideas?" asked Paddy, looking at Hermes and Vulcan. They both said no. "Hermes, get Demeter and Hex."

The god of speed nodded and seemed to vanish. Seconds later, Demeter and Persephone appeared, but Hermes apparently didn't slow down long enough to be seen.

Demeter had more than a little knowledge of many forms of witchcraft and such. "Ryth, darling, I'm stumped. I'm sorry."

Ryth just nodded.

Hermes reappeared with Hex in tow. Paddy brought him up to speed.

The cursed magí did a lengthy examination of the spell circle and shook his head. "Without knowing what was written or having some of the same blood he used, it's too dangerous to try. Ramos undoubtedly booby trapped it, so I could end up killing them." Hex walked over to Sebastian, who was still pinned beneath Pluto's leg. "You're not smart enough to have found the symbols on your own. Where's the book you copied them out of?"

"There was no book. Ramos faxed them to me, and I burned them with the dead babies," said Sebastian.

Paddy told Hermes to get Mosie, but the psychic was completely passed out drunk. Madame Rose was brought in, but her psychic powers weren't up to the task.

"Paddy, what about Gani?" said Hex. Gani was Merlin's twin sister. While not a magí like Hex or Merlin, she had spent over a thousand years studying the various forms of magic. She worked for Nemesis.

Paddy made the call. Minutes later, a shadow grew, and out stepped three women. The one in the center was the raven-haired Nemesis. The white-haired Gani was holding her boss' right hand; the half ogre/half pixie Terrorbelle had the left. As soon as Terrorbelle got free of the darkness, she started dry heaving.

"T-Belle, you okay?" I asked.

"She doesn't usually like to shadowstep. It makes her sick, but when she heard you were in trouble, it wasn't an issue," said Nemesis. She must have been in a hurry because she hadn't even bothered to cover up her giant pixie wings.

Terrorbelle stood slowly, looking awfully green. "I'm fine. Murph, how are you?"

"Could be worse," I said.

"Uh-oh. I don't think you should have said that," said Ryth.

"Why not?" I asked.

"I think my water just broke," said the succubus.

"Guys, get us out of here," I screamed.

"Gani, do something," said Terrorbelle.

"I might be able to whip up something in my lab that might let us read the symbols, but it might take a while," said Gani.

"What's a while?" I asked.

"A few hours, maybe a couple of days," she said.

Ryth screamed with a contraction, and grabbed hold of her belly.

"I don't think we have that long," I said.

Mathew was trying to calm and soothe his wife. It wasn't working.

"We need to speak to Ramos," said Coyote.

"To do that, ye'd have to go into Hell," said Paddy.

"I'll leave now," said the furry trickster.

Pluto picked up Sebastian and threw him to Herc. "I'll go with you." Terrorbelle realized he was the man who had done this, and charged at him. Nemesis had to pull her back to keep her from hurting him.

Coyote looked up at Pluto. "Wouldn't your trespass into another realm of the dead be considered an act of war?"

"Only if we're caught. I can get us to the border. You keep us from getting noticed," said Pluto.

"If that's all, no problem," said the trickster, his voice dripping with sarcasm and a bit of coyote drool. "Any other reasons?"

"I am still in Murphy's debt," said Pluto. I had fed a woman fudge from Hades, which gave her into Pluto's power to punish for killing her husband and child for the insurance money.

"Murphy did not ask for your help. This will not balance your debt," said Coyote.

"I never thought it would, but if he remains trapped or dies, my debt will forever go unpaid," said Pluto. "I do not wish that to happen."

Coyote nodded. "He is alright for a two-legger."

"How are you going to find him? Hell's a big place," I said.

"Where was he last?" asked Coyote. We had run into him as we were fleeing. Other demons had dismembered him as punishment for his failure to beat us. I kicked his own foot in his mouth to shut him up.

Ryth gave him directions. "But there is no guarantee he's still there."

Gani looked thoughtful and walked to Sebastian. "You said you called Hell. Where's the phone, or did you burn that too?"

It was Herc's turn to be persuasive.

"No, it's in my pocket," yelled Sebastian.

Gani made some movements with her fingers, I suppose to check for traps, and pulled out a cell that was about a decade out of date.

"We could trace the call," said Gani.

Both Hex and Vulcan's heads lifted up.

"How, exactly?" asked Hex.

"Ramos is obviously initiating this on his own, or the Horde would have already have Ryth and Mathew. That means he's using his own power without the hierarchy knowing about it. Using similarity…" The rest of the explanation was a bit over my head, and I missed it because Ryth had another contraction. "I need a watch with a second hand or a compass."

Fred pulled his watch off his wrist and handed it over.

Gani held the watch against the phone and hit redial. A voice answered. "Hello?"

There was some glowing, and Gani smiled. Her boss took the phone.

"Ramos, this is Nemesis. Ryth's unborn baby is under my protection. If anything happens to the child, I'm coming for you."

There was laugher on the other end. "I'm being tortured in Hell. What are you going to do to me?"

"If your kind even remembers how, pray that you never have to find out." Nemesis ended the call.

"Do you think tipping off the bad guy may make things harder for Coyote and Pluto when they go after Ramos?" said Hex.

"I'm hoping it may make things easier. If he's scared, he may be more cooperative," said Nemesis.

Gani handed the watch to Pluto. "The second hand will point you to the source of that call once you get into the Pit."

"Nice work," said Hex.

"Very impressive," agreed Vulcan.

"Thank you." Gani walked to a wall, took something out of her pocket and drew something invisible on the wall. An elevator door appeared. "I'll get to work on something to let us read the writing. Would either of you gentlemen care to join me?"

"I'd be honored," said Vulcan.

"I can help more doing something else," said Hex. "Coyote and Pluto's biggest chance of getting caught lies with Nick and the Chief," said Hex, using nicknames for the Devil and Negrel, the head of Hell's secret police.

"What's the best way to avoid them?" asked Coyote.

"I'll distract them," said Hex.

"How?" asked Pluto.

"By making a lunch date," said Hex, pulling out his own cell phone and walking out of the building.

Gani hit the up button on her elevator. The doors slid open and she and Vulcan stepped in. "We'll be back as soon as we can."

Ryth screamed with another contraction.

"In the meantime, it looks like Murphy is going to have to deliver a baby," said Hermes with a grin.

"I don't know if I can do this," I said.

Mathew knelt on the floor as close as he could get to his wife without making contact with the barrier. "John…" Using my first name as a way to get my attention is always effective. "You are the only one who can take care of my wife and baby. I trust you and believe in you. You can do this."

Damn, here I am worried about what I have to do when the daddy is stuck outside unable to help or even hold his wife's hand. I couldn't even imagine what the angel was going through.

"No problem. Dr. Murphy is on duty. Hermes, talk me through it," I said.

"If you want the second best…" Demeter started.

I turned and looked at her to forestall the bickering. Ryth didn't need any more stress. "I expect both of you to guide me through this." My tone indicated I wanted her to behave, and would never have worked on the earth goddess in any other situation.

Demeter nodded. "Of course."

"It looks like she's eight centimeters dilated, so we don't have much time," said Hermes.

I offered Ryth my hand to hold.

She shook her head vigorously. "No, I'll crush your bones into powder when the next contraction hits."

A vision of what she had transformed into earlier would not leave my mind. If that happened now, I could very well be a dead man. I looked at Ryth, and realized she was even more scared than I was, visions of her child dying slam-dancing in her head. I crawled over to where she was lying, pulled her head and shoulders into my lap, and wrapped my arms around her.

"Close your eyes and imagine I'm Mathew," I said.

Ryth smiled. "That'll be hard. He's a lot better looking than you. In better shape, too."

"I'll muddle through, somehow," I said.

"Now breathe like our birthing instructor taught you," said Mathew from outside the circle.

I even tried it. It didn't do much but make me lightheaded.

A few blocks away, Hex made a call of his own to Hell. "Hey, Chief, how's it hanging?"

Negrel was not happy. "Hex, why are you bothering me?"

"Wanted to invite you and your boss to lunch," said Hex.

"Your lunch is not for two weeks," countered the head of Hell PD.

"I had some free time and thought I'd spend it with two of my favorite people," said Hex.

"I see," said Negrel. "And I suppose they were unavailable, so you called us."

"Aw, you stole my line," said Hex.

"Why invite me?" asked Negrel.

"We never spend any quality time together anymore," said Hex.

"We have never spent any quality time together," said the Chief.

"So what better time to start," said the cursed magí.

"And the real reason?" said Negrel.

"Something is going down, and I thought I might get something useful out of meeting with the two of you," said Hex.

Hex could hear the sigh on the other end of the line. "I'll relay your information and get back to you."

"It's okay. I'll hold," said Hex.

Knowing that the Devil afforded Hex more respect than Negrel felt he deserved, the Chief sighed again. Hex heard a click. He figured someone on the other end was monitoring the call while he waited, so he started singing to himself to pass the time.

Five minutes later, the Chief came back on. "Nick said he would meet you in an hour."

Hex smiled. He knew Lucifer's secret name, and because of that, had much sway with the Devil. "There's a new Indian place in Soho." Hex gave the name and address. "I'll be waiting."

"You don't know how excited that makes me," said Negrel in a deadpan voice.

"Just as long as you know I don't put out on the first date," said Hex.

"I'll just have to nurse my broken heart somehow," said the Chief, after which Hex was listening to dead air.

Paddy escorted Pluto and Coyote back to Bulfinche's, and to the underground levels of his garage, where there were nexi that led to other worlds, including the River Styx, which flowed both to Hades and Hell.

Before they could get there, they had to get past Cerberus, the three-headed hound, formerly of Hades. Pluto and Cerberus had a history, little of it good. Pluto had never treated the dog with any kindness, thinking it would make him a better watchdog. He lost the dog to Paddy in a poker game, and the boss treats Cerberus much better. He usually has to be around for the lord of Hades to get safely past.

As soon as he saw Paddy, all three heads began yapping excitedly, but when Pluto got close enough, he growled.

"Easy, pup. Pluto and Coyote need to get past ye. I also want ye to let them pass on their return trip," said Paddy. Cerberus' growls let it be known that he didn't think much of this idea. "Ryth's baby is in trouble." Cerberus became upset at that. The Hades-hound had a soft spot for children of all species. "They are going into Hell to try to help the child." Cerberus yipped in a way that meant he didn't quite believe what he was hearing.

"It's true," said Pluto. "Will you let us pass both ways? Please?"

Two of the three heads tilted to the side. None could remember the lord of Hades ever asking for anything before, only yelling and demanding. The hound looked to Paddy for reassurance, then back to Pluto. All three heads nodded, but none looked happy about having to do it.

Pluto and Coyote moved past, opened the manhole cover, and climbed down. Paddy petted each head and dropped off some food. "I can't stay, pup. I have to go do what I can to help the baby. Thank ye, though. I know you don't like him, but yer doing the right thing."

Paddy was licked thrice, and went on his way. Cerberus lay down, and all three heads turned toward the manhole cover that lead to the Styx nexus and waited.

Once they were walking again, Coyote said, "You don't much like canines, do you?"

"I'm kind of neutral on the matter, but I treated that one badly. He's much better off with Moran," said Pluto.

"That he is," agreed Coyote.

The pair made their way to the banks of the Styx. In the distance, a small boat could be seen anchored, its lone occupant sitting and holding a fishing pole.

"What's he fishing for?" asked Coyote.

"Lost souls and other things best left unmentioned," said Pluto.

"Does he see us?" said Coyote.

"Charon knows the moment anyone gets near his river," said Pluto.

"Then why isn't he coming to get us?" asked Coyote.

"He has issues with me," said Pluto. When I first met the boatman, I mistakenly thought he was afraid of Pluto. He isn't. In his own way, the boatman's more powerful than the lord of Hades, especially on the River Styx. It's just he didn't want to have to hear him complaining, especially about Charon not following tradition.

"You have friends everywhere, don't you?" said Coyote.

Pluto paused before he answered. "Sadly, no." The lord of Hades pulled out a long, thin tube and blew into it.

"You're dog whistle is broken," said Coyote.

Pluto smiled. "It's to summon the boatman."

In the distance, Charon glared at the shore. Taking off his yachtsman's cap, he pulled in his fishing pole and rowed to shore.

"Lord Pluto, I wasn't expecting you for some time. You and the missus feuding? Or is it the mother again?" asked Charon.

"Neither. We need to get into Hell," said Pluto.

Charon's gaunt face stretched as his eyebrows rose. "Why would you need to do that?"

"We need information from a demon," said Pluto.

"Wouldn't it be easier and safer to summon it?" asked Charon.

"This one is banned from Earth," said Coyote.

"Interesting," said Charon, rubbing his chin. "You realize transportation for this is not covered under our present agreement?"

"I do. I also bring you greetings from John Murphy," said Pluto.

"How is my favorite bartender? When's he coming back to fish with me again?" My first day fishing on the Styx is a story for another day.

"He is trapped in a blood circle with a succubus who is giving birth," said Pluto.

The boatman was noticeably upset. "He'll be killed."

"I think not. The succubus is the fugitive Ryth. She holds him in high regard, and will fight her nature," said Pluto.

"I've met her. She braved Hell for him. You may be right. Murphy may survive the birth," said Charon.

"I also bring you greetings from your sister. The unborn child is under her protection," said Pluto, pulling a large bag of gold from the place where gods kept their stuff. "How much for safe passage both ways?"

Charon smiled. "One gold coin each for each direction."

Pluto's jaw dropped. "That is all? I assumed you would want more for all the grief I have caused you through the ages."

"I thought about it, but Murphy's the only one who's been brave enough to go fishing with me in the last century, and Nemesis is family. If the kid's under her protection, I have to do whatever I can to help."

Pluto handed him four gold coins. "Thank you."

Charon simply nodded as the gods boarded his boat.

Pluto cleared his throat awkwardly. "Perhaps, considering all things, you would like to use your motor."

Charon smiled and pulled the tarp off it, pushing the motor into the water.

"And perhaps you would like to use it all the time for your journeys," said Pluto.

"What about tradition?" said Charon.

"We can always make new ones," said Pluto, as the boat sped across the River Styx toward Hell.

Hex was sitting at a table when Lucifer and Negrel arrived. Nick wore a suit that would make a billionaire envious. Negrel dressed like a PI out of an old black-and-white movie.

"Gentlemen," said Hex.

"Daniel," said Lucifer, calling Hex by his given name. Negrel simply sat, straightening a trench coat and fedora that wouldn't have looked out of place on Bogey. "I must say I was surprised to get your invitation. Does this mean you are finally paying for my meal?"

"Dream on, Nick," said Hex.

The Devil stood. "Then perhaps we should go."

"I suppose I might see my way clear to springing for dessert," conceded the cursed magí.

"And coffee?" asked Lucifer.

"Don't push it," said Hex.

"So what is it that you needed to see us for that couldn't wait a mere twelve days?" asked the Devil.

"As I said, something is going down. I thought having both of you here would help me deal with it better." Hex chose his words carefully so that he didn't lie, only misdirect.

Lucifer laughed. "You want to try to get a reading off me or Negrel, do you? Very difficult for any magí, let alone one with your particular problems. Has it ever worked?"

"Once," Hex admitted begrudgingly.

"That's right. I remember, but I took precautions after that. Has it worked since?" asked the Devil.

"Not as well as I've liked," said Hex.

"Or at all. I suppose you have the length of a meal to keep trying. I guess we get a meal and a show. I hope you won't be too disappointed when you fail," said Lucifer.

"Maybe you are the one who'll be disappointed," suggested Hex.

"I doubt it. The Times gave this place five stars. And I will actually be eating my meal," said the Devil. Hex only eats at home or at Bulfinche's. Too paranoid about someone messing with his food. "Shall we order?"

"Where are we?" asked Coyote.

"One of the back doors to Hell. The one Murphy and Ryth used is now too well guarded to risk a try. This one hasn't been used much since the Middle Ages," said Charon.

"But there is no entrance," said Coyote.

"That shadow extends into the Pit. A simple shadowstep is all it'll take," said Charon.

"Which is something neither of us can do," the furry trickster pointed out.

"But I can," said Charon. It was a gift all of Nyx's children shared.

"You? But you never get involved. You didn't help Murphy the first time," said Pluto.

"I didn't know him then. Did you know he actually took over my duties for a day?" said Charon.

"Murphy never was very bright," said Coyote. "He could have been stuck here for all eternity."

"Could have if I didn't actually like my station, but I came back. I may want another day off sometime. If Murphy dies, that's not likely to happen," said Charon.

"And he's your friend," said Pluto.

"That too," said Charon, putting down a ramp and an anchor. The three disembarked. He waved his hand, and the boat seemed to vanish. "Shadowstepping is quite disorienting. I advise both of you to hold onto my hands and not let go. If I lose you in the darkness, I may not be able to find you again. You won't enjoy it there."

Coyote grumbled and changed shape into a two-legged demon. Pluto looked at him. "Camouflage."

Pluto and Coyote took Charon's hands, and the three stepped into the darkness.

"Oh God," I said, meaning the exclamation as a prayer for help. The birth was not going well. Ryth had dilated to more than ten centimeters, the contractions were right on top of each other, and she was pushing. The problem was that I didn't see the baby's head; I saw one set of toes.

"The baby's a breach," said Hermes.

"Murphy, you have to get your hands in there and find the other foot," said Demeter.

"Find foot. Got it," I said. I won't regale you with a description of how I did it. Suffice it to say the miracle of birth had my blood pumping and adrenaline flowing and my hands in need of washing. "Found it."

"You have to reposition the baby," said Demeter, who then talked me through it. "Ryth, push."

The succubus screamed and clawed another layer off the concrete beneath us, unfortunately not enough for us to get out. The blood circle prevented escape up or down.

"Oh no," said Hermes.

"Oh no what?" demanded Mathew.

"The baby's head is stuck. Murphy, is there anything on that tray sharp enough to cut with?" asked Hermes.

"Why?" I asked.

"You are going to have to do a cesarean section," he replied.

"Oh God," I repeated, hoping he was listening. I searched the tray frantically. "There's nothing in here that's sharp."

"Yes, there is," said Ryth. Her hands and feet transformed into claws. "Use one of them."

I reached carefully for her hand, trying very hard not to pass out.

"Lunch was delicious. Wouldn't you agree, Negrel?" asked the Devil.

"Not bad," conceded the Chief.

"Any dessert?" asked the waitress.

"Absolutely," said Lucifer. "I'll have the Shrikhand."

The waitress turned to the Chief. "And you, sir?"

"Gajjar Ka Halwa," replied Negrel.

"What about you, sir?" she asked Hex.

"I'm trying to decide between Seviyan or Rasmalai," said Hex. "Could you give me a chance to decide and come back in a few minutes?"

"Certainly, sir."

Sneaking through Hell was not an easy task, but far from impossible. The place was designed to keep people in, not out. But one mistake would have consequences that could last an eternity.

The trio had been jumping from shadow to shadow in the direction the watch pointed, a task made harder by Charon making sure he could see the next exit point. None of them wanted to step out to find demons waiting for them.

"Stop for a moment," whispered Coyote in his demon form. "My stomach hasn't been this unsettled since I had to swallow a dozen boulders."

"Whatever you do, don't throw up. The smell would give us away," said Pluto.

"I'm doing my best," replied the trickster. "I blame it on the faulty two-legger physiology. In my normal form, I'd be fine."

"Ready for the next shadow step?" asked Charon in a whisper.

"Ready as I'll ever be," replied Coyote.

A dozen jumps later, the second hand on the tracking watch had become huge.

"I think we're there," said Pluto. Ahead, there was a lone head sticking out of the ground, and it was ablaze. "Unless the watch is wrong, that's who we're looking for."

The head would grimace and grit its teeth for as long as it could, then let out a blood-curdling scream, before regaining control and repeating the process.

"There is only one demon guarding him," said Charon as he extended the shadow to cover and hide them. "I guess they aren't too worried about escape."

"He's blocked from returning to Earth. It limits his options. Probably why he noticed the human's call," said Pluto.

"So do we take down the demon?" asked Charon.

"A waste of time," said Coyote. "Finesse is called for. Watch and learn."

The trickster transformed himself again, this time into a larger version of the demon guarding Ramos. That demon looked bored, and barely glanced at his charge.

"Who goes…" said the demon as soon as he noticed he had company.

Coyote smacked him across the face, knocking him down. "Shut up. Why are you still here? Are you an idiot?"

"I'm not sure what…"

"Free souls day. First thousand demons in line get their very own soul to punish for one day." In Hell, souls were currency, food, and entertainment, all rolled up into one. Low level demons could not own souls, only borrow them. They had to dish out the punishment as the hierarchy instructed. Many dreamed of extending their creative sadistic impulses.

"I hadn't heard. Where is the line?" the demon asked.

"If you don't know, I'm hardly going to tell the competition," said Coyote, his demon form running over a hill. The real demon chased him, but once he got to the top of the hill, he couldn't see him. Of course, he didn't look down for the armored cockroach the trickster had turned himself into.

The demon looked in the distance, then back at Ramos, then at the distance. Torturing a demon loses the thrill after a week, but his own human soul to do with as he pleased, even for a day—that would be something special. The demon walked over and examined Ramos. The tormentee looked secure, so the demon made his decision and ran off in the direction he assumed his fellow demon went.

Once the demon was out of sight, Coyote transformed back to his canine self. "Demons haven't gotten any smarter." He walked to the flaming demon head and stopped directly in front of it. "Hello, Ramos."

"Decide already," said the Devil. "It's just dessert, and it's not like you're even going to eat it. And if you haven't been able to read anything off me by now, it's not going to happen."

"Fine," said Hex, subtly acting disappointed. "I guess I'll have the mango ice cream."

"Finally," said Nick. Hex had to stop himself from smiling.

"You want me to use your own claw to cut you open?" I said. "What if I can't stop the bleeding?"

"I don't care. Save my baby," said Ryth, her claw on her belly. "I'll do it myself if I have to."

"It's the only way," said Hermes.

"Do it quickly," said Demeter.

They told me where to cut. I took her index claw and moved it over her abdomen when an idea about knocked me over. "Ryth, transform to your mega-demon form."

"Murphy, with this pain I may not be able to control myself. I'll gut you," said Ryth.

"I'll take the risk," I said.

"Why?" asked Hermes.

"She's nine feet tall and her pelvis is double this size," I said.

"She'd be able to get the baby out easier," exclaimed Demeter.

"Brilliant," said Hermes.

"I have my moments. Do it, Ryth," I said. I added in a whisper, "I trust you."

The succubus bit her lip and made the transformation. I was able to pull the baby out with room to spare, trying to ignore Ryth's screaming and thrashing about with the razor sharp claws. Using my fingers, I cleaned out the mouth and heard a beautiful wailing.

"It's a boy!" I said.

"A boy," said Mathew, and he lit up again, but not so bright that I had to look away.

I cut the cord on a toe claw and cleaned him up as best I could with the linen napkins, then wrapped him in the tablecloth. Ryth still looked scary. There was ichor oozing out of her maw. She was still the mommy, so I placed the little guy into her arms. As soon as she touched him, the demon form disappeared, replaced by her human one.

"He's beautiful," I said.

"Yes, he is," agreed Ryth. "I promised we'd talk when you came out, about how sick you made Mommy with that awful morning sickness and all that kicking, but right now, none of it matters." She kissed him on his little head as he squirmed around.

"Hold him close. Babies need warmth after they're born," said Hermes.

"And human touch," added Demeter.

"So what is the little lad's name going to be?" asked Paddy.

Mathew spoke up. "We had decided if it was a boy we'd name him…"

"His name is John," said Ryth, cutting off her husband. "In honor of his favorite funny Uncle Murphy." I may have cried a bit at that point. Maybe more than a little. "Who we also hope will consent to be the child's godfather."

I probably don't have to add that I accepted the honor gratefully.

Of course, I still didn't know if we'd be out of the blood circle before little John had to go to college.

"What do you want, trickster?" demanded Ramos, his voice crackling as the flames flicked away at his vocal chords.

"Do you really have to ask?" said Coyote.

"I'm not telling you anything," said Ramos.

"Okay then," said Coyote, turning and walking away.

"Wait! That's it? No pleading or threatening? You're just giving up?" said Ramos.

The trickster shrugged furry shoulders. "Like you told Nemesis, you're in Hell. What can I do to you? I certainly won't be able to cause you the same level of pain she will or that you're experiencing now, so why bother?"

"Come on. You have to try something," begged Ramos.

Coyote grinned and cleaned his paw with his tongue. "Nope."

Ramos screamed as the pain again became unbearable.

"Insects devouring your flesh under the ground?" asked Coyote.

"Yes, but it's not as bad as the fire on my head," said Ramos.

"Sounds terrible. Almost as bad as having all your manipulations come to naught by having someone come to find you and then refusing to play by your rules," said Coyote.

Ramos only glared.

Coyote cleaned his other paw. The waiting game went on, neither one saying anything, but with Ramos sure the trickster would break first.

The flaming demon was the one to finally speak first. "They'll never get out without my help."

"Maybe, but you have no idea of the resources Moran can bring to bear. It may already be solved, which leaves you even more screwed than you already are." Coyote used a rear leg to scratch behind his ear.

"I'm willing to help you," said Ramos.

"That's nice," said Coyote, walking twice in a circle and sitting down.

"But I'm going to want something in return," said the burning demon.

"Of course. I'd expect no less," said Coyote while yawning.

"Break me out of Hell," said Ramos.

"Not a chance."

"Have the priest allow me to return to Earth," tried Ramos.

"Not within my power to grant. Two-leggers can be very stubborn on certain points. I doubt after all you've done, the priest would grant your request."

"Have Moran speak to Satan on my behalf," said Ramos.

"You've got to be kidding if you think that'd happen, let alone work," answered the trickster.

"Bow down before me," demanded Ramos.

"Doesn't really work for me," said Coyote. "What else you got?"

"I don't know, but you have to give me something after everything I went through," said Ramos, practically begging. Then he let out another scream. "This fire is more than I can bear."

"I could do that," said Coyote looking Ramos straight in his flaming eyes.

"Do what?" asked the burning demon.

"Put out the fire on your head," answered the trickster.

"You'd do that?"

"Sure," said Coyote. "What are you going to give me? How to break the circle?"

"No," said the demon. "But I will give you what Sebastian inscribed in the blood circle."

"Let me see it first," said the trickster.

"You have a piece of paper?" asked the blazing demon.

Coyote pulled out a large piece of parchment from only he knew where and held it out. Ramos held his breath, momentarily extinguishing the flames in his mouth. He bit his tongue and spit blood on the paper. The crimson dots moved until they formed a diagram of the layout of the blood circle.

Coyote looked and raised an eyebrow. "How do I know this is the real deal?"

"Flip the paper," said Ramos. Coyote did, and the demon spit more blood. This time it spelled out their agreement and signed his name. "My signature on a contract in blood."

"That will work," said Coyote, secreting the paper away.

"So are you going to hold up your end of the bargain?" demanded Ramos.

"Of course." Coyote walked next to the blazing demon and lifted up his right rear leg. A stream of urine shot out straight into Ramos' face. The trickster made a circle around the head, dousing it completely. Wherever the liquid hit, steam rose up, and the flames went out completely.

"Oh, that feels so good," said Ramos.

"Pity," said Coyote as he shifted back to demon form. Before the trickster disappeared over the rise to rejoin his companions in shadow, Ramos' skin was already starting to smoke again.

Everything came together. The Devil and the Chief returned to Hell none the wiser. Cerberus let Coyote and Pluto pass without incident. Gani and Vulcan came up with a lamp that was able to differentiate between two different layers of the same material, as long as they were painted on at different times. Hex and Gani worked together for over a day with the diagram to figure a way to turn off the blood circle. Of course, first they put the paper in a spell circle, to make sure there was no way Ramos could use his blood to do any more damage. They found forty-seven booby traps. Apparently. the demon could function quite well in the corners of his mind, even while being tortured.

We had enough food, thanks to Demeter, and Ryth was able to supply John with everything he needed. We two adults were a little thirsty, until Fred came up with the idea of having Sebastian throw some water bottles in.

Forty-five hours after we were first trapped, Hex and Gani managed to weaken the blood circle. Hercules lifted the cement slab up high enough for Vulcan to get underneath and use a blaster in his walking stick to slowly eat away the concrete until there was a hole big enough for us to climb out. First out was the baby, Ryth handing Mathew his son. I've never seen a happier father. Fred helped Ryth down and out. Mathew wrapped his free arm around his wife and his wings around all of them.

Next Fred helped me out. Before I realized what was happening, Terrorbelle had lifted me up off my feet in an embrace that stopped just short of crushing me.

"I missed you, too," I said.

"Don't scare me like that ever again," scolded Terrorbelle.

"I'll see what I can do," I said. "Besides, I have an entirely new skill. I can deliver a baby. You never know when that will come in handy."

Terrorbelle laughed and put me down. "I doubt that you'll ever have to do that again."

Little did we know.

Mathew came over. Apparently it was his turn to pick me up and hug me. Maybe I should have been selling tickets.

"Thanks, Murphy," said the fugitive angel.

"My pleasure," I said. "I know John wasn't the name you had picked out, so if you want to change it, I'll understand."

"Never," said Mathew.

"Let's get the happy family back to Bulfinche's. We don't know if the Horde is on its way or not," said Paddy. "Best to be in a fortified position if they are." Paddy had kept Herc, Nemesis, and Terrorbelle there the entire time, in case the Horde came before we were freed. Not that any of them were going anywhere anyway.

Hex and Gani incinerated the diagram. Vulcan used his walking stick to vaporize the remains of the spell circle and move it to a pocket dimension.

Hank was at the bar when we got there. I shook his hand. "Thanks, Hank. I don't know how I can ever repay you."

"Double portions at breakfast would be nice," he said.

"For as long as you want," I said. Even though I knew the offer had been made to him many times before, I volunteered to help him find a more traditional place to live, but like Rebecca, he wouldn't hear any of it.

Ryth also thanked him with a kiss on the cheek. First the old man blushed, then he jumped up and down, as excited as a little kid.

"Rebecca, did you see? The pretty lady kissed me," said Hank.

"I did," replied the Mother of the Streets.

"Will you tell Randy? He'll never believe me," he said.

"I will," said Rebecca.

"If you like, bring this Randy by Bulfinche's, and I'll kiss you again in front of him," said Ryth.

"You'd do that?" he said.

"I'd be happy to. You helped save my baby. Would you like to hold John?" asked Ryth.

"Nobody ever let me hold a baby before," said Hank. "I don't know if I could."

Ryth had Hank sit in a chair, and then put John in his lap. The old man made the usual cooing noises. "I think he likes me."

"He does," said Ryth.

John started to cry, so Hank started singing to him. Not only did the baby calm down, he went to sleep.

Hank handed him back to Ryth. "Babies are even better than rats."

Ryth had done her share of morning shifts in the garage when she waitressed here, so Hank didn't faze her. She was used to the occasional odd statement. "You are absolutely right."

Paddy's kids—Shellie, Nellie, and Brian—made a big fuss over the baby. So did BG.

"Nice baby," said BG with a big smile.

"I guess you aren't the littlest anymore," said her mother Toni.

"That's okay," said BG. "I still smaller than Freddy."

"Give it a couple of years," said Dion.

Persephone stood over the proud mother and practically beamed. "Little John is adorable."

"Although if you are going to call him little John, he may want to grow up to hang out with Robin Hood," I said.

"He'd have to go to Faerie to do that," said Hex.

Paddy brought down a crib, and Ryth put John in it. There was no shortage of people willing to watch him sleep. The bar was amazingly quiet while they did.

Paddy pulled the lot of us that were involved in the whole blood circle fiasco into the back room. Sebastian was there, chained to a chair, his mouth gagged.

"We still have to decide what do with this one," said Paddy.

"Even in the womb, John was under my protection. I'd be happy to drop him into the shadows for an eternity of madness and fear," said Nemesis.

"Or we could be merciful and kill him," said Terrorbelle.

"Which would send him straight to Hell," said Hex.

"I can live with that," said T-Belle.

"So can I," said Rebecca.

"The decision is up to the three people he affected most," said Paddy. "Murphy?"

"He wasn't after me. I'll abide by what the parents decide,"I said.

"Ryth? Mathew?" asked Paddy.

"I cannot think of anything painful enough to do to him," said Mathew, his darker side finally showing through, but this man had almost taken away the angel's entire world. There would be no better reason to embrace his dark side.

"No," said Ryth. "Part of this is my fault."

"In no way…" started Mathew.

Ryth put her finger over his lips. "Not for what he did, but why he wanted to. Part of my power was to ruin men for anyone else after they had been with me. I knew that and still I did it."

"You didn't have a choice," said Mathew.

"Wrong, pookie wings. If I didn't have a choice, I wouldn't be here with you. I just didn't care enough to make the right one. I didn't even know there was a right one until I met you. I've done more horrible things than Sebastian has, yet I got a second chance. I vote for mercy," said Ryth.

"You want us to let him go?' said Mathew.

"Absolutely not. We can send him to Ringvue. Gabriel might be able to undo the damage I did to him so long ago, and give him a second chance at life," said Ryth.

"I don't know," said Mathew.

"I don't want the first consequence of our son's life to be the death of another," said Ryth. "Please?"

Mathew looked into her eyes and couldn't refuse. "All right, so long as Gabe makes sure he cannot escape until he is rehabilitated. And maybe even then."

"Thank you," said Ryth, kissing her husband. The two of them seemed to quickly forget the rest of us were there.

"Don't they have to wait six weeks?" I said.

"It's recommended, not mandatory," said Hermes. "Different physiologies heal quicker."

Paddy pointed his thumb toward the exit, and the rest of us filed out of the room. Herc carried Sebastian's chair. Paddy was the last one out, and he shut the door behind us.

"I'll take him to Ringvue," said Hermes. Paddy nodded.

I pulled the god of physicians aside. "Hermes, you examined the baby to make sure he was okay. I was wondering if he was more demon or angel, or half and half," I said.

"Neither," said Hermes.

"Then what is he?" I asked.

"Human."

GRAVEYARD ANGEL:
STONE COLD

It's just business has been used for years to justify evil without placing or accepting blame. People have been saying it so long, it's become a mantra that the masses either believe or accept. It may work on the living, but it doesn't wash with the dead, especially my dead.

My Dad's a small business man who wouldn't be caught dead uttering those words. Coincidentally, he also works with the dead. Our family funeral home is in Sunnyside, Queens. Dad is good with the grieving, and sometimes painfully honest with the living.

I got a call to meet him in his office, and I have to admit I got nervous. When we were kids, any time we got in trouble, we had to discuss what happened in his office instead of upstairs where we lived. We were always on our best behavior in the office, because we didn't want to disturb or disrespect the grieving.

I knew I wasn't in trouble, but I still had goose bumps.

I loved going home, but I hated having to cover up my wings. Mom had to do the same. Most people don't even know what a Lasa is, let alone think we exist. To walk around, black feathers hanging out, would most likely upset the grieving, especially since they'd think the wings were fake. It was easier to cover up with a cape than start explaining. That's why I liked living in Manhattan: I could walk around, wings flapping, and people didn't make a fuss. They figured I was artsy, or doing publicity for something or other.

It was morning, so the doors were unlocked, and I just let myself in. The door to Dad's office was closed, so I rapped my knuckles softly. I could hear a chair move. Dad opened the door. "Mr. and Mrs. Wells, this is my daughter, Moni."

I walked to where the couple sat and shook their hands. I haven't worked full time at the funeral home since I moved out, but I knew these people. They had lost a son, Mikey, a couple of years ago to a drunk driver. Knocked him out of the crosswalk just a few blocks down Greenpoint Avenue. It was very sad. The entire neighborhood showed up, and I came in to help out.

I hoped they hadn't lost another child.

"I asked Moni to join us because she has some experience clearing up matters involving the departed," said Dad. I was intrigued now. Dad played down that Mom and I were guardians of graves.

"Why don't you tell me what's happening. Does it involve Mikey?" I asked.

Janie Wells nodded and got teary eyed. "Mikey still doesn't have a tombstone. We made our last payment to Morton's Monuments almost five months ago, but we can't get them to finish and deliver it."

"I'm not familiar with that business," I said, looking at Dad.

"We typically don't use them," he said.

"Your father recommended we didn't use them, but everything was so expensive when Mikey died. It cost more than a new car. Morton's was a third cheaper than the rest of the monument makers, and they financed us. With the interest, it turned out to be almost the same anyway," said Joe Wells.

"We should have paid the extra, but we just didn't have the money at the time. We should have listened to your father," said Janie. My father's face stayed deadpan. He was never one to tell anyone, even his kids, "I told you so."

"Did you ask Morton for your money back?" I asked.

Janie nodded. "He told us he couldn't because he had already started work. When he showed us Mikey's tombstone, all it had was an M, so he wouldn't take the loss."

Sounded like a nice guy.

"He won't give us a date when it will be done. We've contacted the Better Business Bureau, even the police, but they can't do anything. My son deserves a tombstone, not to lie in an unmarked grave like nobody ever cared about him." Joe Wells was a janitor, an all-around tough guy, and he was crying.

"You are absolutely right," I said. "I'd be honored to help."

I got some more details, copies of their receipts and cashed checks. They left thanking me, and my father shut the door behind them.

"Moni, I want you to do this one by the books," he said.

"By the Lasa book, absolutely," I said.

Then he gave me the piercing father stare, the one that made it very hard to lie to him. Not impossible, just incredibly difficult.

"You know what I mean, Moni Elizabeth."

"On no, not the middle name," I said in mock terror.

Dad smiled. "I know you really don't keep who you are secret, but your mother does. At least in the neighborhood. And I don't want this to affect the funeral home."

I sighed. My father looked on what he did as a sacred obligation. It's one of the things that first attracted my mother to him. She didn't usually go for younger men. Of course, the year of her birth is B.C., but she still lies and tells everyone she's thirty-five. "Fine, I'll try it your way first, but one way or another, that tombstone is going to be on Mikey's grave, okay?"

Dad gave me a hug and a kiss on the top of my head. It still impressed me that his arms were long enough to go around both me and my covered-up wings.

My father made a call, and I had a meeting with Martin Morton. I flew there, but brought and wore the cape. In a business situation, people see a young woman with black wings walk in and they make certain assumptions about her, or in this case my, sanity. Most people assume the wings aren't real and I'm playing psycho dress up party.

He made me wait for forty minutes while he looked at internet porn in his office with the door open with me sitting fifteen feet away in the atrium.

I guess he had gotten his fill of dirty pictures for the morning, so he stood up, walked to his door, and motioned me in with a grunt.

I didn't bother to offer my hand. I told him why I was there.

"Well, I can't be expected to start work until I'm paid," said Morton.

"The last payment was made five months ago," I said in my most businesslike voice. That basically meant I didn't shout or use sarcasm to get my point across.

"I have started work on Micky's monument," he said.

"His name is Mikey," I said. For Lasa, the dead still deserve present tense. "Would you like me to spell it for you? I'd hate for you to misspell it and have to redo all your hard work."

He ran a hand over a messy stack of papers. "I got it right here."

"When do you plan to make delivery?"

"These things take time," he said with a smug smile.

"There has been no engraving done in over a year, and two years for completion and installation is excessive, even for the monument business," I said.

He shrugged and smiled as he muttered the evil mantra, "I don't see what you're getting so upset about. It's just business. Speaking of which, I agreed to this meeting in hopes that it might lead to your father sending me some clients."

There was no way Dad was going to send this scumbag anyone, but I didn't need to say that out loud. "Making things right for the Wells family would go a long way toward that."

"So how many people would he send me per month? I'd give the usual kickback, of course," Morton said.

"I'm afraid I can't give you exact numbers," I said.

Morton shrugged and stood up. "Then this meeting is done."

His attitude pissed me off. "When can we expect the tombstone to be delivered?"

Morton's eyes narrowed and his jowls jiggled as he chuckled. "Definitely before he would have graduated high school."

I had had enough of this nonsense. Mikey was now one of my dead, and nobody mocks my dead. Time to do things my way. Lasa are most powerful on a grave or around the dead. Because Morton's business made grave markers, it was linked strongly with the dead. I wasn't at my peak, but I had enough mojo to make a point by throwing his desk into the wall with one hand. The cheap pressure board broke apart like styrofoam quite nicely.

Morton was shocked, if the sudden paleness of his pudgy little face was any indication. "How the fu...?"

I got up into his face. "You have until the end of business tomorrow to get that stone finished and placed."

"You think I'm gonna take orders from a broad?" He actually used the word broad.

"If you know what's good for you, you will. If not..." I let it trail off. Morton didn't seem too impressed. I guess I'm scarier with the wings out.

"Get out of here before I throw you out!"

I put my hands under his armpits and lifted him off the ground. I instantly regretted it. Not the lifting, just where I put my hands. It was going to take a lot of washing to get all that nastiness off.

"Let me see you try, tough guy," I said. Morton opened his mouth, but nothing came out. Not used to a girl who can bench press him, I guess. I turned and dropped him in his chair. "The end of business tomorrow," I repeated, and walked out the door. Once out of sight, I took off the cape, and was about three stories above him by the time Morton came out to see where I had gone. He looked both ways down the street, but didn't think to look up.

It really came as no surprise that at 5:15 the next day Mikey's tombstone was nowhere near his grave. I waited until dark and flew back to Morton's. The place was empty, but he did have video surveillance—two whole cameras' worth. I used a pair of black men's socks to circumvent them, putting one over each lens from above.

The next part was fun. I found Mikey's stone easily enough, but there were many more. I could read the grave stones, and I don't mean just the engraving. Most were bought and paid for. I could feel their graves calling out for them. Morton was not just screwing over the Wells family, but dozens of others. I couldn't let it stand.

First things first. If it was just a hunk of stone, I wouldn't have been able to even budge it. Fortunately, it was a tombstone, a monument to the dead. That gave me the strength to not only lift it, but fly it to Mikey's grave. I placed it atop Mikey's final resting place myself.

With some more concentration, I was able to use my magic to get rid of the single letter Morton had done a shoddy job on. Then I used it to let my finger carve Michael Wells and his dates into the stone. I even added Beloved Son in my best calligraphy under Mikey's name. I then used my magic to just slightly alter the height and shape of the stone to the style his parents said they would have chosen if they had had the money.

Then I flew back to Morton's. I was getting pretty tired. My magic may have let me carry a tombstone through the sky, but my entire body ached from the effort. This next part of my plan was going to leave me sore for days, although if it had been in a graveyard, it would have just been hours. The tombstones were laid out on what passed for a lawn. There was grass with dirt beneath it, between slabs of cement. With great concentration, I first parted the grass where it met the concrete, and then the dirt; useful ability we Lasa have to check on the buried dead or re-inter them.

I lifted every last headstone on the property and put them in the hole. When I gingerly placed the last one in, I waved; the dirt returned home and the grass moved back into place. The yard was barren as the spot on Morton's soul that should have housed compassion. Morton would never figure out where his monuments went. If things went right, he was going to have a going out of business sale with nothing left to sell.

The next day, my father received a call from Morton. The monument maker spent the entire time screaming about what a horrible daughter he had. I believe whore, thief, and a few other choice words that I'd be hard pressed to repeat were bandied about.

Morton ended the conversation by yelling that he was going to take back what was his. Dad called me.

"I take it you switched rule books?" Dad asked, already knowing full well the answer.

"Mikey's got his tombstone," I said.

"Good girl," he said, without giving me any grief.

I managed to get to the cemetery ahead of Morton. So did a couple of guests I invited, New York police detectives Jason Cervantes and Amanda Walker. We sat in their unmarked car and watched as Morton arrived with his delivery truck. The scumbag drove right up to Mikey's grave and got a dolly out. I knew his type wasn't going to let anyone get the better of him, even if it meant doing something stupid and mean. He actually took the tombstone and put it on his truck.

When Morton climbed out of the back, Cervantes and Walker were there to greet him.

"You mind explaining to us what you're doing here?" asked Jason.

"What's it to you?" Morton snapped back, but his jaw dropped when the pair flashed their badges and identified themselves as detectives.

"I believe Detective Cervantes asked you a question, sir. Would you mind answering it?" said Walker.

"Just picking up a tombstone for repair," Morton said.

"What's wrong with it?" asked Jason.

"Got a chip. Gotta sandblast it out," lied Morton.

"You can't do that here?" questioned Jason.

"Insurance issues," tried Morton.

"Mind showing us the chip?" asked Walker.

"Actually, I do," said Morton, walking past them toward the cab. Which is when he saw me leaning against the truck door. "You!"

I admit I wasn't expecting a pleasant hello and peck on the cheek, but this greeting was more than I had hoped for. Morton bellowed and charged me with his hands outstretched like he wanted to strangle me. On burial grounds, I could have lifted the front of his truck off the ground, but I played meek. I had a video camera on a tripod taping the entire thing. I let him wrap his fingers around my throat, but my detective friends dragged him off almost immediately, knocking him to the ground and cuffing him, then reading him his rights.

"You should be arresting that..." I was described in most unflattering—but fairly creative—terms, although as far I as knew he had never even met my mother.

"Why would we do that?" asked Jason.

"This is my tombstone," Morton said.

Walker looked at the engraving. "You're a ten-year-old who died two years ago? You look pretty good for a corpse."

"No, that's not what I'm saying. I made this, and she stole it from me," said

Morton.

This was going even better than I had hoped.

"Nice engraving," said Jason.

"No, I didn't do that. Only the M."

"So she stole a tombstone and engraved it, then put it on this child's grave?" asked Jason.

"Exactly," said Morton, nodding enthusiastically.

"So, what happened? The family didn't pay for it and you were repossessing it?" asked Walker.

The lights started to turn on behind Morton's eyes, and he began to look nervous. "Uh, not exactly."

"Did the family pay for it or not?" asked Walker.

"Yes, they paid for it," said Morton, his voice practically a whisper.

"I see. They paid for a tombstone for their dead child who passed away two years ago and you hadn't delivered it yet?" asked Walker.

"I suppose," admitted Morton.

"Yes or no," said Jason.

"Yes."

"So this grieving family paid you for a tombstone which you admit you only engraved the first letter on. And magically this tombstone gets engraved and transported to the cemetery," asked Jason.

"It wasn't magic. It was her," said Morton pointing his nose at me. Technically, it was both, but I wasn't about to help stop him from digging his own grave, albeit a figurative one.

"So basically you're claiming she did your job for you," said Walker.

"It wasn't her job to do. She didn't have my permission," said Morton. "Stealing's a crime."

"Yes, it is, but the only one I see guilty of it is you," said Walker.

"What do you mean? It's my monument," said Morton, still not getting the big picture.

"You are taking a tombstone off a kid's grave that you admit is paid for, that you say you didn't finish, yet it's done. I wonder how a jury is going to view this story?" said Jason.

"Jury?" said Morton.

"Probably two," said Walker.

"Two?" echoed Morton.

"The criminal one, of course. Then I figure the parents are going to want to sue you for emotional distress, breach of contract. Juries rarely rule against grieving parents," said Walker.

"But it's mine. I didn't release it to them. She stole it," said Morton.

"As near as I can figure, this poor child's parents are the owners of the tombstone. Ain't a DA in the city who would even consider pressing charges on them," said Jason.

"I've been set up," said Morton.

"That's very original. You know, I don't think we've even heard that one before," said Walker.

"But it's true. She stole every one of my tombstones out of my lot. Almost twenty of them."

"This little woman? She doesn't seem strong enough to move a tombstone. You have any proof?" asked Jason.

"She meets with me and tells me I have to the end of business yesterday to get the tombstone here. It was a threat, but don't nobody threaten Martin Morton, no sir. Then this morning, all my monuments were gone, except the one on this kid's grave. That ain't coincidence."

"You take all those other tombstones off Mr. Morton's property?" asked Jason.

"I did not," I answered honestly. "And I would like to point out something about this tombstone. The parents of Michael Wells asked me to talk to Mr. Morton on their behalf. Our conversation was less than fruitful."

"She attacked me. I want to press charges," said Morton.

"If anyone should be pressing charges, it should be her for the attack we witnessed," said Jason.

"She threw my desk into a wall, smashed it, then picked me up over her head," growled Morton.

"You expect me to believe that she did all that? What is she, a size 4?" asked Walker.

"Actually a 6, but thanks," I said.

"Did anybody see this alleged attack?" asked Jason.

"I saw it," said Morton. "And she knows what she did."

"I'm afraid I can hardly consider a grave robber a credible witness," said Jason.

"It's my tombstone! I can't steal something that's mine," said Morton.

"That's what I was about to point out." I held out a photograph of the tombstone before I got my hands on it. "This is the tombstone Mr. Morton had been preparing for two years. He e-mailed the parents this picture."

Morton nodded vigorously. "That's right, I did."

"It you look, you can see the tombstone that he just took from Mikey's grave does not look like the one in the picture," I said.

"That's impossible," said Morton, but both he and the two cops inspected both.

"She's right," said Walker. "This one is a different shape than the one in the picture."

Jason agreed. "And the M and the rest of the lettering isn't even similar." Of course it wasn't; I took pride in my work.

Even Morton was fooled, if his elaborate cursing was any indication.

"The reason for the deadline was that an anonymous donor—" I certainly didn't want to be identified "—was fed up with the situation. If he didn't make good on his obligations, the donor would rectify the situation."

"Do you think the parents will be willing to press charges?" asked Jason.

"I'm sure that, after all the trouble he's put them through, they would," I said.

"And what about you, for his assault on you?"

"Oh yeah," I said.

"It's only your word against mine. My lawyer will make this all go away," said Morton, smiling.

I smiled back. "We have a little bit more than that. We have video."

Morton practically threw his neck out, snapping it side to side looking for the camera. I took pity on him and pointed it out.

"This is entrapment!" screamed Morton.

"When you called my father and ranted, I got worried about Mikey's tombstone. I called my friends who happened to work for the NYPD, and brought my camera. I figured if they didn't get here in time, I'd at least have evidence that you stole it," I said.

"And Moni is a private citizen, so entrapment doesn't apply," said Jason. "I'd advise a plea bargain."

He didn't go quietly, and added assault on two police officers to the charges.

Morton didn't take Jason's advice. He went to trial, and got six to eight years. He had to sell his monument business for pennies on the dollar to cover his court costs. A friend of my brother bought it, and with my help, made good on all the other tombstones in short order.

As they took Morton out of the courtroom after his sentencing, I made sure he saw me. It took two correction officers to hold him back.

"You did this to me! You set me up!" Morton screamed.

I smiled and winked at him. "I don't see what you're getting so upset about. It's just business."

ONCE AROUND THE PARK

Mosie's hand darted out from under the blankets and picked up the receiver. The phone never even had a chance to make a sound.

"Hi Mom."

"I hate it when you do that. I wish you would let it ring at least once every so often," said Madame Rose.

"Where would the fun in that be?" asked Mosie rather jovially for someone who had been woken out of a deep sleep.

"You're drunk, I assume."

"Of course. Got a bottle nearby and everything."

"Good. I know how you get when you're sober."

"Mom, I have been drunk every day of my life with only a handful of exceptions since I was eight years old. I'm not going to risk being sober without a very good reason. You know that better than anyone," said Mosie.

"I know, but a mother worries."

"So to what do I owe the pleasure of this call?" asked Mosie. He slowly sat up and took a long sip from the bottle ofx Bulfinche's whiskey he kept on his night stand.

Mosie could actually hear the smile in his mother's voice. "What? You mean you don't know?"

"Sure, I could sift through the various time lines and possibilities if I wanted to, but that would be rude. Besides, you did just wake me up, and I'm still sleepy. Just tell me."

"You know the money from your last two winning lotto tickets?"

"We've met, before I introduced it to you, of course."

"Well, I managed to double it," said Madame Rose.

"Again? That's great, but it would have waited until morning. Why wake me up in the middle of the night to tell me?"

"You should be impressed with your mother. I managed to do it in just three days this time. I would have called sooner, but I had some business in some foreign markets to take care of first."

"Was it an IPO?"

"No, those things aren't what they used to be."

"Then I'm suitably impressed," said Mosie, as he stood and he glanced out the window. His Fifth Avenue apartment overlooked Central Park. Mosie liked the park. It was easier to look at than buildings full of people, all of whom had futures that he might not necessarily want to know about. The less populated park, especially at night, suited his condition much better. Still, it wasn't like any place in Manhattan was ever completely deserted for long. Below, a young woman crossed the street toward the park's entrance.

Her immediate future opened up to him, and it wasn't a pretty one. "Uh oh."

"What's wrong?" asked Madame Rose.

"A woman's going into the park and headed for trouble."

"A mugging?" asked his mother.

"No, something far more bizarre. A group called the Hunt Club is going to stalk and kill her. They enjoy using people for sport."

"I've never heard of them."

"Neither had I. Neither has she. Yet," said Mosie, who had already changed into his street clothes.

"You're going after her." It wasn't a question, but a statement of fact. The mother's psychic abilities may not have rivaled the son's, but she hadn't become insanely rich by being a slouch in that department.

"Yes," replied Mosie, putting on his shoes.

"You could call Paddy and let him make sure it's taken care of."

"These scum bags don't need that kind of fire power. I can handle them myself," he said.

"Are you sure?"

"Yes, Mother."

Madame Rose always knew that when Mosie said it, it was true. "So you are telling me that one drunk psychic is going to single-handedly take on… how many armed gunmen? Three, four?"

"Four."

"Four armed gunmen with his bare hands?"

"Technically one of them is an archer. But they only have weapons. I have my ruggedly handsome looks and quick wit."

"If that's all that you have going for you, you might want to rethink asking Paddy for help," quipped Madame Rose.

"Mom!"

"Just teasing. Go help the girl. It would be good for you in more ways than one."

That stopped Mosie short. His mother used to specialize in telling fortunes before she went into the stock market. She still knew how to speak in vague terms, and she was more attuned to the little pictures than he was.

"What do you mean?" asked Mosie.

Madame Rose laughed, but it was a joyful sound. "At times like this, it's a good thing that you drink too much. There are some things alcohol should cloud your vision of. It's about time you were able to enjoy something like a normal man. Now go."

"Is this why you called me? So I'd be up to see her?" asked Mosie. He hated being outpsychiced.

"Hurry. You don't want to be late. Love you."

"Love you, too." Mosie hung up and took another slug of whiskey, making sure it was a big one. It would be a while before he could get another. Grabbing his coat, he rushed out, taking the stairs rather than wasting the extra time he knew the elevator would take. Running toward the door, he waved to the doorman, who was on the phone. His power kicked in, and Mosie paused.

"Stan, don't take the Midtown Tunnel on your way home tonight," said Mosie.

The doorman put down the phone receiver. Mosie had once told him to call his wife to check on their daughter. His daughter had been slipping out their apartment window, and his wife had barely caught her. Ever since, he listened to anything Mosie told him. Stan opened the door. "Thank you, sir. I won't."

"Good. Thank your wife for the cookies," he said.

"I will, sir."

Mosie didn't bother to look as he ran out into the street. His mind had already looked both ways in advance for him. Pealing back time a few minutes, he followed the physic shadow of the woman through the park until he caught up to the real thing.

The psychic was careful to stay back. He knew that if he got too close, the woman, Mitzy, would mistake him for a mugger and speed up, taking a different path. The Hunt Club would kill her before he could do a thing to stop them. Changing the future was a tricky business. There are some things that the Fates wouldn't allow to change, and Mosie had with great regret learned to tell those from the aspects that he could improve on.

These days, Central Park was nowhere near as bad as it is generally made out to be in the media, but it was still no place for a young woman to be all alone in the middle of the night.

"Mitzy, you should know better," whispered Mosie to himself.

Even though it wasn't in his line of sight, Mosie could still see what was happening across the park. The four men had already chosen the first of their intended victims for the night. Mitzy would be their second. The first was an eccentric old man who liked to wander through the streets at night. Hank liked to feed the rats and squirrels instead of the pigeons, and he would sing to himself as he walked.

For hundreds of years the Hunt Club has pulled its membership from some of the wealthiest families on Earth. Nothing had been about to stop it in all that time because they were powerful and careful. On blind luck stalkings, the Hunt Club liked to start with a target they assumed no one would miss. Hank fit the bill.

Mosie saw the future in a world without Hank, and realized that they were right to an extent. Hank hadn't been in his right mind in years. The man was a loner and homeless, without close family. Most of his friends were in the same boat, which meant most of those who would miss him were other street people. As a rule, street people have influence with the authorities almost on a par with the rats Hank liked to feed. But there was one time Hank had been a hero, saving friends of Mosie's from a psychopath who had them trapped in a spell circle. Hank was the only reason a little baby named John was alive today. He would be missed by many more than the Hunt Club could have been bothered to imagine

To let him be killed just so four psychopaths could get their jollies was wrong. Mosie had to stop running to sort through the possible futures in his mind. He kept trying to find one where Hank got to live, but there wasn't any. Even if he called Hermes for help, the Fates would cause a teenage boy to fall through a high rise window as Hermes was passing by. Hermes would catch him, but the boy's throat would be cut a by a shard of glass. The god of physician's would save him, but the boy would never speak again. It would be especially unfortunate because otherwise he would one day have spoken words that would have saved three lives. The Fates were vengeful that way.

This night was Hank's time, and every single outcome had him dying one way or another at the hands of the Hunt Club. By not interfering, Mosie could at least limit other casualties.

"Damn it!" Mosie hit a tree with his fist as he said it. It really didn't make him feel any better, and the punch didn't faze the tree one bit. This was the part of his life that he truly despised: to know ahead of time and be powerless to make a difference. He had tried so many times with far-reaching consequences. He knew this man's death had to be, but it didn't mean he had to like it.

But he still had a chance to save Mitzy. There were actually three variations that Mosie could control which ended with Mitzy alive. In cases like this, three was a huge number. Unfortunately, one of the three ended with Mosie dead, so he eliminated that one quickly. He chose the opportunity that came first, so that if something went wrong, he could still have one more shot.

The chain of events had started minutes earlier. The four men had found the old man feeding some rats a block away from the Museum of Natural History. The four men cornered him and explained their rules to him.

"Listen up, you worthless piece of trash. Tonight you get to meet your destiny and do something worthy for once. You will provide sport for the Hunt Club. This is more than likely the greatest thing that you have ever done," said one.

"The rules are simple: we give you a four-minute head start. You head into the park. If you go anywhere but the park…" said Number Two.

"We kill you," finished Number Three.

"If you manage to make it out the opposite side onto Fifth Avenue, you win. That means you survive. However, if we catch you before you leave the park…" said Number Four.

"We kill you," finished Number Three.

"Any questions?" asked Number One.

"Remembering, of course, that if you have any questions…" said Number Two.

"We kill you," finished Number Three.

The old man was still lucid enough to realize what was going on. Worse, in his psychosis, Hank felt that he was being chased by people who had been trying to kill him for years, but he had believed they could only come out during the day, which was why he took his midnight jaunts. There was no joy in realizing his delusions had been proven true. Dropping the bag of food he fed the rats and squirrels with, he ran in the entrance to Central Park. Hank was elderly and overweight; he couldn't exactly move fast, even though he knew he was running for his life.

"He's pretty slow. Should we give him a bigger head start?" asked Number Four.

The other three looked at each other and answered in unison. "Naw." Whatever else they might have been, the men did wait the full four minutes.

Side by side, the four walked toward the entrance, putting on night vision goggles. Once inside, Number One opened his bag and pulled out a high-powered rifle equipped with a silencer and a laser sight. It took him less than fifteen seconds to put it together. Number Two hunted with a two hundred and ten pound crossbow, complete with pulleys and curare-laced arrowheads. Number Three wore roller blades and held an automatic handgun in each hand. Each, of course, had a silencer. He quickly took the lead. Number Four had set out traps throughout the park. In his pocketed vest he had a lariat, a net, bolos, and various other implements of capture and death. His belt was a whip. In his hand, he held a customized universal remote that triggered the snares and booby traps he had set hours earlier. Lastly, he had a sword at his side.

The old man ran as fast as he could. In logic born of adrenaline and fear, he stayed off the paths, thinking that he would be harder to spot as he crouched low, sprinting across lawns and patches of woods.

Number Three on his roller blades was the first to find that the old man had run off the path. The other three followed the trail while the hunter on wheels stayed on the pavement as near as he could to where his companions were. It didn't take long for them to catch up with the old man. Hank saw them and ran faster, so hard his heart was racing faster than it was meant to at his advanced age. Even if he could find a hiding place, his wheezing would lead the predators straight to him.

The old man tried to cut across toward a path he knew lead to a Fifth Avenue exit. He could actually see buildings in the distance. As he stepped onto pavement, Number Three skated directly in front of him, sliding to a stop sideways. Hank's path was blocked.

"Didn't make it to Fifth Avenue. You know what that means, don't you?"

Hank knew all too well, and started to shiver. "You'll kill me."

"Very good. That's more than I gave you credit for," said Number Three.

The old man turned and ran, but the other three hunters had used the time to encircle him. There was nowhere he could run that one of the Hunt Club wouldn't cut him off.

"Any last words?" asked Number Two.

The old man knew that he was a goner. It was a forgone conclusion. Although he had no friends in polite society, he had plenty of them on the streets. He knew these men would probably prey on them next. They had to be stopped, and so he used his last word to call out her name. "Rebecca!"

"Shouldn't we give him a chance to say his prayers?" asked Number Four.

"Nah, this street vermin doesn't believe in God. Let's just put him out of his misery," said Number One.

There was no need for a countdown. They had done this many times before, in many different cities. The Hunt Club worked as well together as any elite commando unit.

They all discharged their weapons simultaneously.

Number One used his rifle to blow a hole through the man's spine just below the neck. Number Two shot his poison-tipped arrow into their victim's chest. There was no need for the poison—even without his comrades' efforts—the shot went straight to the heart. Number Three fired both forty-fives, blowing off the man's kneecaps, shattering the bone and cartilage underneath. Number Four had assembled a blow gun, and shot a dart—also laced with curare—which landed exactly in the center of the man's left jugular.

The old man died on his way to the ground. The Hunt Club moved closer, pleased with the kill. The man's head was undamaged, and would be a fine addition to hang on their trophy wall. As Number Four raised his sword to slice head from neck, Number One called for their clean up team. Even the best forensic unit would soon be hard pressed to prove anyone had died there. Number Three turned out of habit to scan the area. Through his night vision goggles, he saw the glow of a warm body ducked behind a tree. It was Mitzy. She had a level head; she hadn't screamed out when she saw the slaughter, but moved to hide and was calling 911. When she saw the hunter on roller blades staring at her, she turned and fled, dropping her cell. The other hunters turned in time to be able to make her out as she ran.

"No witnesses," said Number One. Number Three nodded, and skated after Mitzy. It only took seconds for him to overtake and cut her off.

This time, a level head was not enough to stop her from screaming at the sight of the armed man who had suddenly appeared in front of her.

"Do you know what happens to people who are at the wrong place at the wrong time?" asked Number Three.

"They get lovely parting gifts?" stammered Mitzy.

Number Three smiled. "Only if you consider a bullet a gift."

"I called 911. The cops are on their way," said Mitzy.

Number three laughed. "That should give us about twelve minutes to end you and hide two bodies. I've got time to kill."

"Does that type of banter usually impress your victims?" Mitzy asked, trying to figure a way to hurt the hunter.

"Yes. Not impressed?"

"Nope," she said.

"How about this then?" Number Three raised his guns to chest level. Mitsy kicked up in his groin, but the hunter skated backwards out of the way.

Which is when Mosie stepped in, tapping Number Three on the shoulder. Now it was the wheeled hunter's turn to scream, although it was a shorter, more manly type of yelling.

"Where the hell did you come from? How did you sneak up on me?" demanded Number Three.

"It wasn't hard. I just knew where to step."

"That's not true. If you did, you would've stepped away. You know what we do to witnesses?" asked Number Three.

Mosie's stomach flipped and flopped, the sickness pouring straight through to his soul. This close, he could see every last victim this murderer had used that line on. There were dozens, spread all over the world.

"You kill them." The psychic's answer took some of the fun away from Number Three, but he just assumed that Mosie had heard what he had said to Mitzy. "Or in this case, you'll try. It would go better for you if you went with her suggestion of parting gifts."

"There's no question about me succeeding."

"I know," said Mosie, flexing a smile.

Number Three had turned so that he had one gun trained on Mitzy and one on Mosie.

"You might want to use both of these on me, but it still won't be enough," said Mosie.

Number Three just laughed. "You're insane."

"No, just drunk and gifted. However, I will make you a bet: I bet you that, with both of your guns, you won't be able to hit me once."

"You must be very drunk, but I'll play along. What are the stakes?"

"Our lives. And you give the girl a chance to get away."

Number Three considered it. It sounded like it might be interesting sport. "Okay."

"Mitzy, go hide behind those rocks," ordered Mosie.

"How do you know my name?"

"Later. Please go. And keep your head down," said Mosie, knowing that she wouldn't. He turned to Number Three. "You realize that you have the option to simply not shoot and just walk away. You can still forsake this lifestyle of causing death."

"Could death really be considered a lifestyle?" asked Number Three.

"This is your last chance," said Mosie, knowing the decision Number Three would make, but giving him a chance, just in case.

Number Three ignored the suggestion. "Do you want me to give you a head start?"

"Naw, I'm good. Do you actually want me to give you some time for finger warm up exercises?" asked Mosie.

"You are an absolute lunatic, but I admire your cool. Thanks, but I'm good. Do you want a second to say your prayers?"

"No. How about you?"

"I'm confident that I won't need any, but it's good of you to ask," said Number Three. "So, you're ready then?"

"Fire at will."

Number Three opened fire, but Mosie had moved even before the killer's brain could send impulses to his finger. The psychic was no longer in the path of the bullet, and it whizzed by him harmlessly.

"You do realize, don't you, that when I said fire at will, I didn't mean some guy named Will on the next block. I was saying that you could try to shoot me. We are clear on the rules of this game, right?" said Mosie, already in motion.

There were four alternating shots from the automatics, each accented with a pop of air from the silencer.

"That will shut you up," said Number Three, who had begun to lose his own cool. He regained it when he saw the drunken psychic fall. "Sad, pathetic, crazy man, playing a game he couldn't win. I better get back and let the others know the authorities are on the way."

Mosie rolled and stood up, bullet-hole-free. The low tone caused by inebriation had helped him hit the ground without hurting himself. "Why would that shut me up? People have been trying for years, but I just keep rambling on and on and on. The pop, pop from the silencer is really annoying and I prefer not to try to talk over it, so I'll probably wait until you are done shooting, but it certainly won't shut me up."

Number Three fired six more shots in rapid succession. All of them missed their target.

"I thought that you were supposed to be good at this. Shouldn't you have practiced at home before you came out into public? You're embarrassing yourself," said Mosie.

This time, six more shots were fired, all while Mosie moved to the opposite side of the gunman, staying at least a step ahead of each bullet.

"You're not human!"

"Oh I'm very human, trust me. Just drunk and gifted, like I said before." Mosie knew that Number Three had started out with ten bullets in each gun. There had been nineteen shots which had left one bullet in the automatic in his left hand.

The next minute was crucial. Number Three hadn't been able to keep track of his shots. He fired once with his right gun to an empty click. Frustrated, he raised his left hand and gun. Unknown to Number Three, Number One was back in the woods, and his laser sight was currently resting on the back of Mosie's neck.

Psychic fighting is a lot like comedy: timing is everything. Mosie fell flat to the ground a half moment before Number One and Number Three fired at him. Number One's shot took Number Three in the face and kept going to the back of his head, killing him instantly. Number Three's last bullet struck Number One in the throat. He wasn't dead yet, but it was only a matter of seconds.

"Sorry, Paddy," whispered Mosie. Paddy Moran had been the closest thing to a father Mosie had known, and the leprechaun held all life sacred. Paddy believed there was always a way to preserve life. Mosie knew different. The two men who he had just maneuvered to kill each other would have racked up one hundred fifty kills between them in less than a year. Each was a multimillionaire in their own right and one was the son of a billionaire. No law enforcement agency in the world would ever be able to make a charge against either of those two stick. Witnesses and prosecutors would simply be made to disappear. Even if by some miracle they were convicted, they would continue to kill even in prison.

Mosie forced himself to focus back on the current time line. The next member of the Hunt Club he would have to worry about was Number Two. The man was crouched behind some nearby trees, thinking that no one knew where he was. He was wrong twice over. Mosie knew, and the old woman Hank had called to at his death did, too. The Mother of the Streets had snuck behind the archer and made some very quick, subtle rearrangements to the quiver that was on his back. The archer loaded an arrow and let it fly at Mosie, preferring to face his foe from a distance.

The arrow flew straight and true. It would have taken Mosie full in the chest all the way to the heart and out his back, except Mosie knew it was coming. The drunken psychic reached out and plucked the shaft from the air. The arrow stopped three inches from his chest.

Mosie stared right at where Number Two was hiding in the darkness. "If you stop now, you'll live."

The archer cursed silently to himself. How did this unarmed, apparently drunken man manage to take out two of the Hunt Club? The four of them had been together for years. Even though the dead members would be replaced, it would never be the same, although their deaths would elevate him to Number One.

The stranger would be made to pay for that. The archer reached behind him to the quiver on his back to pull out an arrow. Instead of feathers he felt steel, sharp and cold. His own arrow points bit into his skin. Not believing what had happened, Number Two moved his hand in front of his face and stared at it in the darkness. In the shadows of the night, he could see a tiny trickle of blood from his index and middle fingers. His last thought was to wonder how the arrows in his quiver had been turned upside down without his knowing? Number Two fell over, the muscles that let him breathe and pump his blood paralyzed from the poison. And then there was one.

"I don't know how you managed to kill three of the finest men I have ever known, but this stops here," said Number Four, stepping onto the path. Despite the impressive array of more primitive weaponry stashed about his person, Number Four was empty handed. Mosie saw that his ego was urging Number Four to take the drunken psychic on in unarmed combat, in which the hunter was an expert.

Mosie examined futures while he looked down at the poisoned arrow that he still held. Mosie stuck it point first into the ground. He wasn't going to need it.

Number Four wasn't interested in small talk. He simply attacked with a battle cry that would have startled most people, giving him the initial advantage, but Mosie had already heard it long before the cry actually left the hunter's lips.

The drunken psychic sidestepped the attack, and watched Number Four sail past him. The last member of this incarnation of the Hunt Club recovered quickly, attacking with a flurry of punches and kicks. Each was countered and blocked, as Mosie knew where Number Four would strike next, even before the hunter himself did, although it was a struggle to keep the timing lined up correctly. One mental misstep—seeing something an instant too soon or too late—would mean Mosie's and Mitzy's deaths, although Rebecca would avenge them both. It was hardly a comforting thought.

"You're…"

"Amazing," finished Mosie. "Yeah, I know. You can stop all this, turn from your evil ways."

"We're just having a little fun and taking care of a little of the world's surplus population in the process." Number Four attacked again and again without landing a single blow for minutes on end. The dance was tiring both participants.

The last of the Hunt Club backed off to reevaluate the situation. So did Mosie. He realized he wasn't the one the Fates wanted to take care of this man.

"You know that gentleman you and the rest of the Hunt Club killed earlier?" asked Mosie.

Number Four raised an eyebrow that Mosie actually knew who they were. Outside the small circle of potential members and a few conspiracy theorists, the Hunt Club was a well-kept secret.

"Yes."

"What were his last words?"

"He called out a woman's name. So what?"

"The name he called out was that of the Mother of the Streets."

"So what? He called out to some imaginary bag lady who protects the homeless. That's just urban legend," said Number Four, pulling out his machete after deciding that hand to hand was no longer the way to go.

"I know several legends, urban and otherwise, and I can tell you that they are quite real. And many of them consider Hank a friend," said Mosie.

Number Four laughed. "So you're trying to tell me that some bogeywoman is going to come and get me because I did the world a favor and took out some bum?"

Rebecca had been steadily sneaking up on Number Four, and had finally reached him. With one hand, she grabbed his machete, while her other hand reached around to press her own knife against the hunter's throat.

"The bogeywoman's already here," said the older woman dressed in the multi-colored cast-offs of the ages. "Drop the blade."

"Or?" asked the hunter.

Rebecca didn't answer with words. Actions were so much louder. She pushed the deadly blade deeper into his throat until blood trickled out. Number Four realized it wouldn't take much for that knife to go deeper still. The machete clacked onto the pavement.

"So, foreseer, what's the best thing to do with this one?" asked Rebecca. The Mother of the Streets had survived some thoroughly terrible things in her lifetime, and by society's standards, was easily judged insane. It was, however, a rational insanity, entirely functional in the dark corners of the world she lived in. Family was very important to the woman who had lost two of her own. The only person whose opinion she deferred to was Paddy Moran. Because of her respect for him, Rebecca often curbed her own instincts for justice, which leaned toward the an eye for an eye version. In a world without Paddy Moran, Number Four would already lie dead at her feet.

Mosie debated. Number Four was actually the worst of the bunch. He had logged as many kills as his three companions combined, many of whom he had tortured in his little traps first.

"If he chooses to confess to everything, we can give the NYPD a shot at him," said Mosie. He knew Number Four would not confess, and even if they did take him into custody, he would not be there for very long. The death toll of New York's finest during his escape would be three.

"I don't think so," said Number Four.

"Maybe Moran can come up with a solution," said Rebecca, but it would be too late for that.

The hunter reached casually inside his own sleeve to remove a hidden curare-tipped blow dart. With a single thrust, he stabbed it toward Rebecca's wrist. Rebecca felt his muscles moving and simply pulled away her knife hand. Number Four ended up sticking the dart into his own skin below his clavicle. The Mother of the Streets and the drunken psychic watched as the last of the Hunt Club tumbled to his death.

Mitzy, who had been watching from behind the rocks with her head up the entire time, came out. "Are you guys okay?"

"Dandy," said Rebecca, as she walked back across the park to where Hank had fallen.

"What about you?" Mitzy asked her rescuer.

"As well as I can be, considering the circumstances. How about you, Mitzy?" asked Mosie.

"Thanks to you, I'm fine. Thank you so much." Mitzy leaned forward and kissed him on the cheek.

Mosie blushed. "You're welcome."

"Explain to me how you know my name?"

"I know a lot of things. Sometimes they help me to help others like you."

"You mean you knew that this was going to happen? Why didn't you call the police? Or get here in time to save the old man?"

"I only realized what was going to happen to you when I saw you entering the park. The police would have gotten here too late." He wiped at his eye, hoping to get the tear that leaked out before Mitzy noticed, but he was too late. "There was nothing that I could do to save Hank that wouldn't have ended up killing others in the long run."

Rebecca came back holding Hank's body in her arms. "Don't feel bad about the hunters, foreseer. What happened to these men was of their own doing. They tried to kill us; all we did was manage to turn the tables."

"Thanks, Rebecca."

"What are you going to do about the other bodies?" asked Mitzy.

"Nothing," said Rebecca. "Let the cops find them and sort it out. They'd never believe the truth anyway. Those four were important men, at least as bureaucrats and politicians view things. It would be best if you were careful about who you told about this."

Mitzy nodded. Rebecca left the park carrying the fallen form of Hank. Mosie knew that she would see that he was laid to rest properly, burned on a pyre as his fellow street people mourned him. Mosie saw that he and Mitzy wouldn't be the only members of polite society to attend. Murphy, Ryth, Mathew, and their little son John, as well as some of the other staff and patrons of Bulfinche's Pub, would also go to pay their respects to the man who had saved the bartender, succubus, and little child.

"I guess you better get out of here, huh?" said Mitzy.

"We're okay for the moment. The bodies won't be found until morning," said Mosie. "Maybe in the future you should reconsider walking through the park late at night by yourself."

"I've been doing it for years, but maybe. I still have to get home tonight. I live way over on the west side. Would you mind walking me home?"

"I wouldn't mind at all," said Mosie.

It was just then that Mosie caught a glimpse of Mitzy's future. It seemed to involve him, although the details were fuzzy, but pleasant. For once, not knowing had its own appeal.

THE DMA CASEFILES:
THE BEAST WITH TWO BACKS

They called my partner and me in to investigate the beast with two backs. No, we didn't go undercover as peeping Toms; it was more complicated than that. This beast did indeed have two backs, as well as two fronts that were pressed close together. When I say it was hard to tell where one began and the other ended, I'm not waxing poetic. This writhing mass of flesh had at one point been two people, and my best guess was they were engaged in making the figurative beast with two backs before their sexual union turned very literal.

There was a male and female head which seemed to share only one mouth where two sets of lips had fused together. Arms wrapped around torsos, but the hands disappeared, each set of fingers melting into the flesh of the other. At the points where their groins met there was no trace left of sexual organs, just one smooth lump of flesh, as if someone had taken Ken and Barbie and held them together over an open flame.

The pair that were now reluctant Siamese lovers hadn't stopped moving the entire time I stood trying to get a grasp of the situation. Neither paused as each of them thrashed around in pain, desperately trying to pull away from the other. It was a goal they were never going to be able to make happen on their own.

"Isn't this the damnedest thing?" asked Detective Turner. He was one of San Francisco's finest, and had pulled the short straw when it came to this case. "Have you ever seen anything like it?"

"No," I answered honestly.

"How can something like this happen? Radiation?" asked Turner.

"Magic," I answered. The locals never like that answer.

"I don't believe in magic, no offense to the DMA. My superiors called you in," said Turner. The Department of Mystic Affairs is never treated with respect by the locals until some bad mojo moves in and does something they can't explain. We make no effort to hide the fact that magic is real and monsters exist. It's not our fault that most people choose not to believe us until it's too late.

"By the time we're done, you're going to probably want to rethink that," I said.

There was a sound of dry heaving coming from the bathroom. It was an improvement over the sound of the wet ones that had preceded it for the last several minutes.

"Your partner going to be alright in there?" asked Turner.

"Yes," I said.

"Weak stomach or flu?" asked Turner, being polite enough to give her an out for rookie behavior.

"Neither. She's been doing this longer than I have, and I've seen her look at remains where you couldn't tell how many people or what parts of them were left, all without batting an eye. My partner has certain abilities which make her sensitive to emotions, and these two must be pouring out a great deal of terror," I said. Mandi's an empath with propathic tendencies, which means she can send out as well as receive emotions. Usually she can stomach what other people are feeling. This must have been especially bad.

"It's not just the emotional terror these two are churning up. I'm blaming part of this on breakfast at that greasy spoon this morning," said Mandi. She had pulled her long blonde hair back into a ponytail. I guess that helped keep the puke out of it.

"Then I guess you don't want to stop at the all-you-can-eat pea soup, chili, and gefilte fish buffet for lunch? I hear they have a chocolate sauce raw oyster platter that has to be tasted to believe," I said with a smile.

My partner shot me a look. "Keep it up, Karver. I throw up again; I ain't going to the bathroom. I'm aiming for your shoes."

I pulled out a roll of chewable antacids and handed them to her.

"Where'd you get these?" she asked, taking the roll and popping three of the tablets.

"Motel lobby had a machine." Mandi had been in there a long time. I had noticed on the way in, so I ran down at the first sounds from the bathroom. "They also had an assortment of condoms, if you want to stock up."

"I don't know how you can think of sex after seeing something like this," said Turner. "I was hoping you'd know what happened."

"We know," I said.

Turner gave me a cop look. If I had been a suspect under interrogation, it would have meant I was in trouble for an inconsistency.

"I haven't seen something like this, but I know something—or rather, someone—that can do it. It's called a fleshsmith," I said.

"Which is what?" asked Turner.

"It's a mage that can manipulate and mold any type of human or animal flesh," said Mandi. "There's very little we can do for the victims at this point, except calm them." Since Mandi had come out of the bathroom, the painful movements had slowed. Mandi had been sending calming emotions their way in an attempt to relax the couple and block their pain. It seemed to be working.

"What can you do?" said Turner.

"I already called for assistance from the home office," said Mandi. "The Department of Mystic Affairs has its own fleshsmith and he's on his way."

I cursed. "You called Adin?" My feelings toward him fell on the far side of loathing. Adin had been the one to give me my new face when the DMA rescued me from death row. The fleshsmith thought he had a sense of humor, which is the last thing someone who just had a demon use his body to murder more than five dozen people needs.

"How else do you suppose we could separate them? The flesh has changed to the point where, even if a surgeon could separate them, the body parts that should be there, aren't. The doctor wouldn't even know where to begin cutting."

"Fine, you're right, but I don't have to like it," I conceded. "What do you have so far on the victims?"

Turner pulled out his notebook. "To be honest, we're not entirely sure which is which. Neither have any special identifying characteristics. Each of them seems to have a single male and a single female breast. According to the IDs we found, the victims are Barney Diamond and Bambi Boosh. What we've been able to find out, Bambi is an exotic dancer." Turner pointed to a pair of silicon sacks that lay on the floor. "We're running down the serial numbers just to verify. Barney was a partner in one of those dot com IPOs that raised hundreds of millions in capital. He was smart enough to cash out enough of his stock before the bubble burst. He's worth about eighteen million."

"Either of them married or seriously involved?" asked Mandi.

"Diamond is married. His wife's name is Susan. We're trying to find her now," said Turner.

Cheating husband certainly is a motive. "What does Susan Diamond do for a living?"

Turner flipped open Diamond's wallet. There was an entire gallery of pictures of a gorgeous blonde, her features and figure perfect in every way.

"Near as we can tell, she had no outside income." Turner looked at Mandi. "No sexism intended, ma'am, it looks like she was a trophy wife."

"None taken. I'm looking for a trophy husband, myself," said Mandi.

"Yeah, but she has trouble getting them to stay up on the mantle," I said.

Turner smiled. "We've been afraid to move them. We don't want to hurt them, and we don't know what would."

"Good call. Our man will be able to give us a better idea of what has to be done," said Mandi. "Karver, why don't you and Turner go see what you can find out about the missing missus."

"You sure?" I asked. I knew Mandi was using her propathic powers to keep the victims calm, but I also didn't want her in a position that would put her back to praying to the porcelain god.

"I'll be fine. Go."

So Turner and I went, starting with the house, the neighbors, the country club, and a few other places. No one had seen Susan Diamond. Apparently, she was a sight to be seen, from what we heard from the men and even the women. If she had been around, somebody would have remembered and told us, if only to brag.

My phone rang. It was Mandi. After I heard what she had to say, I whispered, "Damn."

Turner looked at me, worry in his eyes. "The victims die?"

I shook my head. "No, our fleshsmith is at the motel. Feel free to take the long way back."

Turner ignored my suggestion and instead turned on the sirens. We were there in record time.

Adin saw me and gave me a perfect smile. Fleshsmiths are notorious for being uber-beautiful people. When you can adjust your looks on a whim, it's not that hard to do. I doubt anyone but me would have seen the sadistic glee in that grin.

"Karver, good to see you," said Adin, rushing up with his hand outstretched to touch mine. That wasn't going to happen. Touch is how their powers work.

I pulled my piece and pointed it between his eyes. "Don't even think about touching me."

"Karver!" scolded Mandi. I could feel the calming waves pulsing off her towards me. They didn't do a thing.

"Pulling your weapon on a fellow agent. That's a suspendable offense there, Karver. I could have you up on charges," said Adin. His perfect smile just kept getting bigger.

"Yeah, maybe I'll get suspended or maybe I'll shoot you. I know where to shoot you that it won't kill you, just hurt like hell until you mold the flesh back into place. However, if I tell about what happened when you worked on a certain new recruit—" namely, me "—I think you'd end up without a job. Maybe even some jail time. You want to continue this pissing contest, or do you want to back down?"

Adin put his hands up in mock surrender. "Fine. I was just saying 'hi'."

"We both know that ain't true." Adin was still too close for my comfort, so I didn't holster the weapon until he took two steps back. Then I put my gun away.

I looked at Diamond and Boosh. "Why are they still connected?" I asked.

Adin's perfect smile faded into a look of embarrassment. "We've run into a few problems."

I was surprised. I didn't like the guy, but he was master level at what he did. "What kind of problems?"

"For starters, we have two entirely separate people that were merged," said Adin.

"We already knew that. It's why we called you in," I said.

"No, that's not what I mean." Adin motioned Turner and me away from the fused lovers. The rest of the conversation, on his part, was a whisper. "When you merge two separate beings, it's common to leave a differentiation point, a clear line where one begins and the other ends. The person who did this just merged flesh without regard for bone, muscle, fat, or whom it came from. I can't tell who belongs to what."

"Can you just guess, separate them, and reform what's missing?" I asked.

"I could, but it could have disastrous results. The two of them have different blood types and different tissue types. If I leave any tissue from the other person still inside, the body will start attacking it. Their own immune systems will kill them. In fact, at this point, I don't think I'd even be able to get all their blood separated because it has mixed so much. And that's going to be a problem, because he's B and she's A. The two don't mix well. Worse, one's positive and the other is negative. If I separate them, we may still have to take all the blood out of both of them and do a full transfusion."

"Can't you just morph the blood into the right type once they're separated?" I asked.

"Too much and too delicate. I can manage a few pints if it's in a jar, but in and among all the capillaries mixed through all the flesh, there's no way; same goes for the foreign tissue. When I worked on you, I changed fat to bone and muscle. But the genetic code in all of them would still be yours. I can't change that."

That's something I hadn't thought about. My DNA was still in criminal databases.

"I'm waiting on two medical teams to arrive. I'm going to separate the pair and have them start the transfusions on the way to the hospital. The problem is that I'm going to have to treat this as an amputation and take the overlapping pieces of flesh away. Unfortunately, they're both in good shape."

"What difference does that make?" asked Turner.

"I can change one type of flesh to another. To do most of my work, I usually use stored fat. Both of them are in good shape and are thin. We may be able to use some of the muscle mass, but it's not going to be enough to grow entire hands and pelvises. We'll just have to see if they survive, then fatten them up and see what I can do later on."

Turner cursed. I concurred. The medical teams Adin was waiting for arrived.

"Anything I can do?" I said.

"Yeah. Catch the sick bastard that did this," said Adin.

"I will," I said. "Can I take my partner with me?"

"Yeah, now that the medical team is here, we're going to sedate both of them. Their eyes are open, and they don't need to see this. I actually had to adjust their eyelids. They were locked in the up and open position. They couldn't have shut their eyes no matter how hard they tried."

I had to agree with Adin's assessment of sick bastard; problem was, the sicko was also pretty creative. That pointed toward intelligence, and a smart monster is harder to catch than a dumb one, human or otherwise.

"Remember, a fleshsmith's power only works through the hands, so don't let this one touch you," said Adin. "Either of you."

"We won't," Mandi said.

The conjoined pair were both being injected in the gluteus muscles, as they were large fleshy areas that neither one seemed to share with the other. In less than a minute, they were both unconscious, their heads lolling to opposite sides, their lips looked as if they were going to be torn apart from the strain. Adin started with the faces, putting one of his hands on each. There was a soft glow, and the space where their lips should have been was removed, leaving a pair of skull-like grins.

I had seen worse. Hell, I had done worse when the demon controlled my hands, but I had no desire to see more. Although I was impressed by the fact that he sealed the flesh that was left behind, and not a drop of blood was spilled. God forbid a seriál demon possessed Adin. There's no telling what kind of destruction it would be able to do. I looked at my partner's face. Mandi had seen what I had seen, but she was turning a little green. Part of it was probably what she ate for breakfast, but part of it was the nausea of everyone in the room who was watching. I went over, put my arm around her shoulders, and led her out of the room, picking up a wastepaper basket on the sly as we left. I closed the door behind us and got her around the corner from where the uniforms were standing guard. We went to the top of the stairwell and I handed her the basket. Mandi started to say thanks, but the end of the word was drowned out by a heave.

Finding one person in a city the size of San Francisco was not an easy thing. Fugitives were able to stay at large for a long time if they were smart. Fortunately, most weren't. Amazing how many are caught getting some nookie at their significant other's abode. Sometimes the only way to catch the smart ones was to put their picture on TV and hope for the best. That wouldn't happen until we had proof that the wife was indeed the fleshsmith – not that it would be effective in this case, with a perp who can change their appearance. It could just as easily be that one of Bambi the dancer's regulars got a little too obsessive and possessive. We decided to check out her club next and ask some questions. The name of the place was the Pole Barn. The door was decorated with cartoons of overly endowed women wearing pasties with hats, chaps, and spurs. We were in time for the lunch rush. When the guy at the door asked us for the cover, we could have pulled our badges. We didn't. Instead we forked over the money. Sometimes it's better if people don't know who you are. The hope was that people might open up more to a fellow purveyor of the fleshy arts. If that didn't work, we'd pull out the badges, go backstage, and talk to the dancers.

We made like a couple out for a little bit of excitement. We weren't the only ones there. Somewhere along the line, strip clubs had gone from a dirty little pleasure to a place to take a date – progress takes all forms.

I sat down on a chair near the stage. Mandi went over to the bar to work her wiles. She came back over with a pair of rum and Cokes.

"What's this? We're on the job," I said.

"Two drink minimum," she said. "I said we were fans of Bambi. Bartender said she hadn't shown up for her shift, and no one seemed to know why. He says the next dancer up is good friends with her. She might be where we start."

There was something a little off in my partner's tone when she mentioned the dancer. Not that something specifically was wrong, but something was up. "What's the dancer's name?"

My partner sighed. "Mandy."

I guess I didn't have to laugh so loud or so hard, but it's so rare that I find something funny enough to laugh at these days that I couldn't help myself. My partner's eyes narrowed, and she frowned. It was her face of intimidation. It only made me laugh harder.

The DJ announced Mandy, and the speakers belted out "Cotton-Eyed Joe." Cowgirl Mandy was energetically swaying some parts, shaking others while making the faces that mimicked ecstasy, but you could tell by her eyes that this was just a job. When her number was done, she came down onto the floor to wander among the crowd to try to separate the patrons from their cash.

Mandi waved a couple of bills to get her attention. "That was great. I was wondering if I could get my man here a lap dance."

Now it was my turn for the face of intimidation. I guess my laughing must have really pissed off my partner, because she knows I'm not good with the touching. It brings back all the butchery, which to the seriál that rode my soul was like foreplay, sex, and orgasm all rolled into one.

Mandi had the right to get even with me, but that didn't mean I was going to let her get away with it. When cowgirl Mandy came over, I said, "I appreciate it, but I can't accept." The stripper gave me an odd look. "She's my mistress. I'm cheating on my wife with her. To let you do the lap dance would seem like I was cheating on my wife with two women, and that would just be wrong."

"I understand," said the stripper. Apparently, this wasn't the first time she heard that line.

"However, you were paid for a lap dance." I handed her another twenty. "I think she could use one more than me."

Mandi's jaw dropped.

"The customer is always right," said the dancer.

"Except when it's him. He's never right," said my partner.

"She's just feeling a little bit awkward because we're in here trying to gear her up for a threesome," I said.

Mandy the stripper was rubbing her bare back and thonged behind against my partner Mandi's front. "I thought you said another woman would be too much cheating on your wife?"

I shot her a smile. "Who do you think the third person's going to be?"

Mandy the stripper swung around, straddling my partner and rubbing her arms up and down Mandi's side. My partner rolled her eyes and stood up, dropping the stripper on her thonged behind.

"Sorry, this isn't working for me," said my partner.

The stripper shrugged. "Hey, I get paid either way. So why are you wearing a gun? You a cop?"

"She's good. Maybe you could frisk our perps that way. We'd probably have a lot less resisting arrest," I said.

"I'd never get the outfit past the director. We do have a dress code," said Mandi. She flipped open her badge and showed the stripper. "We're federal agents. We're looking into the assault of Bambi Boosh." The stripper stopped her playful act. Her expression became one of genuine concern. "Oh my God! Is she okay?"

"No, but if we find who did this to her, there might be a way to undo what damage was done," I said. "Have any of her customers been acting odd of late? Either regulars or new ones?"

The dancer thought about it. "Nobody I can think of. She was seeing this one married guy, Barney Diamond."

"He was hurt in the same attack," said Mandi. "Is there someone else that you can think of? Anybody or anything out of the ordinary at all?"

"No, I'm sorry. I'd tell you if there was. I could tell you about most of her regulars if that'd help," she said.

I pulled out a pad and pen. "It might." I wrote the names down.

The dancer's face got pale as she looked at something over our shoulders. "Didn't you say Bambi was attacked and hurt?"

"Yes," I said.

The dancer pointed to the stage. "She doesn't look hurt. Hell, she looks great. Looks like she got some liposuction and bigger boobs."

Mandi and I jumped up and had our guns drawn.

"Freeze! Federal agents. Don't move."

Either this really was Bambi and she had a lot of explaining to do, or the criminal fleshsmith had altered herself (or possibly himself) to look like her. Either way, she was going into custody.

We had found her easily enough, but she wasn't going to come along quietly. There was another dancer on the stage, who she quickly got behind and lifted off her feet with a single arm around her waist– seemed impressive for such a petite woman, until I realized that she had probably altered the density of her own muscles to make her stronger and faster than any normal person should be. Her other hand touched the terrified woman's face.

"Come anywhere near me, and I'll fuse her nostrils and her lips shut," said the fleshsmith. "I'm not joking."

With her powers, that was a real threat. "I know you're no joke." I took an intuitive leap. "I saw what you did to your husband and his mistress."

I had definitely hit some buttons. "That cheatin' bastard and his whore got what they deserved."

On some level, I suppose that was true… at least from her point of view. Their bodies were her pain become manifest. Problem was, that pain was going to kill them if Adin wasn't able to save them. There's nothing in the regulations that says you have to be 100% honest with a perp in a standoff situation. "It was impressive. It took the Department of Mystic Affairs fleshsmith more than four hours to get them apart."

The fleshsmith swung the dancer around, squeezing her small waist even tighter. The woman was having trouble breathing. "That's impossible! I mixed their bodies so far together that even I wouldn't be able to undo it."

I shrugged. "Well, no offense, but you may not have the same level of skills as the man the government employs. He's been to medical school. Have you?"

"You mean after all that, they're both fine?" she said between gritted teeth.

Mandi had gotten to the side in an attempt to get a clear shot. Our conversation was keeping the fleshsmith distracted enough that she hadn't noticed yet. "Well, as I understand it, he used some sort of radioactive marker that bonded to the specific blood and tissue types to separate the flesh correctly. There were parts he couldn't get," I lied. "So basically, he had to replace the distal parts. Just means neither one of them has much fat to spare at this point, and I think your husband's private parts may be a little smaller than when he started."

"He's just smaller? Oh, that is so wrong!" said the fleshsmith.

"Be that as it may, if you'll just let the woman go, we need to take you in for some questioning," I said.

The fleshsmith laughed. "You think I'm stupid? You think I'm just gonna let you arrest me? Not a chance. I walk outta here, and this floozy gets to keep her face."

"Taking a hostage out of this building will qualify as kidnapping. The death penalty is still on the books for that," I said. I forgot to mention that using magic to kill also carried the death penalty, but that was a law most people weren't familiar with.

"I have a suggestion. Let the woman go, and take me as a hostage instead," I said.

The fleshsmith laughed. "Why would I want to trade a helpless woman for a trained DMA agent?"

"Well you know how we law enforcement types are with acceptable casualties." That was a lie. I knew of no decent cop anywhere who thinks any loss of any civilian is anything less than a tragedy. However, public perception can be different. "We're a lot more hesitant to risk one of our own." The fleshsmith turned so the woman was between her and Mandi. Apparently, she had been watching out of the corner of her eye. "That makes sense, but not you. Your partner."

Mandi had her gun out in front of her pointed at the fleshsmith. "No problem. Let the woman go and I'm all yours."

"First lose the gun," said the fleshsmith.

Mandi looked at me, put the safety on and tossed me her gun. Putting it on the floor would only invite the hostage taker to pick it up and we have some pretty impressive ammo, which would only strengthen the fleshsmith's position.

"So how are we going to do this?" said Mandi. I could feel the waves of calm she was sending with her propathic powers.

"You put yourself in the same position she's in, in my other arm, and I let her go," said the fleshsmith who looked like the stripper Bambi.

"How do I know you'll let her go once you have me?" asked Mandi.

"I guess you'll just have to trust me." The smile on the fleshsmith's face was less than encouraging, but Mandi did as she asked. As soon as her arm was around my partner's waist, she lifted her off the ground and threw the stripper ten feet. The fleshsmith's free hand pulled up Mandi's blouse from her pants so that the hand that restrained her was able to touch the bare skin on my partner's abdomen. I guess her powers wouldn't be able to work through the clothes. Her free hand then came to rest on Mandi's face.

"Now we're just going to walk out of here, and as soon as I'm safe, I'll let her go," said the fleshsmith.

"There's not a chance in hell that's how this is going down," said Mandi, using her emotional powers to try to scare the fleshsmith. It was having a limited effect. "Let go of me, lay down on the floor with your hands behind your head, and you get out of this without being hurt."

The fleshsmith's power pulsed and sealed both of Mandi's nostrils. "I don't think you're in any position to be giving orders Agent."

"You're not leaving. That's non-negotiable," said Mandi with a nasally tone. "Karver, you let her get away and I will never forgive you."

My partner wasn't bluffing, to either of us. Since I wasn't about to alienate the only person I could let down my guard around, I started narrowing my options down to what I would actually do.

"When my partner has made up her mind, that's all there is to it. I'm afraid I'm not going to be able to let you go," I said, lifting up my gun.

The fleshsmith shook her head and let out a raspy laugh. The power surged again, and Mandi's mouth sealed seamless. My partner was moments away from suffocation. At least I saw her take a deep breath when she felt the power surging. That gave her a couple extra seconds.

The fleshsmith rushed towards the stripper she had thrown a minute ago, who hadn't had the sense to get up and run. I shot the perp in the shoulder. It barely slowed her down. She put one hand on the wound. The bullet was pushed out, and it started mending instantly.

I leapt on the stage, running to intercept her. She may have altered her flesh to make her faster than normal, but unluckily for me, the demon that had possessed me had done similar things to my body. Even so, she was going to get to the girl an instant before I was, and I could already feel the power surging in her hands. I couldn't let her harm an innocent. With my free hand, I reached back underneath my suit jacket and pulled out one of a pair of very special knives, about the size of a short sword or machete. I jumped, swinging my blade. I sliced off her right hand above the wrist. It was a clean cut, and bled terribly. She grabbed it with her left hand and started healing the flesh. I could see the palm starting to grow back already.

"Stop," I ordered. Her hands were the same as deadly weapons. As long as she had one, she could hurt somebody else, and if she managed to grow back the other, we'd be back at square one. "Lie down and put your hand behind your head, or I'll slice it off."

"You're a Fed. That would be police brutality," said the fleshsmith, her thumb and the stubs of her other fingers were already back.

"Last chance."

She raised the middle finger of her injured hand, which was already half-way restored, and pointed it at me. I cut it off again, and the other one for good measure. Then I cuffed her wrists to one of the poles on the stage. Normal handcuffs would slide right off. But with the runes that were on the DMA cuffs, they wouldn't go anywhere, and they'd act as a tourniquet for her wounds.

I rushed back to Mandi. She was already a deep red. There was no sign of lips, although the nostrils were still recognizable. I took my other blade out from behind my jacket and held the point up to her face.

"Don't move," I said. With the surgical precision that only an ex-demon-possessed serial killer could have, I sliced two nostril holes where the other ones had been. These bled profusely, but that was dealt with easily enough. I took Mandi's cuffs off her waist and looped them around her nose. The bleeding stopped. It would stay that way as long as the cuffs were on.

I needed help to make sure she stayed okay. Time to call in backup. I took out my cell phone and hit speed dial one. A small purple dinosaur head appeared on my phone's screen.

It was the agent known as the World Wide Spyder. "Karver, what's up?"

"Mandi's been hurt by a fleshsmith, Her face is sealed up. I've got her enough air to breathe, but I need Adin here now to fix her." The purple dinosaur head morphed into the Spyder's real face, something he rarely did, as he was always too busy playing games on the web. As an electronic entity, it wasn't that hard. "He'll be there as soon as he can. Tell Mandi to hold on." I turned the phone screen toward Mandi; she nodded and gave Spyder a thumbs up. It's easy enough to forget that the kid was really just a teenager. Even though we dealt with death and darkness all the time, it's different when it's one of your own.

I may not have liked the guy, but Adin was there in less than fifteen minutes. The DMA takes care of our own. Adin rushed in and ran to where we were on the stage. This caused the fleshsmith who I had cuffed to a pole on the opposite side of the stage to scream about the injustice of having her hands cut off while Mandi only had a couple of holes closed.

"If you like, I can close your holes and see how much you enjoy it," said Adin. The perp fleshsmith shut up.

Adin put his hands on her face and did a quick assessment. "Karver, you did a nice job. The cuts are clean and in the right places. I'll be able to fix the nose easy." He slid the handcuffs off, and the nostrils weaved themselves back together. Not a single drop of red stuff fell. Next, a hole where her mouth should have been opened. Mandi sucked in large amounts of air.

"Mandi, give me your badge," said Adin. He must have seen the odd look I was giving him. "This way I can get her lips to look the same way they did before. Memory's only so good. Unless you'd want some cosmetic changes made?"

"No, the way they were is fine," slurred Mandi. A moment later, you wouldn't have been able to tell that her face had ever been anything other than normal.

"Thank you," said Mandi.

"It was my pleasure," said Adin.

"How are Diamond and Boosh doing?" asked Mandi.

Adin's face dropped. "I was able to get them separated, but it wasn't good. Bambi died. She had asthma, and her system couldn't handle it. Diamond is stable, but he's missing a lot of his pelvis and everything below his elbows. It'll be a matter of time before we find out whether or not he'll survive. He's getting a full transfusion as we speak."

The fleshsmith chained to the pole laughed. "I knew it. The bastard deserves everything he gets for cheating on me."

"What about the woman? She never did anything to you," said Adin.

"She's no innocent. She's the slut who slept with my husband. She deserved what she got."

"So you have no regrets about what you did to both of them?" said Adin.

"None."

Adin smiled and revealed a tape recorder. "That's too bad, but you're going down for what you did." Adin looked at me. "I hope you read her her rights."

I nodded. I did it while we were waiting for him.

I motioned Adin aside. "That was nice work you did there."

Adin gave half a shrug. "It's bad enough what she did to those people, but don't mess with one of the DMA and expect to get away with it."

"Agreed, but that wasn't the only part I was referring to. Thank you for fixing Mandi," I said.

"Karver, you're the one who saved her. All I did was fix the damage the perp did." Adin got a glint in his eye, and grinned every bit of his thousand-watt smile. "Does this mean you'll shake my hand now?"

Adin extended his hand to me.

"Sure." I took it, but I slipped one of my cleaned blades out of the sheath and let it dangle obviously by my side. "Good advice from you about how to take care of a fleshsmith. Cutting off her hands worked great. Now I can take care of any fleshsmith who tries to attack me."

To his credit, Adin chuckled and let go of my hand. "Good. I'll take her in for you guys if you like."

"You sure?" I asked. Paperwork is major on something like this. I'd still have a ton to explain why I decided to perform amputations on a perp.

"Yeah. Give Mandi a little time to collect herself," said Adin. He took her away.

"You okay, partner?" I asked.

Mandi nodded. "I will be. I appreciate the surgery, Karver."

"No problem. To be honest, I think I'm going to miss having you like that. I don't think I've ever seen you be quiet that long," I said, smiling.

"Well, it's not like you can hold up your end of an intelligent conversation," she countered.

"So, you still want that lap dance?" I asked.

"Only if you're the one giving it," Mandi countered. "And I can find a video camera to immortalize you in a g-string."

"Give me the forty bucks," I said.

"For you? I was thinking of digging around for some spare change, and even then, I'm probably overpaying."

"Forget it, then. I have some pride," I said.

"Since when?" asked Mandi.

"Since I got you as a partner," I said.

"No fair. You cheated by being nice," said Mandi.

"Then you can make it up to me by giving me a lap dance. I know you have some experience, but do you think you'll be able to do it without an entire group to perform for?" I teased.

"I guess that's something you'll never know," said Mandi.

"I'll add it to the list."

NEMESIS & CO. :
EQUAL RITES

Amed Shihadid awoke just before sunrise, his day's itinerary already running through his head. His ministry position in the Iranian government had been good to him. There was the prestige, the money, but by far the best benefit of the job was the power. Amed had some control over how things worked, and he was even able to help fix things when they didn't work right.

Life was good. Still, in that state nestled between sleep and wakefulness, he stumbled into his bathroom, intent on relieving the pressure of his bladder. When he reached to urinate in the traditional manner of men, he quickly realized something vital and dear to him was missing. Amed screamed and looked down. He screamed again, and he was greeted by two large breasts that were blocking the view. Not that Amed didn't like breasts. In fact, quite the opposite was true. He was quite fond of them. It was just a shock to find himself sporting a pair.

"Merciful Allah!"

Amed quickly rushed to the mirror and took in his reflection. He could not believe his eyes, but he had to believe his hands as they wandered over the dangerous curves his body had suddenly taken on. He had gone to bed a man, but somehow awoken as a woman. Terror slowly wormed its way into his soul.

It wasn't that Amed had anything against women. As he would be quick to point out, his mother was a woman, and so were his wives and daughters. Current evidence to the contrary, Amed knew he was not one. He would have never risen to his current position if he was. Despite several recent so-called reforms, women were third-class citizens at best. As a woman, his career would be over.

Frantic, he considered disguising himself, but it was hopeless. His hair was now down past his shoulders, but that could be fixed easily enough with a razor. Amed's beard was gone, and he had no idea if he would ever be able to grow one again. A false mustache and whiskers would only help so much. His face was softer, but appeared similar to the way it had before. The lack of his organs of manhood could be hidden as well, but those damn breasts would be impossible to cover.

There was a knock, and the door to his personal bedroom began to open. Amed couldn't be seen like this, especially by his wives. They might begin to think they were equal somehow. Amed rushed forward and slammed the door, almost crushing his wife's fingers between the wood and the jamb.

"Amed? What is wrong? I have your breakfast," said a soprano voice outside.

"Nothing. I just don't feel well. Leave the breakfast outside the door," he answered in an alto tone of his own.

"Amed, you don't sound well. Your voice sounds higher. Are you alone in there?"

"Yes, yes, I'm fine and alone I tell you," he said, making a conscious effort to lower his tone. "Please call the ministry and tell them that I will be working at home today and will not be able to make it into the office."

His wife agreed to do as he asked, and then left. Amed collapsed his female form against the door in nervous relief.

"You shouldn't have lied to her about being alone in here, Amed. Marriage should be built on trust."

Amed's head shot up at the sudden vocal intrusion into his frantic thoughts. Behind him was a woman, dressed scandalously in western attire—black boots, blue jeans, and a purple t-shirt which was actually low enough to show some of her cleavage. On top of it all, she wore a black trench coat. Raven hair cascaded below her shoulders. The woman sat slouched back in a chair with her legs crossed, draped in shadow. Her attitude was casual, as if she belonged in this place. She spoke flawless Farsi.

"What are you doing? How dare you intrude into my personal quarters? I demand you leave at once."

The raven-haired beauty shrugged her shoulders. "Fine, but you'll never find out why you've gotten more in touch with your feminine side then you've ever imagined possible."

The woman got up to leave. Amed rushed over and grabbed the woman's leather coat by the lapels. The woman became still. It wasn't that she simply stopped moving. It was as if she suddenly solidified into a statue and everything around her followed suit, except her eyes. Those eyes bored into Amed's own, and for the first time in his life, he was frightened of a woman. Her eyes broke the stillness by glancing down at Amed's hands. Amed quickly let go of the black leather.

Despite himself, Amed found himself apologizing. Profusely.

"Please, you must tell me why this is happening to me." The woman remained silent. "At least tell me your name."

"I am Nemesis. The reason this has happened to you is simple: it is time for a balancing."

"What are you talking about?"

"Of late, many women in and around Tehran and other cities have been murdered."

Amed chuckled harshly. "Those were not woman, they were prostitutes. And their deaths were not murder."

Nemesis frowned, and Amed took a step back, cowering from that simple act more than he would have had he been facing a half dozen secret police.

Amed felt he had to justify himself to this woman, although woman didn't seem the right term. She was like no other female, in fact, she was like no one he had ever met before. "By the holy teachings, one can not murder one who is a waste of life. A woman who debases herself by becoming a prostitute can be considered nothing but a waste of life."

"You condemn a woman who, in order to survive, turns to something she may find horrible and distasteful. Her greatest crime is wanting to live. But I guess that's why the so-called Serpent's actions have been so popular that no one in your government seems overly concerned with trying to capture this serial killer."

Amed swallowed harder than he liked. "I am not this Serpent."

"No, you're not. He is just the gun, and will be taken care of later. You are the one aiming him."

"I do not know what you are talking about."

They both knew that Amed was lying. With the shock of a hand slap across the face, Amed realized that somehow this Nemesis knew the truth, that he and several of his cronies at the ministry had decided to rid some of Iran of some of its surplus population. They found and easily manipulated a zealot, supplying him with police records, including mug shots of the prostitutes. Their puppet killer would find the women and end their existence. There was no sincere effort underway to stop the killings, except for a lone woman in the legislature demanding something be done.

"No more innocent women will die, strangled by the green scarf of the Serpent."

"If you have him killed, we will simply find another."

Nemesis smiled. At first Amed thought it was a cold, humorless thing, but as he stared at her, he realized there was humor there, of the dark variety. It was as if she was laughing silently at a joke only she knew.

"You are responsible for the deaths of these women." Her eyes dared him to argue the point. Amed's spirit was not up to the challenge.

"Why do they matter to you?"

Nemesis did not explain her own history. Did not explain that, despite having divine power, despite being able to slaughter gods, she had suffered greatly. She didn't even bother to try to explain what the Council of Thrones was, that Death and the Fates themselves sat on the seven seats of the Council, hearing grievances and setting wrongs right. Neither did Nemesis explain that the Serpent's last victim, a devout Muslim, had learned of the Council's existence and had invoked them with her dying words. The invocation was fueled by the lifeblood that was spilled by a small cut made by the strangling scarf. There was no mention made of how her slain spirit pleaded her case and that of the other victims to the Thrones or how the Council listened and answered her pleas by sending their enforcer, Nemesis, to see justice done.

Nemesis clarified none of it. She simply said, "There are those who care. I am one of them, and it is my job to convince you to set right what you put wrong. You personally have supplied files which allowed and encouraged this Serpent to choose his victims. You know who he is, and you will stop him. You have one week."

Surely this woman is mad, thought Amed. She couldn't possibly expect that he would ever entertain doing anything of the sort. Still, he was not foolish enough to say so out loud in her presence.

"You cannot prove any of this."

"I don't need to. The proof of my threat is that you will remain a woman until tomorrow morning, at which point you will awake in your usual body. Use the next week wisely. If this killer has not been brought to human justice, you will face mine."

"What will happen to me?" Amed told himself he really didn't take the threat seriously, but just wanted to know for curiosity's sake. There was a little part in the back of his mind that he was unable to silence; it told him that he was a liar. He ignored it.

"One week from today you will reawaken as a woman. That change will be forever. Then you will reap what you have sown."

A knock again sounded at the door. The feminine Amed walked to the door and said, "What?"

His wife answered. "I called and told them."

"Good. I will be staying in here by myself the entire day. Wake me up tomorrow morning as usual."

"All right. Is there anything you need?"

"No. I'm fine. Now leave me," said the female Amed, turning back to the raven-haired visitor, but Nemesis had gone just as she had come; without a sound, without a trace. All that was left was the shadow over the chair.

Amed decided that he'd been given an unusual, unparalleled opportunity, and spent the rest of his day exploring his new body.

The next morning, Amed awoke as a man. The previous day's events could easily have been dismissed as a dream or a hallucination. Amed didn't. He had had the foresight to use his digital camera to take pictures of himself, and looking at them was the first thing he did upon rising. As he stared at the pictures, he determined that the woman in them was amazing. If it hadn't been him, she was someone he would have gladly bedded, even wedded.

Amed went about his activities as if nothing had happened. He did worry about the woman's threats, but he did not fear them as the little part of the back of his mind warned him he should. In his work with the Serpent, he was doing the will of Allah, therefore he knew Allah would allow no harm to come to him. Of course, he had no reason for this conclusion, other than his own ego and misguided notions of what the divine creator wished of his children. He assumed that the divine would obey his wishes, instead of realizing it should be the opposite.

On the seventh day, Amed woke, curious but unafraid, until he looked in the mirror and saw the beautiful woman staring back at him.

This morning, his first wife did not knock, but merely opened the door with his breakfast on a tray. When she saw the naked woman standing before her, she threw the tray and its contents crashing to the floor. She began to scream as she reached down to pick up the metal tray, and chased the female Amed around the room, pounding on her shoulders and head with the tray.

"Stop it, woman! This is no way to treat your husband."

"How dare you speak of my husband, you harlot! Get out of my house. Get out now!"

Amed realized there was no reasoning with his wife. He had to flee his own home, still not having come to grips that he was now a she. Amed barely even managed to grab a flimsy dressing gown so that he—now she—did not have to run through the streets naked, subject to the penalties that could bring. Amed spent the next month on the streets. Penniless, without a friend in the world that knew her, Amed was faced with some tough decisions. She tried to contact family and friends, but none believed her. Her own iman cast her out as a madwoman. Worse, since Amed the man had vanished and Amed the woman was the last one seen in his quarters she soon found out she was wanted for questioning regarding her own supposed death.

Amed fled to Zahedan, but she knew no one in the smaller city. Without identification, there was no way to be considered for a wife or even get a job. There was also the risk of the police finding her. Her options few, Amed fell into the oldest profession, the one she had condemned the practitioners of as a waste of life. But Amed found that she, too, did not want to die, and would do anything to live, as had so many others before her. She lived in squalor, even suffered the indignity of arrest but had changed so much physically that the police did not even recognize her as a murder suspect from Tehran. After many weeks on the streets—turning tricks in the back alleys of Zahedan—she found himself with a man who looked vaguely familiar, although she would not realize why until it was too late. The man led Amed to a back room in a run-down building, which had little more than a table, a cot, and a single bare light bulb over head. Amed didn't dare complain. She had seen worse in her short time as a woman. Amed did her best to try to ignore what was happening until the transaction was done. The man ordered Amed onto her stomach. There was nothing unusual in the request, and Amed complied. Suddenly a flash of green blurred before her eyes, and a green scarf was around her throat. As the man pulled back, Amed found herself drowning on dry land, unable to breathe. She struggled to the surface to no avail. The serpent was much stronger than Amed's female form. As the world started to go dark, she made one last effort to throw off her attacker. It was more a flail than a punch, and it managed to knock a file to the floor. Amed's head dropped to the side, and she saw police photographs of her first arrest, along with information on how to find her. It was the type of file she was all too familiar with. Before her eyes went forever dark, she made a silent wish and prayer that she had listened to the raven-haired woman. Amed's last thought was that it was unfair that there would be no one avenging her.

The following morning, Amed's superior in the ministry, the man she had taken orders from when still a man, awoke to find that his maleness was gone, replaced by an abundance of womanhood.

The raven-haired beauty visited this next link in the Serpent's chain, hoping he would be more reasonable than the last.

HEXCRAFT:
VAMPIRE UNDER GLASS

I'll admit freely that I'm really a dog person, but there was something about the tomcat that caught my attention. Maybe it was his odd brown color, but more than likely it was the way his feline shape coalesced from a cloud of mist.

Mind you, I was hidden behind a dumpster, doing my best to hold on until the aspirin kicked in to get rid of my curse-over. It's a lot like a hangover, but instead of being caused by alcohol, I get it from using magic. It takes different forms depending on what I do, but it all stems from a curse which gives me pain for any use of magic. It's something I try to keep under wraps, otherwise the bad guys wouldn't be afraid of me, and I'd be much closer to dead. So in the interest of maintaining my rep, I was in that alley leaning against the wall when the cat appeared.

As if becoming solid wasn't impressive enough, the large tomcat walked over to me, put his front paws on my chest, and looked me in the eyes.

"Please help me," he whispered.

This was unusual, even for me, but he had said the magic words. Another effect of the curse prevents me from using magic to interfere in any situation that doesn't directly involve me.

"What do you need?" I asked.

Before he could answer, a voice from above shouted, "I found him." When I looked up, I saw another large tomcat perched on a fire escape. This one was black, and his eyes were glowing red. Both cats had especially pronounced incisors.

The cat on my chest turned back into smoke, unfortunately at the same time I was taking a deep breath. An instant later I retched up everything in my stomach. The smoke rose up above the fire escape and again became a cat. The brown tom dropped on top of the black one, claws and jaws flashing, fighting with all he had. The talking black cat was soon hurt and bleeding. Too bad for brownie that his opponent wasn't alone.

A man in a brown trench coat with a bit of a belly came into the alley. The guy had long, scraggly hair and a beard to match. In his right hand was a containment bottle. They were used to imprison spirits and other things immaterial, such as, I was guessing, a certain transforming cat.

"Get in the bottle," intoned the mage, his tone part of the spell. I read his umbra. The guy was a trapper, a type of mage whose powers lean toward imprisonment. Handy to have around if you are trying to capture a demon or jinn or the like. Nasty if you are on the receiving end.

The brown cat hissed and extended the middle finger of his paw, the claw popped up. He then dropped from the fire escape onto the bearded mage's head and proceeded to scratch the hell out of his face. The man fought back, grabbing him behind his neck, and then pressing a ceremonial looking blade to the tomcat's throat.

I stood unsteadily. "Put the knife down and step away from the cat. There's easier ways to get your favorite Chinese food dish. This is your only warning."

"Take care of him," the bearded mage said. I was hurting enough from the curse-over that I forgot about the black cat, who also could take the form of a vomit-inducing cloud.

I was sick a second time, falling to my knees until I was heaving dry. The black cat then took the shape of a man. When he stood over me in a dark shadow and smiled, I saw the fangs. Great. Another breed of vampyre, and one I know nothing about. I thought I knew all the breeds in New York. You learn something new every day. I just wished for once that what I learned wasn't trying to kill me.

The mage pushed the blade into the brown cat's throat, so the cat turned into a mist to escape the blade. The trapper opened the bottle, and it sucked the mist in until the vamp was gone.

I readied a hand spell. Spells by gesture hurt me more than spoken ones, but I wasn't convinced I could speak without vomit interrupting me. Bad thing to interrupt a spell, and a gesture spell would probably knock me unconscious at this point, but it would be worse to do nothing and let this guy kill me.

As I made ready to fry both of them, the mage spoke. "Norman, leave the homeless man alone and come and get your reward."

I must have been looking bad if he thought I was homeless, but the vamp obeyed and turned his back to me. The vamp leapt into the air, transforming into his black cat form and landing in the bearded mage's outstretched arms. The mage kissed him on the mouth, and the cat licked the man's lips. I was guessing they were close. The mage then pricked an index finger with the knife and offered the digit to the cat. The vamp feline started lapping it up, then began to suck on it like he was nursing. I caught a stray thought that he had taught a god how to do this, to use his blood to control others, but couldn't get any more.

I could feel the pain of the vamp they had trapped in the containment bottle. I had to help him, but when I tried to stand, my knees buckled and I threw up some more. They were walking out of the alley, so I did the only thing I could think of. I snapped a picture with my cell phone.

"Help," I sent mentally. A moment later, two of my roommates were with me, a spirit wolf and a spirit coyote. I knew they would stand watch over me, so I let myself pass out behind the dumpster.

I woke up before sunset, but not by much. I had been left alone, which may in part be due to Mordi and Sly's innate ability to be invisible to the mortal eye unless they willed otherwise. They extended that to hide me. With one on either side, I was functionally invisible.

I got home, showered, and changed. The rest of my horde of roommates fussed over me. I tend to take in strays, but that may be because, in a lot of ways, I'm a stray too. My other two spirit wolves licked my face. Jeeves, a golem who I rescued from slavery, insists on acting the part of butler, despite my telling him he doesn't have to. He considers it his rent. By the time I got into the shower, he had a fresh pair of jeans and my blue bandaged crescent moon t-shirt laid out and ready for me. Bollywog is a pixie who I saved from a vengeful queen of the fairies. She buzzed around like a hummingbird, and I had to insist she not watch over me in the shower. For her, it's a giant peep show.

When I got out, Jeeves had supper ready—soup, iced tea, and brownies. For someone with no taste buds, Jeeves is a great cook. He is also big into the internet and computers. The golem had already printed me ten copies of the picture from my phone.

Now I just had to find the bearded mage and the two vamps. My first stop was Plasma. I figured somebody at the vamp club would have a clue as to the type of vamp I was dealing with, and maybe even know where to find this particular one.

It was a bit after sunset, but well before opening. This time of night was a vamp's morning.

I knocked on the door. Barber opened it, his massive body dwarfing the frame. "Hello, Hex." The bouncer opened the door, and I went in. "What do you need this time?"

"What makes you think I need something?" I asked.

"You're not working tonight." I help out as an extra bouncer when the creatures of the night get extra unruly. The owner and I go way back. "And Layla didn't mention she was expecting you."

I shrugged as Barber shut and locked the door behind me. I showed him the picture. Barber looked at it without saying a word. He wasn't sharing anything without a reason. I decided to give him one.

"The guy with the beard is a trapper. He took a vamp prisoner, but I'm not familiar with the breed."

Barber chuckled. "About time you admitted ignorance about something. You figure Layla or I might know more?"

"Pretty much. They can turn into cats which can go out in sunlight. They can also become a cloud or mist that makes people violently ill. The black cat is working with the trapper."

"Who's the one in the bottle?" asked Barber.

"Jake." Up until he asked his name, I didn't realize I knew it. Being a cursed magí is like that. Sometimes the magic works under the curse's radar and gives me info I'm not consciously aware of. "He's fighting his entrapment. He won't obey the bearded man, and he hasn't been able to break him. I think he may decide to take the bottle and throw it away. It was already done decades ago." The magic again. "He just let him out to see if Jake's spirit had been broken. It hadn't. I have to rescue him."

Barber nodded. "They're Bajang. That breed gets used as a familiar sometimes. Hadn't seen that one since disco was big until a couple of nights ago." Barber's been around over three centuries. "The black cat's named Norman."

"That's what the guy in the beard called him."

"Heard talk behind the velvet rope that he was back in New York with a mage."

"Any idea where?" I asked.

"Layla'd know. She's getting ready for a meeting tomorrow night that Norman set up with some people who wanted to make her a business proposition."

We went into the back office, the one no patrons were allowed in. Incense burned a pleasant lavender scent. Most vamps have a heightened sense of smell, which is not always a good thing. Incense helped drown some of the more unpleasant scents. Barber rapped on the door.

"Come in," she said. She saw me, smiled, and stood to hug me. "What do you need, Hex?"

"Am I that transparent?" I asked.

"At times," she said, motioning me to sit.

I explained the problem. Layla mulled over giving me the information versus what it might cost in business. She made the right decision. She always does.

"I'm supposed to meet with some Stormer high ups. They claim they've figured a way to juice up animal blood so it's more potent that the human variety. It could be worth a fortune and save lots of human lives. They want to test market it here. If it goes well, I get the exclusive distributorship for the tri-state area, they get my endorsement for the rest of the country," said Layla.

"That's troubling. Paddy Moran banned Stormers from New York City." The nationwide gang's Manhattan chapter made the mistake of hurting his adopted kids. Paddy flipped out and tore down a building, then basically exiled them.

"I didn't know that. Moran is one of the last people I'd want to alienate," said Layla, worried. The owner of Bulfinche's Pub not only sat on the biggest concentration of raw power on the continent, but he was a billionaire. Paddy would put everything into saving a single person, but he'd also tear down anyone he thought deserved it. Unlike me, he didn't always give one warning.

"I will not do anything against Moran," said Barber. Paddy had once been a conductor on the Underground Railroad, using Faerie as an in-between route. Barber's human family had been among those the leprechaun saved. Paddy tends to inspire loyalty that lasts a very long time.

"What should I do?" asked Layla.

"Maybe talk to Paddy. If their product is everything they say it is, it could save lives, both human and vampyre. That's something he could get behind. I doubt he'll let the Stormers back in, but he might allow the deliveries," I said.

"I better call him," said Layla.

"Good idea. Now, where can I find Norman?"

"The Stormers are in Jersey City." Layla gave me the address. "But Hex, these guys are serious gangbangers with weapons and at least one vampyre. Even you aren't going alone, are you?"

Layla knew about the curse.

"I'll take Barber if he'll come." The black vamp nodded that he would.

"Fine, but you're leaving me without any muscle bouncing tonight," said Layla. She had a team, but the others were regular-strength vamps, nowhere near Barber's class of power. "If you take him with you, I need a replacement."

I thought about it a moment. My first thought was Hercules, who bounces at

Bulfinche's, but that might expose Layla to problems if she hadn't contacted Paddy about the Stormers first. I needed someone with enough muscle to keep order and who wouldn't be intimidated by bloodsuckers. Two people jumped to mind.

"What if I could get Nemesis or Terrorbelle?" I suggested.

"You could get the enforcer for the Council of Thrones to watch the door at my bar? That would be more intimidating than even you, Hex," said Layla. "Failing that, Terrorbelle would do nicely."

I tried not to be too offended. More people in New York knew who I was, but those who know both of us tend to be more afraid of her. The lady is known as a godkiller, after all. Still, she was a good friend, despite the fact that I had once dated her mother. I like older women, and Nyx predates this universe's emergence. And Nemesis and I owed each other favors.

It was worth a call. I had her direct line. "Nemesis, it's Hex. I was wondering if you or Terrorbelle would do me a favor." I told her what I needed.

"Terrorbelle will do it. What time do you need her?" I told her, mentioned the dress code, and asked her to thank T-Belle for me.

Barber and I made a quick side trip to an Army surplus store a few blocks away, then headed to the PATH. I could have body slid or otherwise teleported us to Jersey City, but I was already hurting from yesterday. Besides, the trapper would probably feel the power surge, and the element of surprise would be lost. So we took the train. There are times people who don't know me will unconsciously or otherwise move to avoid me in a crowded subway. There was nothing subtle about people avoiding Barber. He was more massive than a linebacker and didn't much go out for smiling. Other than me, there was nobody within a seven-foot radius of the vamp. In a crowded train car in New York or Jersey, that is highly unusual.

Once we were in Jersey City, it didn't take long to find where the Stormers were. They tended to take over a business through any means available to them, and some of those they used as meeting places. They weren't as big as the Crips or the Bloods, but it wasn't for lack of trying. They even had a business portfolio, and there was actual talk at one point of them offering an IPO, but nobody could make the legalities work.

This time, they had taken over a tax business to facilitate identity theft, and had trained, well-dressed gang members to do the returns during business hours. We were definitely visiting after hours. I could sense Jake and his bottle had been inside recently. The other vamp, too, but not the trapper. I also sensed the faded presence of a minor god, but I couldn't get a handle on which one, not even which pantheon. Probably the same one the trapper was teaching blood games to.

We'd try subtle first. I knocked on the door, and kept knocking until someone responded.

A teen dressed in shirt and tie answered in a surly tone. "We're closed. Please come back tomorrow."

I wasn't expecting polite.

"We're here to see a man about a cat. He's the one in the bottle with the waggily tail," I said.

The Stormer glared at me and slammed the door. Normally, I would have stuck my foot in to block it, but normally I didn't have Barber.

"That was rather rude," I said.

"Very," agreed Barber.

I tried knocking again, but was ignored. Well, not exactly. Everyone inside was grabbing guns.

"This doesn't seem to be working. I must be knocking wrong. Would you mind giving it a try?" I asked.

Barber, the original strong and silent type, simply nodded and hit the door once with his hand. It splintered into tiny shards. Barber didn't bend or turn as he went through the door, making a wider opening in the process.

I waited outside while the gangbangers emptied about two clips each at Barber. He's the only vamp I've ever met who is actually bulletproof. Barber's a first generation vamp, having ticked off the son of Adam himself. He doesn't have a breed named after him because, as far as I know, he's never turned anyone.

"Anyone who fires another shot will piss me off," said Barber. He lifted a desk and crushed it accordion style to accentuate his point. Guns hit the floor as fast as gravity could slam them down.

I walked in. The entire office was covered in bullet holes, glass was shattered, and sheetrock was turned to powder.

"Love what you've done with the place. Very gangsta chic," I said.

"We know who the big guy is. Who the hell are you?" demanded a gangbanger in a suit. He actually wore a nametag that said his name was Gary.

"Well, Gary, the name is Hex," I said. "Mr. Hex to you."

"I've heard of you. Now leave. The two of you are trespassing on private property. Get out before I call the cops," said Gary.

"Yeah, right, because concerned citizens always open fire with automatic weapons first, then call the police. I'm sure Jersey City PD will love just how many bullets are in these walls. Do you actually think they won't assume there is a dead body because of all the shots? I imagine they'll be going over the entire building with a fine tooth forensic comb. They find one drop of blood and they will be DNA testing it to every unsolved murder and missing person case in the tri-state area. I wonder if they'd find any blood?"

I had meant it as a rhetorical question, but Barber sniffed the air. "They will."

"Then what do you want? I thought the Stormers were going to be working with Plasma to move some choice hemo," said Gary.

"That was before we found out that you were banned from the city by Padraic Moran," said Barber. Gary looked sheepish, and I got a vision from his past. "Not that any of you necessarily were involved." Barber was being diplomatic, in hopes of not blowing the blood deal for Layla.

"Gary here was, although he went by Turk at the time. Very into ballet, apparently," I said. Paddy and the rest had dressed Turk up in a pink tutu before they tore down his building. There were some chuckles from Stormers who caught my reference. Turk glared at me, murder in his eyes. "So he knew and didn't care. Either very brave or very stupid. Guess which one I'm betting on?"

"What do you want?" asked Gary.

"Norman and the vampyre in the bottle," I said.

Gary narrowed his eyes when he glared at me. "Why?"

"Because he's being held prisoner against his will," I said.

"That's it?"

"That's it," I said.

"I tell you where to find him and you walk away?" asked the tax preparer formerly known as Turk.

"If you mean will I tear this building down on top of your head—not unless you lie to me or otherwise screw me over," I said.

Turk looked at Barber. "Could he do that?"

Barber nodded.

Gary the Turk wrote down an address and handed it to me. "They're there."

"Thank you. Was that so hard?"

Turk's parting words where impressively vulgar.

"If you think we're still doing business with Plasma, you've got another think coming," yelled Turk to our backs.

Barber turned and walked to within three inches of Turk, who cowered into the wall. "That is too bad. I was going to approach Mr. Moran and try to broker his blessing on this deal. Since there is no deal, I will simply tell him that Stormers were in New York."

"I'll call and tell Daks you're coming," said Turk. Daks must be the trapper's name. Barber shrugged, pulled out his cell phone, and did just what he said. So did Turk.

When Barber hung up, he smiled. "I'd advise you to vacate the building."

"They're in Manhattan. Even without traffic, it'll be a half hour before—"

Which is when Hercules came through the roof like a cannonball, his lion-skin trench coat wrapped around him. When I say cannonball, I mean both the metal ball and the type people do off a diving board. It was especially impressive when you realize we were in a five story building. Hermes had obviously dropped him from way up.

The Stormers went for their guns on the floor, but they had already vanished courtesy of Hermes.

Paddy walked in the front door like he owned the place. "Hello, Turk. A pity we have to meet again. This time it won't go so easily for you." The white-haired man turned to us. "Thank you for the tip, Barber."

Barber nodded. "Layla's fine?"

"She'd be regardless. She wasn't aware, nor were you." Oh boy, these guys were in trouble. Paddy only loses his brogue when he's royally pissed. "Hex, do you need any help?"

"I have Barber."

Paddy smiled, and turned his attention back to Turk, who was now in a pink tutu without a leotard; he was apparently cold, scared, or both. Dion and Demeter were watching the exits as we left. We exchanged pleasant nods all around.

"This Daks knows we're coming now. Mind if I body slide us there?" I asked. The Stormers were being piled naked outside the building, and I could hear it rumbling at its foundations.

Barber nodded his assent. As I aimed us, I heard the building crumble, and turned just in time to see the roof settle on the rest of the rubble.

I phased us out of sync with existence for a moment and used the available forces—gravity, momentum from the Earth's rotation, revolution around the sun, and so forth—to shoot us sideways across reality. We ended up in Daks' living room. Alone, I would have landed outside—body sliding always takes me a few moments to recover—but Barber was fine. Norman attacked, and Barber laid him out with a single punch.

Unfortunately, I was a little slower. Daks was indeed the mage with the beard. He was holding a containment bottle and chanting. Before I could mount a defense, I was sucked in, and my world went black. I barely had enough time to concentrate to keep my body's molecules together. Normally, that particular spell would kill a human, leaving only the spirit trapped in the bottle to do Daks' bidding. Of course, staying trapped forever was also an option.

I couldn't figure a way out. I couldn't even feel my body, see, or hear. It was total sensory deprivation.

I had no idea how long I had been in there when I heard a blessed pop and my spell to manage my body unwound. Suddenly I was standing back in the room, the containment bottle at my feet.

Barber had obviously opened the bottle, but the trapper managed to catch him in a spell circle, one of many he must have lined the floor of the apartment with.

"Freeze," I ordered.

"What do you want, Hex?" asked Daks. As his jaw was unable to move, the words came out slow and stunted.

"I'm here for Jake," I said. I focused on the spell circle around the vamp bouncer. It was a basic model, easily broken so I intoned, "Open."

Barber was free again. "Thanks."

"Just returning the favor, big guy," I said. I might never have gotten out of that bottle by myself, which made me wonder, "Why didn't he suck you in?"

"He tried. Didn't work. I don't move unless I want to," said Barber. I was impressed.

Daks apparently less so. "How do you even know about Jake? He's been in a bottle for decades."

"Hex is the homeless guy you wouldn't let me finish off," said Norman bitterly, rubbing his jaw where Barber had slugged him.

Daks did a double take. "Hex is homeless?"

"I partied too much, and was trying to sleep it off," I lied. Had to cover up the curse.

Norman shifted into mist form, and headed toward me by way of Barber. He wasn't real bright. Vamps don't need to breathe, so Barber stopped, and the mist named Norman came for me, but this time I was ready. It wasn't even going to take magic. I put on the gas mask I had picked up in the army surplus store.

"Nice try," I said. The cloud pooled above me, and Norman solidified into his black cat form, intending to drop on my head. I whipped up my trench coat, slipping out of it as I caught the vampire cat in it like a sack. I proceeded to smash the cat in the coat against the floor several times, then gave the package to Barber to hold, but not before getting in the last word: "Bad kitty."

Now I turned to the frozen trapper. "Where's Jake?"

"I'm not going to tell you. And even if you do find him, you'll never be able to free him."

"Yada yada yada," I said. Magí are more powerful than the average mage. We can work any kind of magic; it's just a matter of knowing how, which isn't as easy as it sounds. Containment bottles are easy, however. Daks was still ranting about how we could never undo his mighty magics, blah, blah. I wanted him to shut up, but didn't want to waste magic on it. The immobilization spell was already making me stiff, as if I had worked out for two hours straight. The guy actually had doilies on his coffee table, so I picked up the biggest one, crumpled it into a ball, and shoved it into his mouth. Without the use of his face muscles, he couldn't spit it out.

Now it was just a matter of sniffing out where he had put the bottle. Daks was good. I went over the apartment three times and didn't find a thing. Either Jake's bottle wasn't here, or I was slipping. Asking Daks anything was going to affect my bargaining strength, although I could have Barber beat it out of him. I didn't want to do that either. Believe it or not, Barber was a rather gentle soul.

I was stumped, and about to break down, when I saw a single key on a ring in the middle of the kitchen table, the kind used in a bicycle lock. And then it came to me.

"Barber, watch them," I said, and headed out into the hall. I stopped an older woman who was carrying laundry. "Excuse me, where is the building storage area?"

"In the basement, next to the laundry room." She gave me an odd look, because I hadn't taken off the gas mask.

"Thanks," I said, running down the hall and taking the mask off. I passed the stairs and had to backtrack, which got me a stare from the woman. I went down the four flights in hopes the exercise would loosen me up a bit. It didn't, so I popped more aspirin.

I found the storage room easily enough. The woman with the laundry came out of the elevator and watched me strangely as I struggled with the outer door. The key didn't fit, so I had to force it. The building supplied a storage area a little bigger than a walk-in closet for each apartment. The woman followed me in and watched as I tried the key in each of the locks. It opened the fifth one.

"You don't live in this building, do you?" she asked.

I opened the door and went in. "Just visiting."

"You're stealing something, aren't you?" she said from outside.

"What makes you think that?" I said and again someone answered my rhetorical question, only this time in great detail about my suspicious behavior. I ignored her because I found the containment bottle. It was on a shelf next to some old porn.

A lot of power goes into making a containment bottle, but it doesn't take a whole lot to undo one. Either opening or smashing it will do the trick. Of course, sometimes they are booby-trapped to discourage that kind of thing. As near as I could tell, this one wasn't.

If I just opened it, it could be reused, so I smashed the thing. Jake came out as smoke, then solidified into a man lying on the floor. He wore baggy pants, white shirt, suspenders, and an old style cap. He got himself to his feet, looking around.

"How long has it been this time?" he whispered.

"Less than a day, Jake," I said.

"How do you know my name?" he asked.

"Long story. I'm Hex."

"I know you. You were the bum in the alley I asked for help."

"Did I really look that bad?" I had about a week's worth of face stubble. Maybe it was time to shave.

"I don't know how you did it, but thanks," said Jake, shaking my hand.

"My pleasure, and the fun's not over yet," I said.

The woman with laundry was now banging on the storage door. "I have my cell phone out. I have the super on speed dial. That area belongs to Mr. Daks in 3B. It's a great apartment, one of the nicest in the building, but you don't live there. You better come out, or I'll call the super and the police."

I rolled my eyes. "Jake, I'll explain everything, but first, would you do me a favor?"

"You just freed me. What do you need?"

"Turn into a cat and follow my lead," I said. Jake did as I requested, and I picked him up and stepped out.

"Ah, a kitty!" said the woman reaching out to pet Jake, who cringed back.

"He's shy around new people," I said. "Daks couldn't find him, then realized he must have been locked in here earlier."

The woman gave me a beady eyed look. I guessed she was the busybody of the building and knew everyone's business better than they did. "Mr. Daks has a black cat."

"He adopted this one from the shelter last week," I said. "And he's been cooped up for a while. I'm going to take him upstairs and feed him. Bye." I ran into the stairwell, not waiting for a reply.

On the first floor landing, Jake became a man again and ran alongside me. I explained what I could. When we got to the apartment, I introduced him to Barber. Seems Jake had been trapped during the Kennedy administration by Daks' uncle, who couldn't control him enough to have him kill on command. Norman had turned him into a vamp against his will, as a toy for the adolescent Daks to play with. The family had used Bajang for generations, but they couldn't control Jake. Daks had put the bottle away and forgot about it until recently, when he tried to break Jake again. Jake wasn't any more amenable after over four decades in a bottle, but managed to escape briefly.

Jake was angry, and moved to hit Daks. Then he stopped. "He can't move at all?"

"Nope," I said.

"Hitting him doesn't seem right," he said.

"He stole your life, had you turned into a vampyre, and locked you in a bottle," I said.

"When you put it that way…" Jake kneed him in the groin. Even the doily in his mouth wasn't enough to muffle Daks' scream.

"That's it?" I asked.

"Ain't right to do anymore with him unable to defend himself. Now, if you'd like to free him or wake up Norman…" Jake smiled and cracked his knuckles.

I shook my head at Jake's suggestion. "Not a great idea. But I do have one I think you'll like." I lifted the containment bottle Daks had used on me. Jake took one look and dove behind the couch. "Jake, this isn't for you." I reset the bottle with a chant of my own, paying for it with a splitting headache. "It's primed and ready to be used on anybody."

Jake came out smiling. "Even them?"

"Yep," I said. "Mind you, it might kill them."

"Could it have killed me?" he asked.

"Yes," I said. If he hadn't been in mist form or tried to change to escape.

"Seems a fair risk and solution. An eye for an eye, an eternity in darkness for an eternity in darkness. How does it work?" asked Jake.

"Pull the stopper, point the open end, and it'll suck anyone in."

Jake picked up the unconscious black cat and laid it out on Daks' immobile arm, then flicked the cat's ear with his finger. "Wake up, Norman. You don't want to miss this."

The black cat opened one eye. Before the second one was open, Norman was racing away, but Jake had already opened the bottle, and the trapper's own magic pulled them in.

"Put the top on quick," I said.

Jake did. "What do I do with the bottle?"

"Your call," I said. "But if you break it, they'll get out."

"I'll have to think about it. I'm also going to have to figure out a place to live, and some way to make a living. During my short-lived freedom, I figured out that I've been gone for a while."

"I can help with the living arrangements. I own a building, and I have a few empty apartments."

"Really?" he asked, shock and gratitude seeping from his tone.

"Sure. I already have a graveyard angel and the former empress of the world living there. Why not a vampyre? You're probably going to get along well with Peaches. She's the empresses' cat."

"Empress of the world? No more USA?" Jake asked.

"Not exactly. It's a long story."

Barber chimed in. "Think you can bounce?"

"Like at a bar? Sure."

"We'll ask Layla if she'll hire you," said Barber. What he didn't mention was that, if he was recommending someone, they pretty much had the job.

"So it's your first night as a free man." Or vamp, depending on your viewpoint. "What are you going to do?"

His face got real sad. "I'd like to find my Ma if she's still alive. And look up my girl, but she probably moved on. Might even be a grandma by now."

It might take magic, so I couldn't offer to help without being limited to mundane means. Hopefully, he'd think to ask.

"I'm going to go home and get some sleep. Pack some things, and I'll take you to your new place," I said.

"Pack what? All I got is the clothes on my back," said Jake.

"Go through Daks' stuff and take what you want. He won't be needing it, and it's the least he owes you," I said.

Jake packed up a bunch of stuff, then stood in front of the big screen, flat panel TV. "What's this? A way to talk to spaceships?"

"Nope. That's a television." I turned it on, including the sound system. Jake was dumfounded. "Want it?"

"Oh yeah." He was grinning ear to ear.

When we had everything together, Jake looked around. "How are we going to move all this stuff?"

I picked up Daks' keys. "Take his car. I can forge his signature on a bill of sale."

"I think my driver's license is expired."

"Layla can help with that," said Barber.

As we were loading the car, the nosy neighbor watched us the entire time. She finally came downstairs as Barber was finishing tying some furniture on the roof.

"Where's Mr. Daks and his roommate, Norman?" she demanded.

"Can you keep a secret?" I asked, knowing full well she couldn't.

"Absolutely."

"Turns out they were terrorists. They've been sent down to Guantanamo Bay for questioning," I said.

"They didn't look Arab," she said.

"You think only Arabs are terrorists? These two are the ones that knocked down that building in Jersey City," I said.

"I saw that on the news. They said it was a gas main leak," she said.

I leaned in to whisper. "That's the cover story, of course. Not that I could ever confirm what I'm telling you, you understand, but you look like a loyal and trustworthy American citizen who'd never leak a word of this."

"Of course. I won't tell a soul."

She had called into a talk radio show before we even got Jake to his new home.

TERRORBELLE:
OPEN DOOR POLICY

It's nights like this that make me want to ask my boss for a written job description. I'm pretty certain that it wouldn't list filling in as a bouncer for a Goth vamp club as a favor from my boss to the magi Hex.

Nemesis could have asked Rudy, but no she came to me. Rudy is the daughter of Thor and more than capable to work the door at Plasma. Rudy is even stronger than me, although she's not half the fighter I am. She's only played at soldier. I've been the real thing during my time as a Daemor in Faerie. This was a grunt job, which meant Nemesis wouldn't bother with it. Gani can handle herself in a fight, but sometimes magic's only so good up close and personal. That left Rudy and me. Nemesis knows the valkyrie princess doesn't like getting her hands dirty, so does she even ask her? Nope, she goes straight to Terrorbelle without a second thought.

It really bugs me. Did Nemesis ever even bother to consider that I might have plans? It didn't matter that I didn't. It's the principle.

I don't even like being around vampyres. By nature they're all predators, even if some of them fight it. Being in a Manhattan club full of them was like being back on the battlefield—no way to relax, always assuming an attack was coming from somewhere and trying to spot it before it guts you.

I took up my spot at the door, getting ready to open it.

"Terrorbelle, I appreciate your help filling in," said Layla. The owner of Plasma was tall, thin and beautiful, the exact opposite of me. Well, I was tall and built like a brick outhouse, but it was an oversized building. My mama was an ogre and there is only so much my daddy's pixie blood could do to counteract those genes. "Is there anything you need?"

"I'm good," I said.

"That's what Hex tells me." Nice to know the magí speaks well of me. "We don't always have problems here, but when we do, the blood really hits the fan. Usually, just the presence of Barber is enough to keep the riff raff at bay." Barber was a big, black vamp that made me look tiny, although he leaned toward the quiet side. "I call in Hex when a situation looks like it may spin out of control. Since he's the one who commandeered my head bouncer I insisted he get someone to fill it. He suggested Nemesis or you would be the best candidates for the job. I guess Nemesis was busy." Layla's smile let me know she didn't think the enforcer for the Council of Thrones was all that busy tonight either.

"I guess." I was surprised that I was personally requested for this job. True, I was the second choice after my boss, but that's pretty standard. "What do I need to know about working the door?"

"We have a strict dress code." Layla smiled as she looked at my outfit. Hex had mentioned that I should dress to impress. I wore form fitting black pants and shirt with neon pink trim, belt and holster. I topped it all off with a bright fuchsia trench coat. "We get a lot of black, not much hot pink. You'll stand out."

"I will anyway," I said. My shoulders would give a linebacker pause, but my bras have to be specially reinforced to do their jobs. My chest is the part of my anatomy people notice most, at least without the trench coat.

"It's not a bad thing. You have a unique look and a pleasing face," said Layla. I nodded to acknowledge the compliment. People always feel the need to point out how attractive ugly people are. I don't buy it from any of them, except maybe Murphy. Sadly, I'd probably buy two of anything he was selling. "Please feel free to hand the coat in the check room."

"It helps cover a few things," I said.

"No one will mind the wings here. Moni comes in often with hers unhidden," said Layla. I didn't bother to point out that the graveyard angel had beautiful black angelic wings. Mine were pixie shaped, but razor sharp and harder than steel. "Thanks, but it'll be too easy to slice someone accidentally and I get the impression that fresh blood will make my night much more difficult."

Layla laughed. "It might."

"Plus, I'd have to find another place to put my gun."

"Whatever makes you happy. The bouncer at the door sets the mood for the place. Vampyres get highest priority. Best dressed are the first in the door. That holds for both vampyres and humans. People will try to tell you anything to not have to wait in line. They will say that I said to let them in or that Barber always does." Layla handed me a small walkie-talkie and a clipboard. "If there is any question about my blessing on a customer not on that list, call. If they are lying, they don't get in. Period. Barber is not here tonight, so it's your call. I will back your play. If a vampyre looks ragged or hungry, screw the dress code. Call me and I will bring them in and make sure they get fed."

Normally that statement would trouble me, but Layla has turned bloodletting into a business. She gets the Goths, college kids, and other assorted oddballs to donate or sell their blood. She in turn sells it to the vamps. It saves on a lot of unnecessary attacks and if she happened to make a few bucks in the process, so be it.

"You need anything, you call me," said Layla.

"Will do," I said, opening the door and taking my place as the guardian of the crimson velvet rope. There was already a line about forty feet long. I had no special ability to tell a vamp from a human, but it was pretty obvious in a lot of cases who was the real deal and who were the wannabes.

One genuine vamp pushed his way to the front of the line, decked out in a black silk suit with a pair of shoes that cost more than a month's rent on my apartment. He had a human woman on each arm, a blond and a brunette. Each had large enough saline implants to raise the water at the South Street Seaport to flood levels. Sadly, they each sported bejeweled chokers, undoubtedly covering matching blood hickeys. This vamp expected to just walk past me without any problem. My hand on his chest seemed to surprise him a great deal.

"Where do you think you're going?" I said.

"Inside," he said, looking down his nose at me. "I'm expected."

"That's nice," I said, but didn't move out of his way or check the list.

"I'm going in," he said.

"Ah, but you forgot to say May I. You'll have to go to the back of the line," I said.

"Do you know who I am?"

"Nope, but I have a sinking feeling you're about to tell me," I said.

"I am Baron Fields."

"Sorry to hear that. Maybe the harvest will be better for you next year," I said. The blond giggled, not noticing the glare the Baron gave her.

"That is my station."

"Mine's Columbus Circle or sometimes 50th, but a Metrocard ain't getting you past me," I said.

"I will not be treated this way by a human woman!"

"Oh, you think I'm human. How sweet."

Baron Bozo took a mental step back at that one and gave me the once over. All he could tell is I wasn't a bloodsucker. Apparently not being terribly impressed he trudged on. "I'm going in there with my guests. You can either step aside or face my wrath."

I put one hand on my chin as if mulling it over. "I'll go with choice B." Baron Bozo bared his fangs. "I hope you and your wrath have a good dental plan."

Next he made eye contact. Not all vamps have the same abilities, so not all can swing mind control mojo, but Baron was trying without much success. First off, he was gearing it for a human, which I'm not. He probably didn't even know Faerie existed, which is fair because most people didn't believe in vampires. Add to that as a mixed breed, my mind has its own unique qualities. Plus I was wearing my Daemor medallion as a belt buckle. The black raven on a silver circle had several built in charms, including one to make the wearer resistant to mind control. It wasn't total protection, but with a strong will it made it very hard to take over a mind and there aren't any weak-willed Daemor—too hard to get in the all-female fighting force for someone of that mental persuasion.

Still he was trying so hard to impress the ladies that I decided to play along and see where he went with it. I stared glassy eyed out in front of me. Baron Bozo smiled.

If he had just tried to walk past me, I might have been nicer, yelled boo and checked the list. Instead he laid his hands on me, attempting to hurt me. Most vamps were used to superior strength being enough and had no skills in hand-to-hand combat. I grabbed his offending extremity and twisted it behind his back. Lifting him over my head, I heaved him over the waiting people. He landed at the back of the line.

"Wow," said the blonde.

"That was wild," said the brunette.

"It's all in the wrist," I said. Now that Baron Bozo was taken care of, I noticed that the pair of bimbos were staring at my chest. I wasn't sure how to take that.

"You have the most amazing boobs I've ever seen," said the blonde.

"Thanks," I said.

"Who did them? I'm thinking of upgrading again, but that size would make me fall over forward," said the blonde.

"They're natural," I said. Ogre size and pixie tone made them hold their shape pretty well.

"No way! Can I feel them?" asked the blonde, reaching out.

Her friend was doing the same. "Me too."

I caught both of their hands. "Just take my word for it."

"You can feel mine if you want," said the blonde.

"Mine too," said the brunette.

A young man in the line said "All right!"

I looked at him and said, "Shut up." The shouter took a step back and decided looking at his shoes would be a good idea.

At the back of the line, Baron Bozo had stood and dusted himself off. Just when I thought he couldn't annoy me any more, he began motioning to the girls, snapping his fingers like they were a pair of trained cocker spaniels. They sighed, put their heads down and started to go to him.

"You two can do better," I said.

The blonde shrugged. "But vampyre sex is so hot."

Baron Bozo had vamp hearing and practically preened at the words.
"With any vamp?" I asked.

The blonde shrugged. "I'm not sure. Baron is the only one we know."

I looked at him. "And he was that good?"

Both girls looked back at him, then the blonde whispered, "He looked a lot bigger than he felt. And for all those muscles he was kind of soft." Glamours are wonderful things for looking at, but they only go so far when it comes time to get down to business.

"The biting thing was sort of hot, but these hickeys are kind of embarrassing. We're not teenagers anymore."

No, they weren't.

"So if I said you both could go in, you'd rather go to the end to keep him company?" I asked.

"You'd let us in?" they said in unison, smiles showing off all their pretty caps.

I unhooked the end of the rope. "Sure. You want in?"

"Yes!" they shrieked in bimbo unity and rushed inside. I could hear Baron's grumbling as he watched them dump him to get in the club. I smiled and winked at him, then got the line moving.

It wasn't hard. I had to frisk a few people and take away some weapons, even a cross on a gold chain. Inside that piece of jewelry would be a weapon. Everyone then went through a metal detector just to be on the safe side. My sidearm was spelled to not set them off. One of the benefits of working for Nemesis. It also shot mystic ammo. I could control which kind with a thought. It also held the equivalent of more than a dozen normal clips.

Hopefully I wouldn't have to pull it tonight.

Some of the vamps were going to Plasma to fight their addictions. I could respect that. Others were just going because it was a hot club. Layla had rules, which included no fighting inside and no hunting within a three-block radius. With Barber and Hex around it didn't have to get enforced often.

I didn't have to like any of the vamps I let in. I just had to make sure they didn't hurt anyone else, vamp or human.

A little after midnight, five vamps came strolling up the side of the line, dressed in leather pants, with black straps loosely designed to take the place of a shirt. There were four men and one woman, each of them trying to out glamour the next. Even the other vamps in line took second and third takes as they went by. Their mystically enhanced beauty wasn't what had me staring. It was the five humans crawling on all fours, dressed in rags with choker chains around their throats. Back in Faerie, Thandau and others had slaves.

I spent some time in a slave camp. The Daemor fought to free them. When I saw these people, I saw slaves and it made me very angry.

Now all I was going on was my gut reaction, but it rarely steered me wrong. Still, I needed more than just that. A lot of people were into bondage, domination and the like. When they find out vampyres are real, that sort of thing turns a lot of them on. Some of them do it in hopes of one day getting turned themselves. I needed to be sure of their status before I interfered.

They seemed surprised to see me at the door instead of Barber.

"Names?" I said. The vamps told me and they were on the list. "Go on in."

They moved, leading their human pets by the chains.

"Excuse me, but what are their names?" I asked.

"They no longer have any," said the one calling himself Heston, who acted the part of leader. "They are our guests."

"Sorry, there is no plus one on the list," I lied. Heston had a plus one, but none of the others did. "They can't go in."

Heston looked me in the eye, trying to work the same mojo Baron had. Heston was better, trying to feel out my mind and shift his energy accordingly.

"You will let us all pass," he ordered.

I jabbed him in the eyes with two fingers. He yelped and grabbed his face. "No, I won't. If you try that on me again, the next time I poke you and pull away my hand, your eyeballs will be impaled on my fingertips, understood?"

"What are we supposed to do with our… companions?" Heston used the term as if it were a joke.

"Leave them out here," I suggested.

"Very well," he said. The five vamps brought the humans over to a parking meter and fashioned the chains around the metal bars like cowboys leaving horses outside a saloon. "You will all wait here until we return."

There was no answer from the humans, no indication they had heard, but they stayed even after Heston and the other four went inside.

A human girl dressed all in black was the saddest vamp wannabe I had seen all night. She walked past the line and to me at the front. "Hi, I'm Tashana. I'm on the list."

She was, so I frisked her and let her in.

By this time, Baron was halfway to the front. He may have ticked me off, but at least he hadn't mind mojoed either of the bimbos to make them be with him. They were both willing.

"Hey Baron," I said. As near as I could tell, he was the last real vamp in line and I didn't need any vamp looking over my shoulder during what I was about to try. There was a simple way to get rid of him.

"Yes?" he said.

"Go on in," I said, lifting the rope.

Baron brushed past me with a curt nod.

I walked over to the chained people. There were three women and two men. All of them looked almost anorexic, with blood hickeys all over their bodies. I was sick to my stomach. I tried to pull the choker collar off the nearest woman, but she reached up and pulled it back on, whimpering and curling up into a ball. One of the men looked at me and I swore his eyes were begging for help. I moved to remove his collar. He made a token effort to stop me, but I got it off.

I pulled off my Daemor medallion and took the man's hand and wrapped his fingers around it. His body shuddered as its magic broke the mind control link and he fell to his knees.

"Help me," he whispered.

That was enough to prove to me that Heston and company had enslaved these people. I put the medallion back on my belt and pulled out my cell. To call the boss I only needed to push a single button.

"What is it Belle?" asked Nemesis.

"I need you and Gani down here at Plasma now," I said.

Nemesis chuckled. "Can't handle the vampires?"

"I can handle them just fine and I'm about to handle five of them. I need Gani to EVAC five enslaved people and free their minds," I said.

A shadow in the alley twitched and out stepped my boss. Shadow stepping is pretty close to teleporting. Since she knew where I was and had been here before it was easy. Without that, it wouldn't have worked.

"What do you need me for?" asked Nemesis. She was dressed in a low cut purple t-shirt, black leather slacks and a dark as shadow trench coat.

"To make sure none of them sneak out and get away to do it again," I said. Bad vamps are too powerful and dangerous to let live.

My boss nodded. "You worried about offending Layla or Hex?"

"Not terribly. Hex'd do the same thing and Layla said she'd back my call," I said.

"Okay, Nobody gets out," Nemesis said. "You need anything, holler."

"Will do, but I won't," I said.

"You're a little too hard headed sometimes, Belle," said Nemesis.

"One of my best qualities." I banged on my noggin with my knuckles. "When's Gani coming for EVAC?"

"She's bringing the elevator. She'll be inside." Gani had been to Plasma before and it had been fun watching her carve invisible sigils into the wall without anyone noticing.

I turned to the enslaved humans. "Come with me." Only the man who asked for help even tried to move. I shook my head, grabbed their chains and led them inside.

I saw the elevator door materialize on a far wall and made for it. Heston spotted what I was up to and made a beeline for us, but there were a few hundred dancing vamps and humans between us.

I hit the up button, but down would have worked as well.

"Hello, T-Belle. Heard you called for a ride," said Gani. Her snow-white trench coat matched her long hair. White hair tends to make most women look old, but not Gani. She'd pass for a young forty, which is impressive since she wasn't exactly a teenager when she served as a mage in Camelot.

"I did. These five are under vamp mind control." I pointed to the male who had spoken. "Already started undoing it with him using my Daemor badge."

"Any idea what kind of breed of vamp?"

"None. Is it important?" I asked.

"It'd help," said Gani, helping me get the people inside the elevator.

Heston had made it through the crowd and was rushing toward us. I pointed my thumb over my shoulder. "He's one of them."

Gani looked at him and tilted her head while she read their umbras, a fancy term for the shadow of a soul. "Hmm, probably Dubbelsuger. Tend to suck blood and energy from groups. You need any help?"

Gani could probably incinerate the lot with a fireball or lightning, but that wasn't the way this was going to go down. "No thanks, I'm good."

"What do you think you are doing with our chattel?" demanded Heston.

"After I fix them up? By the looks, I'd say hitting the food court," said Gani.

"Come out here!" Heston ordered triggering the mind control. Four of them started to move.

"Be still," ordered Gani. The four froze. While her brother sleeps, she is able to tap into some of his power and Merlin is a magí same as Hex. They are both supposed to be in the same power category. Gani knows more than either of them, which makes her as effective, if not as powerful. The snow-haired mage waved as the doors closed. Heston charged and pounded on them. A few seconds later they glowed and vanished, but Heston was still pounding so hard he put a hole in the wall.

"Don't you hate it when someone won't hold the elevator door for you?" I said.

"You will bring our property back," shouted Heston. The dance floor had pretty much cleared by this point and his four vamp friends had moved in a semi-circle around me.

"Not going to happen," I said.

"Then you will replace them yourself," he said.

"So are all Dubbelsuckers…" I intentionally mispronounced the name assuming Gani had correctly ID'ed the breed. "Delusional or is it just you?"

"You think one lone woman can beat five Dubbelsuger vampyres?"

"You're right. It is unfair. Do you have any other friends who'd be willing to help you out?" I said.

"I'm going to enjoy feeding on you. The things I'm going to make you do will make you beg me to let you meet Death," ranted Heston.

Layla had moved to watch. I looked at her and she nodded. Heston was about to violate both the no fighting and feeding rules. I was doing this anyway, but it was nice to know I had the management's blessing.

I pulled out the two-way radio.

Heston laughed. "So you are calling for help."

"Nope." I pushed the talk button. "Lock this place down." The other bouncers did as instructed.

Heston charged me fangs first. I reached out and pushed him back by his face so hard he landed on his butt ten feet away.

"Wait a second. This coat is silk." Over the armor coating anyway. "Do you know how hard it is to get blood out of silk?"

I slid my coat off and laid it over a nearby chair. Now my wings were revealed and they gleamed in the club lights. I stretched them out to their full size. It felt good after being cooped up for hours.

"What the hell are you?" asked Heston, nervous for the first time.

"Remember when you told me I'd beg you to meet Death? You have it mixed up. You are about to meet the Reaper and I'm going to play matchmaker," I said.

"Big talk for a woman with a gun," said Heston, apparently thinking if I was talking to him, I wouldn't notice the two other vamps sneaking around behind me.

"I won't need it. Trust me."

The two vamps behind me charged. Dumb move. Behind is where I'm most dangerous. I sliced out with my upper wings and both their heads were severed. I reached out and caught them by the hair before they hit the ground.

I held the heads in front on me and spoke to them. "Slaver vamp numbers one and two, meet Death, Death meet slaver vamp numbers one and two." Heston stood his ground, but the other two vamps took a step back. "Come on, people. The Grim Reaper doesn't have all night and neither do I."

The other two attacked me from the sides. They were assuming they were faster than me. They were, but not by much. Luckily they telegraphed their moves and I was able to smash both of them in the temples with the heads I was holding, but dropped them in the process. Blood is very slippery. While they were stunned, I bent over and grabbed each of them by an ankle, inverted and spun them hard and fast. When I stopped I flung them up so their heads smashed together somewhere above me. Luckily, Plasma had high ceilings. I followed this by smashing their heads on the floor, then above me again. I admit I was showing off which was stupid. I also assumed none of the vamps would have any weapons, but I was wrong. I was so concerned about the human slaves that I hadn't personally searched Heston or his friends. Considering his outfit I figured the metal detector would catch any weapons, but they don't work on ceramic guns.

Heston had my head lined up between his sights. I was already moving, both trying to get me out of the way and the vamps in front of me as a shield. Even as I did it, I knew I wasn't going to be fast enough. I hoped he had bad aim or the gun would backfire and blow up in his hand.

Neither happened, but he didn't manage to shoot me thanks to the blonde that had come in with Baron. She smashed a chair over his gun hand and the shot went low into the floor. I spun and my right wing sliced him at the wrist. The hand and gun dropped to the floor.

He started to spout something, but I wasn't in the mood. I sliced the heads off the vamps I was holding, then lifted Heston up and did the same to him.

I picked up the radio and hit talk. "Cleanup." I knew from past experience that the bouncers could dispose of vamp bodies. Part of me wanted to feel worse than I did, but if I let them live they would have only hurt more people. The DMA might have gotten them to trial, but if they had good lawyers they might have gotten off. Vamps live a long time, so even thirty years wouldn't be enough. They'd just get out and do it again. This was the only sensible way.

Layla was annoyed, but she handled things with class, especially after I explained about the slaves. Layla was all about protecting people, both those with and without fangs. I apologized about letting the ceramic gun slip through.

"Don't let it happen again," Layla said.

"Again? You want me to come back?" I said, surprised.

"You did a good job and after tonight, no vamp is going to mess with you. You want an occasional part time job?"

I thought about it. "On one condition."

"Which is?" asked Layla.

"The blonde that helped me out gets put on the A list and doesn't pay for a drink."

"An alcoholic drink. For three months."

"Deal."

I excused myself and went over to talk to the blonde. I realized I didn't even know her name. That was going to change.

"I wanted to thank you," I said.

"No biggie. It was the right thing to do."

"I can't argue with that," I said, extending my hand. "I'm Terrorbelle."

"I'm Sydney."

I told her the deal I worked out with Layla on her behalf and she thanked me. I also handed her my Nemesis & Co. business card with my cell number on it. "You need anything, day or night, call me."

"Wow, thanks," Sydney said and got a big smile. "You know what I'd really like to do?"

"Nope," I said. She reached for my chest. "Oh, no."

"I'm not a lesbian, unless you count that one time in college. I'm just jealous and curious," said Sydney. "Please?"

I sighed. She had saved my life. "Make it very quick."

She was. "They feel even better than they look."

"Thanks, I think," I said.

Sydney opened up her top and revealed a black push up bra. "You want to compare?"

"I'd rather not," I said. Sydney covered up.

"Those wings are awesome. And your arms and abs are unbelievable. You must have a mind-boggling workout program," gushed Sydney.

It was kind of intense. Just the wing hovering alone was exhausting. "You've gotta come clubbing with me some time," said Sydney.

"I'm not really a clubbing kind of gal," I said.

"Come on, just one night," she pleaded. "It'll be fun."

"Maybe," I said. The rest of that night at Plasma was easy.

My night out with Sydney, not so much.

CRIMSON MIDNIGHTS:
EBB AND FLOW

Layla danced among the silver moonbeams that cascaded down on the sleeping city. Every moment was a revel in her ability to still walk the night streets unnoticed, to pass for a human among humans. Just the simple act brought back memories of a more innocent time which, sadly, was gone forever. But if that past hadn't led her to her present, Layla probably wouldn't dare to be out alone on streets so dark and deserted. Without the blood curse that had claimed her, she would have been helpless prey. With it, she was the most dangerous predator on the streets tonight.

The light of the full moon cast an illusion of tranquility. Layla let herself fall under that illusion, basked in it, enjoying her night of freedom. She rarely got any alone time anymore. It was her gift to herself.

The darkness came alive for her, almost knocking Layla down with the beautiful, sweet, sticky scent of fresh blood. Smell lit up her world these days as much as sight ever had, maybe more. Scent bypassed the conscious centers of the brain and traveled beyond to something more primal.

It didn't take her a second to determine the source of the crimson smell. A barely open window, seven floors up. Layla's breed of vampyre was Mora—Mora can't fly, but they can climb—and she scaled the wall in seconds.

The window was tiny, barely big enough for her to squeeze through. The point was moot, as she had not been invited in. The aroma was making her crazed. Riding the night air, alongside the scent, were the soft sounds of music.

The window opened into an immaculate bathroom, aglow in candlelight. To the left side, a man relaxed quite leisurely in a full tub of warm water. In one hand was a lit cigar, the other, a snifter full of brandy. The bottle lay, a third empty, on the side of the tub next to a bloody knife. Twin rivers of red poured out of his open wrists.

Layla made no effort to hide herself. In a moment the man, Jerry by name, noticed her.

"Hello," said the man with a sad smile. If Jerry thought it odd to see a woman's face staring into his bathroom, he kept it to himself.

"Hi," Layla said, letting go of the ledge with one hand so she could wave. "Interesting way to spend the evening."

"There was nothing to watch on TV," Jerry said, barely smiling at his own joke.

"Things will get better," suggested Layla. It was her way to teach that philosophy.

"No, I've seen the new season. It doesn't get any better." He gave a weak laugh.

"I meant life will get better."

"True. In about twenty more minutes, it should be all over with."

"It doesn't have to be."

"I want it to be. Listen, if you're going to be bother me, you might as well come inside."

Layla didn't hesitate to take him up on the invitation, and squeezed her way in, warping the window frame in the process.

"Do you always invite strange women into your bathroom?"

"Do you always hang out outside strange men's windows?"

"Touche. You want to talk about this?" Layla asked, silently cursing herself a moment after the words escaped her lips. That was the old her talking. The new Layla didn't get involved.

"If I wanted to talk, I wouldn't have done this. I would have called a hotline, left a note, told a friend," Jerry explained.

"You have a disease or something?"

"No. I'm in perfect health. You're pretty nosy. You a social worker or something?"

"I was." Layla's voice was tinged with regret. The old her wasn't dead, just half buried in a grave of blood.

"What are you now?"

Layla hesitated for a moment before answering. "A vampyre."

"Yeah, right."

Layla lashed out with her right fist, smashing the toilet tank, then smiling wide to reveal ivory fangs.

"Glad I went before I climbed in here," he chuckled morbidly, sipping the brandy. "I guess you could be a vampyre."

"Thanks for your permission. So what's the deal here? You get dumped?" asked Layla, still unable to leave well enough alone.

"Nope. Have plenty of interested women."

Layla looked his well-muscled body up and down. "I can believe that."

Jerry raised an eyebrow. "You find me attractive?"

"Attractive? Hell, I want to drink your bath water."

Jerry chuckled. "Help yourself. I only brought the one snifter. Use one of the paper cups over the sink. If we get bored you can ask me some of the riddles written on them."

Layla shrugged her shoulders and took a cup. Lifting up Jerry's left arm, she held the hand over the cup and let the blood pour out. "I prefer it from the pump, if you don't mind." Layla was practically drooling.

"Not at all. Help yourself."

Layla filled the cup, then drained it. She went back for a refill, pausing a moment to admire his handiwork. "You did it the right way."

"What?"

"The cutting. Went up and down, as opposed to side to side. You'll bleed better."

"Good. Hate to think I did it wrong. I also took a dozen aspirin to make sure I didn't mess things up by clotting."

"Seems like you thought of everything, except living."

"What do you care?"

"I don't," Layla lied. "But all the same, is there anything I can do to talk you out of this?"

"Nope."

"It's such a waste."

"What? The blood?"

"I meant your life, but the blood's a waste too. What you're throwing away could feed a dozen of my customers. You are wasting a fortune."

"Fortune?"

"I make my living brokering blood. I own a club called Plasma. Caters to the goth crowd. You know the type: dress in black, pretend they're vampyres. I get them to donate blood to my clients, real vampyres. The goths get to hang with the undead, the vamps get to feed, and I make some cash. The donors are never killed. No dead bodies means no hunters or cops seeking revenge. No revenge means those I look after survive to see another sunset."

"Sounds like a sweet arrangement." Jerry reached over with his right hand. "Why don't you try the other side?"

"Thanks."

"Hmm."

"What?" asked Layla.

"Just thinking. A vampyre could do whatever she wants. Who could stop you? You have great freedom."

"Definitely."

"But it comes at a price, I imagine. Do you hunt?"

"For food? Not as such," Layla admitted with embarrassment. Part of her longed for the hunt, the power of predator over prey, but another, slightly stronger part held her back.

"So you haven't become a monster, running wild on the dark side of the night. True?"

"Perhaps," was all Layla said, very uncomfortable with the subject.

Contrary to popular belief, becoming a vampyre does not transform the cursed into an evil, killing machine. The vampyre chooses her path, same as a person. Most take the easy one, caving into the blood lust. Layla found it hard to condemn those who did. The blood lust sometimes seemed overwhelming, but she knew it could be controlled. Layla likened it to a reformed smoker resisting cigarettes, only easier. Layla could still enjoy her addiction, she just did not have to kill for it. It was her choice, and it was not an easy one. Layla had no desire to share that fact, or the fact that she clung to what little humanity remained in her soul with every ounce of strength she had. It was not a thing that a vampyre admitted.

"Of course it's true. Otherwise why bother talking to me? Just drain me and be done with it. Thing is, I think part of you wants to 'save me.' Won't work, though. It's too late. I've lost too much blood."

"Maybe. Maybe not. There is another way to save you." Layla had never turned anyone, but something in this man's eyes tempted her to offer, extending her hand. Jerry slapped it away.

"You mean become a vampyre? Forget about it. I hated the thirty-five years I've already spent on this planet. I ain't going to spend eternity here."

Layla felt a sense a loss, the same loss she felt whenever she lost a client back in her days of humanity. "Are you sure?" Her voice was steady, but her eyes begged with force.

"Absolutely."

"That's it then."

"You're giving up?"

"Back when I was a social worker, we used to say that if someone really wants to kill themselves, there's nothing you can do to stop them. It was true then, it's true now. I can see into your thoughts and dreams. You really want to. I can't stop you, only delay you."

"You are a woman of rare insight." The music stopped. "I knew I should have brought a MP3 player, but I enjoy vinyl. Do me a favor: flip the record over."

"Sure." Layla looked at the record. "Cab Callaway?"

"Great stuff. Love 'Minnie the Moocher.'" Jerry drained his glass. "Love brandy, too. This is the good stuff. Five hundred bucks for this little bottle. The cigar's a Cuban. Money was no object. Figured I might as well go in style."

Jerry's smile was starting to fade, his eyelids flickering as they grew heavy and fell shut.

"Parting is such sweet sorrow," Jerry said in a horrible British accent, projecting weakly towards the ceiling.

"Last chance to back out," offered Layla, in a voice barely louder than a whisper.

Jerry shook his head weakly and whispered, "No."

Jerry opened his eyes for the last time. The end had arrived, and he knew it. He greeted death with a smile. Layla never knew if death smiled back. She felt his spirit leave and, just like that, Jerry was dead. Layla didn't bother to check for a pulse. If there was one thing she knew, she knew dead.

Layla shook her head and again muttered, "What a waste."

Taking the brandy snifter from Jerry's limp left hand, Layla dipped it into the warm, crimson bath water. Raising the full glass she said, "I hope you're in a better place."

Layla drained the glass dry before smashing it against the wall of the tub. With quick, graceful movements of her hands, she closed the dead man's eyes before leaving by the same window she entered.

Layla still spent the rest of the night dancing between moonbeams, but, try as she might, Layla couldn't shake away thoughts of the man who had thrown away what had ripped out her heart to lose.

STORMERS BREWING

As he ran by the young woman, James Pratt's hand snaked out with a razor blade and sliced her face. He concentrated hard to make sure the slashes made the form of a simple lightning bolt. It wasn't because he was worried about what the Stormers watching his initiation would think or say, but if it wasn't a recognizable lifemark, they'd make him do it again. That thought made him sicker to his stomach than he already was.

James was a Department of Mystical Affairs agent, sworn to honor, watch, and defend. Having to harm an innocent had been making him physically sick for days, but there was no way around it, no other way for him to complete his deep-cover assignment to get inside the Stormers. The gang had grown to have chapters not only around the US, but around the world. They dealt in drugs, prostitution, and extortion, which would have normally put them under the jurisdiction of other federal agencies, but they also appeared to be dealing in magic. They were rumored to be juicing up animal blood somehow so that it had the same kick as—or maybe even more than—the human variety. The new designer drug they were distributing was said to have a mystic component, making it the most addictive high on the streets. Most notably in terms of leaving a paper trail, they had been blackmailing small desert towns and communities near harvest time. If the farmers or town halls didn't pay, it didn't rain. If they paid extra, there was enough rain to grow anything they wanted.

The change in weather patterns was playing havoc around the continent. Most people were blaming it on global warming, but the DMA suspected it was something else entirely, which was why they had assigned James Pratt to infiltrate the gang. He was twenty-four, but could pass for sixteen without any help from a fleshsmith. Like many DMA agents, he was a mage—specifically, a bug. His powers had nothing to do with insects. He had the power to pick up conversations, electronic more than normal. As his magic was of the receptive variety, it was hard to detect. Knowing what was being said around him was a huge advantage undercover. It wasn't enough to make arrests, because he couldn't record what he heard, but it was enough to get warrants and, hopefully, keep him safe.

The woman screamed, and then sobbed as the tiny blade sliced through the tender skin on her face. James didn't even stop to inspect his handiwork. He didn't want to see what he had wrought, although he promised himself he'd find out who the woman was, and make sure the DMA fleshsmith took care of the scar.

He disappeared as fast as he could around the corner into an alley.

"Nice job, Bug." As coincidence would have it, he was given the same handle as his mage classification. "I've never seen a nicer bolt from a first timer, except maybe mine," said Stripe, named for the lightning streak of white he dyed into his black hair.

"Thanks. I've been practicing," James said, his nervous relief at being done mixing with his self revulsion to make him say more than he should have.

"On who?" Stripe said with a questioning look.

James tried to look embarrassed. "Watermelon."

"Must be a hell of a lot easier than the real thing," said Stripe.

"No doubt," said James.

"Well, you did it. You in," Stripe said, slapping him on the back.

"'Bout time," said James.

"Don't be getting all uptown on me. You get what you get when you earn it, not before," said Stripe, handing him an envelope. "Here, you earned this."

Confused, James opened it, half expecting to see cash. Inside was a bus ticket to New Mexico. "I'm relocating?"

"Temporarily. You're going to Stormer orientation," said Stripe.

It sounded more like what happened when you got a job with a Fortune 500 company, certainly not what he expected when he joined a gang.

"Orientation? I don't understand," said James.

Stripe laughed. "Stormers are way organized on every level. You gotta be trained. You'll start at the bottom, but you can work your way up pretty quick. You'll be there a month and learn everything you need to know."

"You mean like guns and stuff?" asked James.

"That's only a little. It's going to open your eyes to so much it'll blow your mind. Enjoy it, cause in five weeks you'll be back on the streets earning."

While on route, James checked in via his cell phone with the World Wide Spyder to let him know where he was headed. After a seeming eternity, he arrived in New Mexico. There was someone waiting at the station holding up a sign with "Bug" written on it, a lightning bolt tattoo on the inside of his right wrist. The Stormer mark.

He walked over. "I'm Bug."

"I'm Speedway. You're the last one." Which was news to James. Speedway took him to a row of lockers and waved a wand over him. "You'll have to leave the razor blade, gun, and cell phone here." He was handed fifty cents. "Pick a locker."

By no means did he want to leave his best means of defense and calling for help, but he couldn't see any way around it. Normally, he could be tracked by his badge, but it was too dangerous to carry it undercover. Still, maybe he could let Spyder know what was going on.

"Can I call my Moms first? She worries," said James.

Speedway laughed. "Sure." Of course, the Stormer made no effort to leave or give him any privacy.

James hit a special number. Spyder knew to answer pretending to be his mother if he dialed it.

Speedway leaned forward to listen in.

The phone rang twice before an older female answer. "Hey, baby, how's Mama's favorite boy?"

"Mom, I'm your only boy," said James. Covering the mouthpiece he whispered "Five sisters." Speedway grinned. "I'm just calling to let you know I got that job I was trying for."

"Baby, that's wonderful. I'm so proud of you. What are you going to be doing?"

"I'm not sure exactly. I'm starting at the bottom and I have to go to an orientation for a month."

"Are they paying for it?"

"Yes, Mom. It's just the place only wants their people to concentrate on work, so cell phones aren't allowed. I'll call if I get the chance, but I didn't want you to worry if you didn't hear from me for a while."

"You just worry about doing a good job and impressing your bosses, okay?"

"I will." Speedway was motioning him to speed things up. "I gotta go."

"I love you, baby."

"Bye Mom."

"You aren't going to tell your Momma you love her?" Spyder was playing his part to the hilt.

James made sure to look embarrassed. "I love you too, Momma."

"Bye baby."

Speedway was chuckling. "New job, huh?"

James shrugged. "Seemed the best way to explain things. She's my Moms."

"No problem," said Speedway, taking the quarters back, putting them in a locker, and opening it. Making sure he used his shirt to cover the gun, James put everything inside and reluctantly closed the door. "Your chariot awaits."

The ride awaiting him may not have been a chariot, but it was a Hummer super stretch limo, complete with every amenity from wet bar to stereo. Speedway opened the door and James got inside. There were two other recruits waiting.

"Hey, I'm Bug."

"I'm Brickhouse," said a beautiful girl whose figure lived up to her name. James tried not to stare.

"They call me Slick," said a boy who could almost pass for a man, Stormer colors of blue with gold bolts proudly displayed on his do-rag.

"Anybody have any idea where we're going?" James asked.

The partition between passengers and driver slid down. "Don't worry about where. Just know you're going to meet your new family." Speedway made what at first glance appeared to be the sign of the cross, but on closer examination was the zig zag motion of the Stormer bolt—a touch to the lips, right shoulder, left breast, belly button. "May Coco Joe watch over and protect us. You may want to buckle up. The trip normally takes about three hours. I'll have you there in one and change."

The partition went back up, and the limo lurched, throwing all of them backwards. Brickhouse landed on top of James in what, at other times, might be considered an intimate position.

For a moment, their eyes locked, and all thoughts of his mission momentarily rushed out of James' head.

"Sorry about that," said Brickhouse with a smile that could melt ice, and slowly eased herself up.

"Don't be. Any time you want to land on me, feel free," said James.

"I'll keep it in mind," she said.

"And they call me Slick."

The trio settled back. James noticed that the tint on the windows was so dark that they couldn't see outside, so they'd have no idea where they were when they got there. Drinking and eating in the back of a limo was a much better way to travel than blindfolded or knocked out in the trunk of a car. James was able to pick up a single cell conversation where Speedway told someone he had picked the new recruits up and that they were on their way.

The trip took just over the promised hour. Speedway opened the door. "Welcome to the Stormhold."

They were met by a man who could pass for a drill instructor. James fully expected to be put through the start of some sort of boot camp. Instead, the man came over and greeted them with the Stormer handshake—each person grabbed the other's wrist with the index finger alone on top pointed forward.

"Welcome to our Stormhold. I'm Top Dog. Tomorrow your orientation will begin. Tonight we welcome our latest brothers…" Top Dog looked at Brickhouse and smiled, "and sisters with a celebration fit for Stormers. First I'll show you to your quarters. The rest of your class is already here."

The men were shown to what could pass for army barracks, with all the beds in a single room. They were told the women had similar quarters. As none of them had had any notice that they'd be traveling, they had nothing to unpack. James was able to pick up subliminal messages being broadcast in the soft music that played in the background. It was typical cult programming stuff. The usual propaganda— Stormers are the only ones who care about you, the only ones you should care about, and something about the greatness of someone named Coco Joe, which was the same name Speedway had invoked on their way here.

James guessed they also probably limited sleep, and constantly broadcast their message. They probably controlled who the members spoke to, where they went, and what they saw and read. Pretty soon the members would become converts. It was why deprogramming had to be done in so many cases when people left cults. He had never heard of a gang using these techniques, but there was no reason why it wouldn't work as well for them.

James listened to the air. Someone was having a phone conversation saying their New York problem had followed them to Jersey because Stormers had set foot in Manhattan. They were unsure how to deal with the situation, and hung up to consult with someone higher up. James was also barely able to pick up the faint signal of an oldies station broadcasting from far away. He made a mental note to concentrate on that signal, in order to not fall prey to the Stormers' programming. After all, if he couldn't hear it over ancient rock and roll, it wouldn't cloud his mind.

As soon as they had their bed assignments, they were taken to the cantina. One area was set up like a cafeteria crossed with a four-star restaurant. There were linen table cloths, real silverware, and crystal drinking glasses. James met the rest of his class. There were twenty-six men and eighteen women. They served themselves, so no one was put above another. Top Dog explained that they would each be working in the dining hall and kitchen one day a week. They sat down to a meal that was easily one of the best James had ever had.

The strategy the Stormers were using made sense to James. Most of these kids came from poor or broken homes. They'd never been treated like they were important or really mattered. They came here and got the red carpet rolled out for them. It made an impression. Loyalty not through violence or fear—these kids had lived that their whole lives, and it hadn't taken so far—but through kindness and generosity. Excellent psychology. Added to the subliminal messages, it was undoubtedly an effective combo.

Immediately following dessert, they were lead into another section of the cantina set up like a swanky nightclub, the kind most kids dreamed about going to but usually got stuck outside of, waiting beyond the velvet rope. There was a stage with a DJ, a lightshow that would make most touring pop stars envious, and a huge screen twenty feet high by thirty wide. There were already fifty Stormers in the club.

The newest class were brought to the stage and, one by one, their faces splashed on the giant screen as the DJ introduced each of them to thunderous applause. James was impressed by how good the cheers made him feel, and his were only a fraction of what Brickhouse got, mostly from the men.

The party got started. Each of them was made to feel special. They jumped into the mosh pit and were carried above the crowd to the dance floor, where they were gently put back on their feet. Drinks and snacks were free, any songs they wanted to hear were played.

James ended up dancing with Brickhouse. After several drinks, he realized that they had been spiked with something, as he felt his inhibitions fading fast and his spirits rising with a euphoria beyond anything he had ever known. Another part of him started to rise as well, and Brickhouse could feel it as they grinded together on the dance floor. She became as excited as he was. It took only seconds for their lips and tongues to find each other. He could feel the drugs pushing his rational tendencies far away, and he couldn't have cared less. Brickhouse's amazingly hard body was all that mattered. Barely able to control himself, he led her behind a five foot tall stack of speakers. As he pressed her body up against it, the bass made her vibrate with every beat. It was a race to see who could tear off the other's clothes first. He won, but just barely, because she stopped for a moment on her knees to do something that almost brought him to his. Their lovemaking became surreal, with the music pulsing through their bodies like a third lover, the lights doing things to the way her naked and bare body looked that didn't seem natural. Brickhouse returned his every thrust with an equally frenzied parry. James had never experienced anything quite like it. Thanks to the drugs, he honestly couldn't tell if they were one person or two. His climax seemed more powerful than every other one in his life combined together. Brickhouse's screams momentarily drowned out the music. Instead of being exhausted, they were both invigorated.

The drugs had taken control of more than his body and libido. They also took over his tongue. "I think I love you."

Brickhouse smiled. "I certainly loved that. Wow, Bug you were amazing."

James smiled. "Back at you, Brickhouse."

After a few more passionate kisses, they hurried to get dressed again, and returned to the party proper. They noticed several of the other new Stormers had the same idea they had had, some not even bothering to leave the dance floor. The logical part of Bug's mind struggled to the surface. For sex like that, the Stormers would be able to get almost anyone to do almost anything. The thought was sobering, especially when he realized he was probably the only one who even cared.

Once everyone was done and back on the dance floor, the music fell silent and the lights went off, plunging the room into darkness.

"Ladies and Gentlemen, Stormers all, I give you our guiding light, our leader, and our very god—Coco Joe!"

The applause was thunderous, even from the newest Stormers, who had never even heard of Coco Joe. The drugs were a wonderful thing, letting them ride the biggest emotional waves any of them had ever experienced.

The leader's name alone made James' mission a success. The DMA had been trying for months to find out who was the leader of the Stormers, but every investigation reached a dead end. Every Stormer brought in for questioning invoked their right to remain silent, even when faced with serious jail time. Even the mob had wise guys willing to rat out their bosses to avoid prison, but not the Stormers. Not a one squealed.

James now had a pretty good idea why. He would carry this memory to his grave, realizing that without those drugs, every other day would be pure drudgery when compared to the magic of this night. What wouldn't he give to feel like this again, over and over? He realized not even his soul was out of the question, and it scared him. The adrenaline countered some of the drugs' effects.

On the pitch-black stage, a man appeared. On wasn't exactly right. He hovered fifteen feet over the stage, lightning crackling all around him, brightening the darkness. He seemed to appear from nowhere, but James knew this Coco Joe hadn't. Seconds before, he had picked up a wireless cue radioing the Stromer leader to get ready. Even so, it was damned impressive the way the electricity crackled around him. James realized the drugs in his system were heightening even this.

He tried to focus on the oldies broadcast. It helped, but only a little. James tried to focus on why he was here, hoping it would help more, but it was so hard to concentrate on anything other than the sparking man in front of him. Deputy Director Sarge Winston had briefed him about speculations that maybe the gang had a weather deity working with them. Coco Joe, whoever he was, wasn't on Sarge's list, but he was obviously in charge. Worse, he seemed to be cultivating worship from the Stormers, which was how a god got power. This god was minor, maybe even forgotten, but he was making a power play in the here and now. And it was working. Coco Joe didn't care that he was affecting weather patterns, throwing parts of the country into turmoil with record hot summers and sending winter on a path a drunken sailor would have a hard time following.

James Pratt knew he was outclassed, but he was a DMA agent. He'd see his mission through for the four weeks, then report back to the DMA, who would bring in the big guns to take apart the god of the Stormers. All he had to do was get through his orientation, and how hard could that be? And it might not be all bad. Maybe he'd enjoy a few more parties and lots of liaisons with Brickhouse in the meantime.

"Welcome, my Stormers," said Coco Joe, his voice booming like thunder, but to James it had a slight echo. The god was using a speaker system to project his voice. "And welcome to the newest members of our ever-expanding family. You have all proven yourselves worthy to be here by your actions. The Stormers are now your only friends, your only family, your new religion, your reason for living. Now and forever, your fellow Stormers will be looking out for you, as you will be looking out for them. In turn, I will be watching over all of you. Many of you may have been brought up in various false religions that demanded your faith in a god or gods that you could never see, let alone meet. I am not that kind of god. You can pray to me directly and if I choose to answer your prayers, you will know it. Remain loyal, and you will be rewarded, both in this life and in the next."

Even drugged, James knew a con job when he heard it. Still, he had to force himself to care, using every technique the DMA taught him for resisting mind control. The same training included what gods could and couldn't do. After all, they had had to arrest more than one. Most members of pantheons had distinct specialties. Most afterlife deities had trouble staying long among the living. The cheers from the throngs showed the Stormers couldn't see the same things he could. Then again, the drugs were making him cheer just as loud. The longer he did, the more convincing Coco Joe seemed. The music started playing in the background helped; James couldn't completely block out the subliminal messages telling him how wonderful Coco Joes was, how smart, powerful, and caring, too. It helped make the god's words ring with the most absolute of truths.

"Together, we will cut a place for all of us in this world, where we will all be treated like kings and queens, and those who oppose our order we will strike down like lightning before we crush them beneath our heels."

Everyone was on their feet, hollering. Suddenly, they had gone from being life's underdogs and castoffs to being important, and what made them important was belonging to the Stormers. And the Stormers, understand it or not, now belonged to Coco Joe.

"And tonight, you will receive your first sacrament. You will drink not water and wine that your imagination is supposed to convince you is divine…" James also knew from his training that most major religions, Christianity among them, had legitimate connections to the truly divine, unlike this snake oil salesgod. But even armed with that knowledge, he still wanted to believe so badly that it hurt him to his very soul. "You will drink the blood of a real god. Who among you will be first?"

The newest Stormers rushed forward, but Brickhouse got there first. Coco Joe stroked her cheek, and a tiny bolt of electricity jumped from his left hand to his right pinky. A spot of blood pooled on the fingertip. The storm god held it out, and Brickhouse thrust it in her mouth. She sucked on it even more passionately than she had on a different part of James back behind the speakers. And she moaned even louder. What effect would drinking the blood of a god have on a mortal? Probably bind her to him forever, a bond that would not even break under threat of prison or death.

He took his finger from between her lips. "Kneel before me."

Brickhouse obeyed, prostrating herself on the floor at his feet.

"Rise, my daughter, and give me your right wrist."

Brickhouse obeyed, and sparks flew from him to her, burning the Stormer bolt forever into her skin. It should have been incredibly painful, but Brickhouse smiled as the tears ran down her face.

So it went for the next five. Ten. Twenty. Thirty. James had spent the entire time trying to figure a way out of this, but he was coming up blank. He was number thirty-nine, and figured he'd be the first one to have a problem, but number thirty-six beat him to it.

It was Slick. He was sweating, shivering in terror. James realized he hadn't touched the drinks, at least as far as James had seen, which meant he alone was operating here without chemical interference in his brain.

Coco Joe called him forward, and he froze. The god repeated his request, this time in a harsher tone.

Slick replied in a whisper. "No."

"You would deny my gift to you?"

"I'm a Baptist. Maybe not a good one, but I believe in the real God. I've asked Jesus into my heart. The bible tells us we shall have no other gods before God. I won't do it," said Slick.

"That is most unfortunate. You see, your god isn't here."

"Wrong. He's everywhere."

"Be that as it may, I doubt he will call down lightning to destroy me." Coco Joe laughed, and it wasn't a pleasant sound. "Nor will he rescue you. Will you drink my blood? I will not ask again."

"No."

"Then I'm sorry. You are no longer a Stormer," said Coco Joe.

"Fine, I'll go," said Slick, moving toward the door. A sea of bodies blocked his path.

"Leaving is not an option. In all religions, there are sacrifices, usually the unbelievers and the heretics. You qualify as both."

James watched as Top Dog pulled out something that looked like a cross between a tub and a surgical table.

"My people the Zapotec once practiced human sacrifice, until the Aztec and Spanish wiped them out. It's a custom the Stormers have brought back. I have to tell you, I've missed it."

Top Dog and three other Stormers grabbed hold of Slick and dragged him to the sacrifice table.

Breaking cover was no longer a big worry for James Pratt. DMA rules state the safety of civilians is paramount. The problem was that the odds were over a hundred to two. James considered briefly maintaining his new identity and testifying to the crime later, but he was ashamed by the thought, even if it was the smart thing to do.

James briefly considered yelling for them to stop, but tactically, it would be a mistake. Instead, he moved in, knocking out Top Dog and one of the other men before anyone realized what was happening. Slick joined in with a kick to a third man's groin and an elbow to the back of his head.

Attached to the table were three ceremonial knives. James tossed one to Slick and took the other two for himself.

"We're getting out of here now," said James. "Stay out of our way and nobody else needs to get hurt."

The crowd didn't move forward, but didn't back off, either.

"Slick, we're leaving, back to back," said James.

"You got it, Bug," said Slick.

They moved toward the door. Hands reached out to grab them, but they slashed out, cutting gashes in hands, wrists, and arms.

"Enough!" shouted Coco Joe. "You will not hurt any more of my Stormers." With that, the storm god floated up, lifted up by winds that almost knocked all the mortals down.

James saw Coco Joe's hands start to sparkle. Before lightning could strike, he threw the knife, aiming for the god's heart. His aim was off, instead piercing Coco Joe's left shoulder. The storm god bellowed, and lightning flashed out from his right hand. James Pratt's world faded to black.

When he woke later, his limbs were bound to the sacrifice table, and every muscle in his body screamed in agony. Two open wounds where the lightning coursed through him bled, one in his chest, the other in his left ankle.

Looking around, he saw the Stormers standing in a circle with him at the center. Coco Joe lounged in a throne on the stage.

"So the bug has awakened," said Coco Joe.

"That's Agent Pratt to you," he said.

"Ah. DEA or DMA?"

"DMA," replied James.

"Figured it would happen sooner or later. It's why we don't allow amulets or cell phones. Well, Agent Pratt, I offer you an option, the same one I offered the late Slick."

"The late?" said James, panicking when he realized he had failed.

"Yes. You slept through his sacrifice. An impressive accomplishment, considering how loudly he screamed." Coco Joe held up a spike driven through the center of Slick's decapitated head.

"You sick bastard," said James.

"Sick? You think so? I lean toward it being practical. We put the head out front to discourage more traitors. Of course, one never knows when the stray plane or satellite goes by overhead, so maybe indoors would be best. In a way, I almost admired him. We couldn't get him to renounce his beliefs, and we tried. Pity. If we could only have turned that loyalty to where it would have done some good," said Coco Joe.

"Toward you? Who would that be good for, besides you?" asked James.

Coco Joe smiled. "For him, of course, because he'd still be alive. Although his sacrifice helps me as well."

"What kind of god bleeds?" said James.

The storm god rubbed his left shoulder. "My skin was only pierced because the knife had a small portion of my power in it, so don't give yourself too much credit, Agent Pratt. Now, I have a proposition for you, but I'm honestly not expecting much. So, either denounce your former life, take my sacrament, and join the Stormers body and soul, or you will be sacrificed."

"You are a murderer. I'll see you pay for what you did to Slick," said James.

"Agent Pratt, you really aren't in a position to enforce any threats or promises. I take it that you refuse my offer?"

"If you were closer, I'd spit in your face," said James.

"I believe you would. A shame. The inside track on the DMA would have been useful. Any last words?" asked the storm god.

James had several, none of them kind.

"Agent Pratt, I may have to file a complaint with your superiors over such a disgraceful display of language," said Coco Joe.

James laughed, but it sounded hollow even to his ears. "Doesn't matter. Your cultists saw what that knife did, and some of them are going to wonder. Whatever happens to me, I still made you bleed."

"I'm going to make you bleed worse," said Coco Joe.

"Won't change the fact that a mortal hurt you, false god."

"Maybe, but tomorrow I'll be healed and you'll still be dead," said Coco Joe.

"Then just kill me and get it over with," said James, his options down to going out whimpering or with bravado. There would be plenty of time to be afraid when he was dead.

"I think you misunderstand. I don't actually do the sacrificing. It's unbecoming for a god to make sacrifices to himself. The power of the slain life doesn't go to the god then. Otherwise, gods would constantly be going on killing sprees instead of fading away to oblivion. One of my followers always does it. I believe you know your executioner quite intimately."

A woman stepped forward, a large ceremonial dagger in her hands which she cradled to her breasts.

"Brickhouse?"

"Hi Bug," she said with the same smile she used when she fell on him in the limo.

"You don't have to do this. You can tell him no. He can't force you to kill," said James.

"You misunderstand. Your lover volunteered for the task," said Coco Joe with just a hint of sadistic glee.

"Why?"

"Because Coco Joe said he would raise me up in the Stormer ranks to one of his lieutenants if I did," said Brickhouse, running her hand down his bare chest. As he followed her fingers, James realized for the first time he had been stripped naked before they tied him down.

"Killing someone changes you forever," said James.

"I know. I killed my stepfather when I turned sixteen. I told everyone he had been molesting me. I even videotaped it so I had an alibi, but I really seduced him. My Mom grounded me and wouldn't let me go to a party, so I slept with her boyfriend," said Brickhouse.

"In fact, the young lady killed her lifemark, making the bolt right through his jugular," said Coco Joe.

"I've killed nine times before. You'll be my perfect ten. I'll remember you always, Bug," said Brickhouse, leaning forward to kiss James. As her tongue darted in his mouth he bit it hard enough to make it bleed. Brickhouse's face went dark, and she raised the blade up and plunged it into his chest.

Top Dog stepped closer, ignoring James' dying screams. "Move it down to cut through the bone. Nice job." He moved in with surgical tools to separate the rib cage and expose the heart.

As she had been instructed, Brickhouse used the dagger to slice around the heart, then reached in and tore the still-beating organ out of his chest. James's eyes glared accusingly at her, but she ignored their charges, and they went dead and glassy without being answered.

Brickhouse ran up to the stage to get the heart to Coco Joe before it stopped beating, and bowed before him, lifting the hunk of dying muscle above her.

The storm god took the offered organ from her and took a bite, ripping the still-moving meat with his teeth. "Thank you, my dear. They are always best when they are fresh. You have served me well. We must begin planning, because the Stormers will soon return to New York to destroy those who have stood against us in the past, and who attack us in the present. But that is talk for another day. Tonight, we celebrate."

And the Stormers did, into the wee hours of the morning, stopping periodically to play catch or soccer with either of a pair of severed heads.

THE SWORDS OF THE DAEMOR:
LUCKY DAYE

Sometimes you just get lucky, but it's not always of the good variety. There had been rumors circulating for a while that some woman was impersonating a Daemor. Very bad move on her part. Mab is fighting a losing guerilla war against Thandu's forces to free Faerie from the tyrant. One of the strongest things she has going for her is the reputation of her troops, especially the Daemor. We're the elite, the best of the best. And we're all women. Mab's got some serious issues, but then I can't talk. I'm a banshee that kills people, which is not exactly a traditional role for a caoineag. A Bean Sidhe is supposed to warn of the dark embrace, not hasten it. It's made me an outsider among my own people. My given name is Daye, but I've heard them call me Dark Daye in frightened whispers. Most are too afraid to call me that to my face.

Mab has a death edict against anyone impersonating a Daemor. If the people can't trust us, then we have no hope of victory. I get to enforce her orders.

Lucky me.

Taking care of impersonators takes up a good piece of my time. Not that there have been that many after the first dozen; most of those, Mab punished herself. Very old school, as Kande—a human Daemor—likes to say. Even though they are few in number, they don't exactly walk up to me and say "Kill me." Finding someone in Faerie can be a tremendous task.

I can't say I don't like my work, mainly because I get to kill the bad and I'm considered exceptional at what I do. If my job helps me work out some anger issues, it's a bonus.

A rule of thumb for an assassin: Never go in blind. Know your prey, a good trick when all you have to hunt are rumors. I typically travel incognito, and I strive very hard not to repeat disguises. The locals aren't stupid. They talk about anybody new in town. If a certain type of person were to regularly show up right before a killing, gossip would eventually get me caught when I showed up somewhere. The price Thandau has on the head of any Daemor is sizeable. The bounty on Mab is enough to buy a small kingdom. The reward for my capture is almost as high.

There is one cover identity that I have repeated time and time again: that of a widow. There are too many of them of late. Thandau forcibly drafts the able-bodied males. Many don't return, which leaves a small population imbalance. Probably the most practical reason for Mab's recruiting choice.

A lot of rural widows come into town to get drunk when they get the news. Normally, they're too busy out on the farm to bother. With the current state of affairs in Faerie, nobody even notices a new widow. There's another one almost every day.

Besides, I like wearing black. Mab says it matches my personality, which may be true, but I can lay legitimate claim to the right to wear the ensemble. Thandau took my husband and my son. My husband came back in a wooden box. My son never did. One day I'll make the bastard pay. Until then, my fury will be wasted on those willingly giving aid to the enemy.

Taking on the look wasn't hard. I just let down the walls that I kept up the rest of the time, and the crying came. The experience is actually quite cathartic. It's the only time I allow myself the luxury of tears. There will be time enough for weeping and wailing for the dead once Thandau is among their number.

My hair was dyed blue. I don't bother with glamours; there are far too many people roaming around with the means to see through the illusion, and that would set me apart from the simple villagers. Poor farm widows can't afford glamours.

The first tavern I went to was called The Club and Foot. It was busy. I made my way in to the barman, making sure to pause and look around warily. Farm widows are nervous types in new places. I pulled out a pair of copper coins, hiding them unskillfully.

"How much for a grand ale?" I asked. The price quoted was much more than my cover identity would have. "What do you have for a copper?"

The barman looked at me with sympathy. As he moved toward me, I could see he was missing his right leg above the knee. He had a wooden one with a locking hinge, skillfully carved, but not magically enhanced. Thandau doesn't take good care of his wounded soldiers. The injured are not much use to him, so he discards them. The man probably had to make the leg himself.

"Stout," he said, then leaned forward and whispered, "But I'll fill the bigger mug in honor of your loss, missus."

A soldier honoring the dead. I could respect that, even from the opposite side. I touched his hand. "My thanks."

He nodded and gave me a sad smile that spoke volumes, followed by the drink.

I meekly stood and raised my glass to make a toast. The room at large ignored my soft words. Remaining in character, I tried a second time with no more luck than the first. The barman took pity on me, or maybe it was just good business. If glasses were drained, they'd have to be refilled. He banged a couple of tankards together and yelled, "Respect for the missus."

The room got quiet, even the cutthroat types. Everyone had their dead in these wars.

I nodded my gratitude and raised my mug. "To the finest husband a lass ever had! I miss and love you, heart of my heart. Until!" Short for *until we meet again.*

Glasses raised and more than didn't said, "Until!"

"May those that caused your death die a thousand times."

Glasses raised again, but not as high. It was unclear if I meant those who drafted him or those that did the actual killing. Speaking out against Thandau could be a death sentence. My words were chosen carefully, but caused many to be wary. Raising a glass in memory was fine and good, but speaking out against the ruling power was flirting with suicide. A banshee knows all about the many faces of dying. Suicide seems like a cute one from a distance, full of promises and a way out of trouble. Up close, you can see the ugliness, and see that his promises are false. But if you've already allowed him to kiss you, it's far too late to back out of your final date.

Most of Faerie had seen too much death of late, ironic for a world that lets life go on for so long. Death from disease is minimal, but killing each other has always been popular, although never like this. Fey don't reproduce quickly. My husband and I weren't blessed with a child for over a century, though it wasn't for lack of trying. It will take centuries for the population to recover. Goblins and humans have shorter life spans, but reproduce so much faster, maybe because they aren't natives. Not that most Fey believe in Earth or humans any more that they believe in us.

I left my toasting at that. A widow daring to speak out directly would be too memorable. One soft stepping around it was common. An angry woman's little jab at an unfair fate would not stand out.

I found a table in the middle of the room and sat. It made me uncomfortable to have people behind me, but the tables in the back corners and along the walls are always the first taken.

Which is when I got lucky.

Most fey don't evolve off into gentry like leprechaun, pixie, or ogre. Many look a lot like humans, except in a greater variety of colors and sizes, with the occasional pointed ear, chin, or nose. Even Banshees don't stand out too much, as long as we keep our mouths shut when it comes time for an endsong. Normally, I have snow-white skin and ivory hair with coal-black streaks. I make an effort to tan, but it isn't easy. Sometimes I just resort to skin dye.

A fey woman walked in wearing armor, a broadsword, and something nestled beneath her breasts that she never should have had—a silver medallion with a black raven's head. It was the emblem badge of the Daemor. It had been faked in the past. We had been trained to recognize the real thing. This one was the genuine article, which should have been impossible. No Daemor were missing or should even have been near this town. If one were killed, the medallion would have sent a signal so we could locate the body and bring it home. I know every Daemor on sight; I have to, so as not to make a horrible mistake.

This woman wasn't one of us, but the medallion was real. That meant I couldn't just kill her. I had to find the Daemor she took the badge from. If she was alive, I'd rescue her. If she was dead, I'd avenge her. Slowly and painfully.

The question was how. Luck was still with me. The imposter stood up in the center of the barroom and started ranting, not two jumps from me.

"Now is the time to rise up and cast off the shackles of tyranny. I'm looking for a few brave souls to join me in a vital mission to strike at Thandau's very heart." Interesting. She was using our reputation to weed out sympathizers. I doubted her intentions were good. She went on for a while, trying to rile the crowd up. Most tried to ignore her. A few looked like they wanted to tell her to shut up, but a Daemor's reputation was dangerous enough that none dared.

After her impassioned speech, she marched outside, and the room returned to normal. A pair of youths with more guts than hairs on their chins tried to casually sneak out. It was made more obvious by the trying. I waited longer, finished my stout, and returned my mug to the barman.

"My thanks," I said, touching his hand.

"My sympathies," he returned. He seemed a good man. Many others have tried to prey on my supposed vulnerability to have their way with a distraught widow. Nice to see that there were still some decent men left in the world.

I left and scanned the area outside the Club and Foot. The imposter would want to lure would-be traitors to Thandau into her trap. She would not go far. In fact, she was right behind the stables. Four men were hiding nearby, doing a fairly good job of it. Most people wouldn't have noticed them. A Daemor would have to be near passing-out drunk or suffering a still bleeding head wound to not have seen at least three of them.

The youths were strutting and trying to impress the woman. As they told their tales of imagined bravery, neither took their eyes off the cleavage the armor was designed to enhance and prop up. One of the reasons we built it that way. The woman was extremely well proportioned—nothing like my fellow Daemor, Terrorbelle, but still impressive—especially next to my meager chest. Perhaps that was part of the reason she was chosen to play the part of the siren leading them to their doom.

When I stepped around the corner, the males jumped and turned on me, ready to growl. They relaxed noticeably when they noticed I was a woman. The impersonator remained cool, but then, she knew she had hidden backup.

"Welcome," said the impersonator.

I played the meek card. "I heard what you said. Thandau took my husband from me. How can I take something from him?"

The pretender smiled. "I will bring all of you to a Daemor stronghold first, where all will be revealed. Let us wait to see if any other brave souls join our campaign."

We spent an hour lurking, but no one else took the bait.

"Let's move out. Keep up," ordered the imposter.

"No problem," said one of the youths, whose name was Han.

"Absolutely," said the other, not wanting to be left out. His name was Wok.

I just nodded and trotted after them into the woods. The quartet hung back, following at a discrete distance.

The pretender was careful to avoid a marked Faerie path. Smart. Wandering on a ramble path can get you lost in time and space or worse, especially if you step off at the wrong spot. In the Daemor, we have a pathmaker, Tralla, who has drilled maps of the majority of the paths into our heads. It's one of our greatest tactical advantages. We can get into and out of places quickly and quietly, while the enemy is hesitant to risk life and sanity by following. I had actually come in on this path.

We trod on for a couple of hours. Occasionally, Han and Wok would attempt some witty banter, but the pretender would shush them, claiming the need for stealth. I got the impression she didn't want to be bothered listening.

We finally arrived at an empty campsite. With a wave of her hand, she lit the pile of wood in the center. Simple survival magiks, but it impressed the youths. Probably neither knew anything beyond basics like translation spells.

The imposter kept us busy while her companions surrounded us.

"The Daemor is a secret organization." Hardly. We simply hide to survive. The impersonator lifted up her stolen medallion. "This gives me great power." Not true. It's the woman wearing it that has the power. The badge has some communication and tracking functions, a few protective wards, but that's about it. Its real power is in the symbol and what it stands for—the hope of freedom for all of Faerie and the death of tyranny. "What I need all of you to do is swear an oath to me that you will dedicate your lives to fighting Thandau."

"I so swear," said Wok.

"Me, too," quickly chimed in Han, not to be left out.

The imposter looked at me for my oath. "I'd like to know a little bit more about your plan before I swear an oath." Faerie is a magic world. Promises and oaths can become almost tangible things, and should not be entered into lightly.

"You are not fully committed to the fight?" asked the pretender, with a tone both scoffing and filled with condescension.

"What fight? All you've done is go on about a fight that you have said nothing about. I wouldn't agree to kill an animal without knowing the how and why, let alone swear an oath to it," I said. As I spoke, the men in the woods were moving in. One wasn't even trying to be quiet. Han and Wok were oblivious.

"She doesn't need to swear the oath," said the noisy one. Han and Wok jumped at the sound. "Just by being here, that's enough to justify conspiracy. For women, we get paid the same either way."

"What's going on here?" said Wok.

"Bounty hunters make a living by taking in traitors," said Noisy.

"That's what we were doing," said Han. "We were going to get the drop on the Daemor and bring her in for the reward."

"Sure, laddie. That'll hold up in the Ax Man's Court," said Noisy.

Ax Courts were set up around the land to dispense death with only a passing nod at justice. The resultant heads kept Thandau's pikes decorated.

"You're no Daemor," I said, feigning indignation and surprise.

The impostor laughed. "You got me. Not that you were smart enough to figure it out before it was too late for you."

"I knew it. That medallion doesn't even look real," I said.

The imposter lifted it up and held it toward me. "Oh, it's real all right. I took it off a Daemor myself."

"She must have died before she'd give it to you," I said.

"She's not dead yet. Ax Man's Court will take care of it tomorrow, though. You'll probably get to watch. The woman was dumb enough to try to come to my rescue. While she was defending me, I smashed her in the back of the head. We got a pretty price for her, and I got to keep this trinket. Enough talking."

I took deep breaths to control my anger. My hair tends to float on its own and my eyes tend to get on the fiery side, which would be counterproductive.

Two of the others wheeled a cart that had been made into a rolling cell. The cart had a balance spell on it, which made it easy for anyone to push it. No beast of burden was necessary. We were all forced into the cell. Although I could have fought back at any point, I let myself be put inside. A Daemor was in danger. That was my first priority. I could kill the bad later.

The ride was bumpy and uncomfortable. I spent the time studying the woman and the men. You can learn much about how well someone can fight by watching them move and walk. This lot could handle themselves, but they were far from experts.

I also wanted to memorize everything about them, as I would have to find them later.

We got to a Graycoat outpost jail before sunup. My luck was still holding—it wasn't a Destroyer outpost. The Destroyers were Thandau's elite. They'd be much more thorough searching prisoners, and there was an outside chance I'd be recognized even with my disguise.

We were handed over without incident. The bounty hunters were given their due. Han and Wok spent the entire time arguing about their innocence. I just wanted in to the jail. I ignored as much as I could to keep control of my temper.

The pair of Graycoat guards searched the two of them thoroughly. My search consisted less of looking for weapons than feeling out my womanly attributes. Fine by me. I'd suffered worse indignities, and they missed all of my weapons in their groping enthusiasm.

They threw Han and Wok in the first empty cell. I was taken to the back, where they kept the female prisoners. The three incarcerated there weren't treated well. In fact, it seems the Graycoat guards thought of them as their own personal brothel, without even granting them the respects of pay or consent.

A pair of guards escorted me, laughing about my upcoming strip search. I ignored them, but they didn't seem to notice. Probably thought I was mute from fear, instead of trying very hard not to kill them.

The last cell held six men. Five held down a woman by her head and limbs while the sixth raped her. She was fighting like a griffon. Judging by the state of undress of the others, he was the third on this shift to do so. I moved so I could see her face. It was Marra, one of the first to be called Daemor. She was a Leanan Sidhe, a member of the gentry. They have often been mistaken for vampyres by mortals, but they have no bloodlust. They can feed off the spirits of others; the energy can be taken or offered. They have been known to inspire poets, musicians, and artists, and can feed off the creative energy they give off without harming them. At least in the short term.

They were planning on putting me in the same cell. I waited until the door was opened. An instant later, a pair of needle-thin brain-picks separated the pair of guards' frontal lobes from the rest of their brains. They fell, their spirits fled before their bodies made contact with the floor.

I worked my magic with the picks twice more, on the pair holding the arm and leg closest to me. I got the pair pinning her other limbs with a poisoned dart each.

It hadn't taken three blinks. I could have taken the guards at her head and womanhood in a fourth and fifth blink, but I didn't want to hog all the fun. Marra had suffered much at their hands. She needed a little revenge. It always makes me feel better.

With fewer attackers, she could focus better. The rapists didn't stand a chance once she got her natural magiks going. With her hands free, she reached up, pulled the guard holding her head down and locked lips with that attacker. The physical contact triggered an energy drain, and Marra rode the wave as it surged. The drain grew to include the current rapist who hadn't been quick or bright enough to pull out when he saw four of his fellows drop dead. He tried now, but he was too late. Marra wrapped her legs around him, and he had no hope of escape. Minutes later, the pair were withered corpses, and Marra was revitalized, if shaken.

I remained silent until we went down to the guard office and retrieved her armor and weapons. Once she was dressed, she finally looked at me. I could see what it cost her to meet my eyes.

"I was taken down like an amateur," Marra confessed. "They got my badge."

"I know. It's how I found you. We'll get it back, but first we have a job to do," I said.

Mara nodded. We both knew standing orders. If an opportunity presents itself to hurt the enemy, do it.

First we freed the other prisoners. Han and Wok couldn't stop gushing gratitude. The women were hurt badly, both in body and spirit. They would be a long time healing.

I took point. Our exit was clear, and I gave Marra the signal to bring the others out.

We got to the edge of the compound without detection. We crouched low as a pair of Graycoat sentries moved on their rounds. Han stood and shouted, "Daemor! I've got two Dae—"

Marra slit his throat before he finished his betrayal. I reached and downed both Graycoats with my picks before their swords cleared leather.

Marra and I got on either side of Wok. He fell to his knees. "We were planning to capture the other one for the reward, but you rescued us. I wouldn't have turned on you."

I didn't believe him, but it didn't matter. Someone had to live to tell the tale. We tied him in the upper branches of a tree, and I used a dart coated with paralyzing venom. He wouldn't be able to move or speak for at least a day. I pointed his head toward the compound.

We ran out back into the woods. There was another ramble path a quarter of an hour's journey away. We got the women on it and brought them to our nearest camp—normally four days away—and handed them over to our medics for healing. One day, they might choose to become recruits for Mab's army, or possibly even Daemor, once they've proven themselves.

We had a path into a Graycoat compound we didn't know existed a day ago. We had little time before an alarm was raised, if it hadn't been already. I took a squad of Daemor back with me.

We hit the compound running, and my luck held. No alarm was raised. We hit the Ax Court and wiped out every last one of the murdering bastards. A lot of Graycoats fell, but Daemor aren't murderers—excepting me of course—so we let the wounded flee. Hard to tell the draftees from the volunteers, as they all wear the same uniform. There has to be something that separates us from our enemy. After that, we burned the compound to the ground.

I stopped in the tree where Wok, unable to even close his eyes, had watched the carnage.

"That's what happens when you mess with the Daemor. Tell everyone you meet. I will come back one day looking for you, and if I do not hear this tale from others, it will not go well for you," I said. I knew he heard and would obey.

My final stroke of luck was when we went to search the town nearby. This one had a tavern called the Rusty Mug. Rust is dangerous poison to fey, so the name let passersby know it wasn't for the weak of heart. A quick recon found the imposter and her crew drinking to their good fortune inside.

I had changed to my Daemor uniform before the battle, including my armor and badge. I even used a small token of

power to return my skin and hair to their natural colors.

Daemor guarded all the exits, down to the windows and cellar doors. That's when I let out my endsong. A banshee's wail is known as an omen of death throughout Faerie. It can't be sung unless the final darkness approaches.

As expected, all those assembled within the bar tried to get out. It didn't work, as they all found armed Daemor blocking their paths. No sense in making an example of someone if nobody is there to see. I walked in, Marra at my side. My power was flowing, and I could no longer pass for ungentryfied fey. My hair flew, my eyes bled fire, and my voice summoned the reaper.

When I turned toward the imposter and her compatriots, they were left alone and deserted by those who had been toasting with them moments before.

"You have ignored the edict that none shall falsely claim to be a Daemor, upon penalty of death. Your lives are now forfeit," I proclaimed.

The five of them jumped up with their swords. As I predicted, they could handle themselves, but Marra was far better with a blade that the lot combined, and claimed the four men in less time than it takes to tell.

By right, the imposter herself fell to me. She held her sword out to defend herself. I screamed. My vocal range is quite good, and my shout was focused on the pretender. Instinctively, she raised her hands up to protect her ears, and as she did, I plucked the sword from her fingers.

Legends abound in Faerie. There is one that claims banshee can claim a life with a single spoken word. I like to encourage that belief.

"Those who do not wish to join the bodies on the floor, shield your ears," I said. Most did as I recommended. The pretender tried to, but I grabbed her right wrist with my right hand. "Except for you." I leaned in to whisper in her ear.

"Die."

That wasn't the word. The problem with using the word is how to keep from hearing it yourself. How do you learn the proper pronunciation without practice? Not to say it can't be done, but it's not easy or safe, and there were too many Daemor nearby with excellent hearing.

I pricked her behind the ear with a tiny poisoned needle that dissolves after contact with blood. This particular venom molded the face into a frightened expression that stays as a death masque. It also induces almost instant rigor mortis, which meant she kept her feet until after she was dead. I plucked the Daemor medallion off her chest, then pushed her forehead with a single finger. She fell like a cut tree.

We left without another word. The message was clear, and the bad were dead.

TRICKSTER IN CHAINS

The screams shook the rock walls with the force of an earthquake as the trickster god was boiled alive with acid venom. The serpent was tremendous, towering over the chained god. The scaly beast seemed to be enjoying the torment it was inflicting, proving that sadistic tendencies were not limited to humans or gods.

For a god who had the reputation of being able to hear grass grow or see farther than it seemed possible, Heimdal knew what Loki was being subjected to long before he was close enough for either participant in the ring of torture to be able to sense him. It wasn't the guardian of the rainbow bridge's first visit to see the trapped god of mischief. Fate had tied them together. They were destined to slaughter each other at Twilight. The Twilight, Ragnarok, the end of all.

It was only natural to study the man who you knew would one day kill you. After all, Heimdal had to do the same to Loki. It wasn't wrong to gloat at how far your future murderer had fallen; the watchgod had, multiple times, and had never once thought about it being wrong, never had a pang of guilt.

That had changed.

The watchgod made his way slowly down the cliff walls, moving carefully so as not to alert the beast. Its intelligence wasn't much, but its appetite for pain was insatiable. The target didn't matter much. On his back, Heimdal carried a shield, a quiver, and a bow. He was certain he could defeat the beast, but did not want to arouse Odin's anger by killing Loki's tormentor. He had to be careful.

Once on the ground, he notched an arrow dipped in poison. It flew true, and buried itself in the scaly hide. Four more arrows followed in quick succession. The serpent was so large that the poison was only enough to knock it out, not kill it.

The snake reared its head, bellowing in pain before it fell atop the trickster's chained body. Heimdal moved to its tail and pulled, dragging the beast slowly back. It took awhile to get it far enough away that, if it woke, Heimdal would have enough time to plunk more arrows in the snake's hide before it attacked him.

"Murphy?" said the trickster, his bare skin still smoldering from the venom. In places, it had eaten away enough flesh that his muscle was exposed to air. "I wasn't expecting you for weeks."

"No, not Murphy," said Heimdal.

The voice made Loki involuntarily twitch against his chains. The trickster was as familiar with his destined killer as his killer was with him.

"Hello, son of eight mothers." Heimdal had had a most unusual birth. "To what do I owe this unexpected pleasure?"

"What, I can't drop by to visit a member of the family?" asked the guardian.

"It's not that you can't, but I've been here a long time, and you never have before. At least not since you helped bind me here," Loki smiled. It was a disconcerting sight, because half of his lips had been scorched from his face, and that part of his grin appeared partially skeletal.

"Things change," said Heimdal.

"Do they?" asked Loki.

"It's what I've been hearing."

"Hearing is something you are noted for. Listening, not so much," said Loki.

"I'm listening now," said Heimdal.

"Are you? Very interesting. I wonder how my burning flesh must sound to you. Much like meat sizzling on a skillet, I'd imagine. Is it easy to hear it over the pounding the pain makes my heart do?" questioned the trickster.

"I can separate one from the other," said the watchgod.

"Must be handy, although here there is not much besides stone to listen to. No pesky vegetation growing or insects buzzing to give you headaches."

"Sounds pleasant."

"Oh, it is. I'd be happy to switch with you," offered Loki.

Heimdal chuckled. "I'm sure you would, but I'll pass."

"I suppose the damned serpent would ruin the ambience for you. I know it makes my time here most challenging," said the trickster.

"It's not meant to be a holiday. You have much to atone for, Loki," scolded Heimdal.

"I am well aware of that, Heimdal," replied the trickster. "But the Christians have a saying: Let he who is without sin throw the first stone. Not one of my Aesir brethren would be able to toss a pebble my way if we held to that rule."

"You killed Balder," shouted Heimdal.

"You know what he did to me and mine," whispered Loki, spittle flying out of the side of his mouth that was still lacking most of its skin. A tiny border had started to grow back, but it was barely the width of a sheet of paper.

"We have only your word on that, lie-smith," said Heimdal.

"I swore on my power that what I said was true."

"Balder said you lied."

"You asked him but once and asked of him no oath. You took him at his word and dismissed my oath." The trickster yelled the last word. "I, who saved Asgard more times than even Thor. My oath meant nothing. No other Aesir would have been dismissed so easily."

"We had reason," said Heimdal.

Loki was silent a moment, contemplating the watchgod's words. "Perhaps you had. But you should have given me the benefit of the doubt. After all, what was Balder besides a pretty face? I actually had to work for what I achieved."

"Balder was more than that. He was brother to us all," said Heimdal.

"Really? Then tell me one great deed he did," said Loki.

"Why he… Balder… There were many," said Heimdal, but he squinted his eyes, as if to jump-start his memory.

Loki laughed. "Even now, his power works upon your mind. Thor, Odin, even you have done things bards sing of, and are remembered even today. Balder was nothing but a pretender with a talent to make others see him as he wished."

"All creation loved him so much that it swore not to harm him," said Heimdal.

"We both know that was just what the mortals were told. The poor baby said he had a dream that he would die, and went crying to his mommy. Frigga was so upset that she gathered the morphogenic secrets of most organic matter and wove them into her son, so that the darling boy of Asgard couldn't be harmed. She just couldn't crack the DNA on mistletoe, so he was vulnerable. And magic rarely allows absolutes. There is always a fatal flaw."

"Law of nature. You exploited it."

"He deserved it. He hated me because his natural charisma didn't work on me or mine. Balder used to mock me, knowing full well none of you would believe me or even consider taking my side. He even told me he made up the whole story about dreaming his death."

"Why would Balder lie?"

"Oh, I don't know. To be able to live forever, maybe? We live long because of the apples, but we will die eventually. Think about it. Did he ever claim to have a prophetic vision that did not in some way protect or benefit him?" Heimdal did not answer, because he could not remember a single instance, and he did not want to give Loki the satisfaction. "Frigga spent over a century putting all of that together. She could have spilt it among all the Aesir, or even given part of it to Thor so that Asgard's mightiest defender need never worry about a frost giant getting the upper hand. Have you even wondered about that?"

Heimdal's brow now creased. "I have to admit, I had not. It is strange."

"Balder told her not to. He did not want to share his invulnerability with the rest of his family. Selfish bastard," said Loki.

"Balder would not do that," said Heimdal.

"And yet he did. And I told you he did."

The watchgod tilted his head. "You did?" Loki simply raised one eyebrow, and the embers and ashes of the other. "You did, but it was so farfetched it had to be false. You are the lord of lies."

"So you came here to flatter me and tell me how unbelievable I am. Well, at least you knocked out the serpent. Did I thank you for that?" asked Loki.

"You have not."

"Did I also not thank you for transforming one of my sons and forcing him to slaughter another of my sons, his own brother? Where pray tell is Vali? Have you seen the rabid wolf you transformed my son into?" Heimdal looked away, for the moment unable to meet the trickster's eyes. "Then transforming my dead son's small intestine into rope to bind me with? Who came up with that idea? If I remember, you were the one who wrapped me up in it. Even Thor didn't have the stomach for that, but you managed okay. None of you even bothered to clean his blood off first," said Loki. "I could smell it for decades."

"It was part of the binding magic. His blood was of your blood, so it prevented you from changing shape to escape," said Heimdal.

"Couldn't you have just made a gash and taken the blood?" asked the trickster.

"We could have, but Narfi was part of your conspiracy," said Heimdal.

"No, he wasn't. I acted alone. All Narfi was guilty of was leaving his knife out where his father could find it and carve a mistletoe dart. The lot of you slaughtered an innocent boy. I hope that makes you proud," said Loki.

"We could have just killed you," said Heimdal.

"Dragonshit. Odin never would have allowed it. It might have triggered Twilight instantly, and the old man has spent his entire life trying to come up with a way to stop it. The best he's managed to do is postpone Ragnarok."

"Woton will find a way around destiny," said Heimdal.

"You can't cheat fate. The Norns are too sharp for that. But I guess I do owe you for the respite from the serpent, so thank you."

"Excuse me?" said Heimdal. "I was barely able to hear you."

"You want me to repeat it?" asked Loki indignantly.

Heimdal nodded. "I would like that, yes."

Loki grumbled under his breath. "Fine, but I'm not saying it any louder, so you better move in nice and close, because I won't say it a third time."

Heimdal leaned in, putting his ear up against the trickster's mouth. Loki sighed and took a deep breath. With a mighty bellow he shouted loud enough for rocks to fall from the pit wall. "THANK YOU!"

The watchgod doubled over in pain from the sound in his sensitive ears.

Loki laughed. "I can't believe you fell for that."

Heimdal rose to his feet and wrapped his left hand around the trickster's throat. With his right he stood ready to pummel Loki's face.

"Sorry, but I couldn't resist," said Loki. "Don't just stand there looking tough. Hit me and get it over with. Trust me, it won't be as bad as acidic venom or being wrapped in the guts of my dead Narfi, but it may make you feel better."

"What did you say?" said Heimdal. It was not an angry statement. It was one of clarification.

"Hit me."

"Before that."

"I couldn't resist."

"Before that."

"I'm sorry?" said the trickster.

"Yes," said Heimdal. "I've never heard you utter a simple apology before. When you've gotten caught, you utter the most inane, long-winded pieces of drivel while you try to weasel your way out of whatever it is you did."

Loki tried to shrug, but the chains held him too tight. All that happened was his shoulder and neck muscles tightened. "I'm not the same person I was then."

"That's what I hear," said Heimdal.

"Oh, really?" said Loki coyly.

"We've all been wondering why Murphy and the rest have been coming up here in shifts to keep the venom off you. Murphy and the tricksters you've met, but I've never known you to be close to any save Padriac Moran."

"Paddy's a good man," said Loki.

"He is the one who arranged for your freedom on Hallow's Eve." Unbeknownst at one time to the watchgod, Paddy also broke the Norse trickster out of his prison each year on April Fools' Day to compete with the other tricksters.

"He feels he owes me a debt."

"You told him what to tell Woton in order for him to be gifted with apples of immortality. I asked the All-Father for the same thing and was refused," said Heimdal.

Loki's face became thoughtful. "I hadn't known that."

"I spent most of Prohibition working for Paddy and his wife. I loved Bulfinche too, and would have done whatever I could to prevent death from claiming her. I failed. Thanks to you, Paddy almost succeeded. Had he been but a few minutes earlier, your actions would have saved his wife."

"But she wasn't saved. Most people would have written off the debt because of that," said Loki.

"Paddy is not most people," said the watchgod.

"No, he's not," agreed Loki.

"As far as he is concerned, his debt is the same to you regardless. I even warned him about you. He did not listen," said Heimdal.

"Lucky for me."

"Yes, it was. And apparently for many others, as well," said Heimdal.

"I'm not sure what you are talking about," lied Loki.

"But you do, yet you keep silent to protect others. It is very unlike the you I know," said Heimdal.

"If you say so," said the trickster.

"All is known, Loki. We know how you helped save Faerie. We know that you saved a defenseless world from invaders bent on enslaving them. We also know that you had a chance to run, but didn't. I have heard how Murphy had tried to bargain for your freedom and Woton offered you a deal. You turned it down."

"The price was too high," said the trickster.

"One mortal life put at risk if you disobeyed Woton's orders."

"I know my nature. I would not allow Odin to put Murphy at risk."

"But the bartender offered freely and without coercion," said the watchgod.

"Which is exactly why I refused."

"You're not going to say anything about the rest?" asked Heimdal.

Loki gave his best half-eaten stone face.

"I'm not searching for information. Mista overheard Terrorbelle mention something about it recently," said Heimdal.

"Ah, yes, during the dark stag hunt," said Loki.

"How do you know that?" asked Heimdal.

"My name was mentioned. With focus, I can see and hear wherever my name is spoken. Focus helps distract from the pain. Murphy did quite well then."

"You speak of him with pride in your voice," said Heimdal.

"He is one of the few I would dare call friend. And one of the few who would not be shamed by the calling," said Loki.

"Mista told Woton. He and Paddy are pretending like they each don't know the other knows, but there will come a reckoning when Moran's freeing you for the Fools' Day contests is brought into the light."

Loki laughed. "Old One Eye must not be happy."

Heimdal chuckled. "Not hardly. But what calmed him down was Mista pointing out that you went willingly back to confinement all those years."

"I would not betray Moran."

"And yet betrayal is in your nature."

"There are sides of me you've never dreamed of," said Loki.

"I've begun to realize that. This explains the tricksters, the trolls and goblin, and even the garba that have come to watch over you."

Loki actually looked embarrassed. "I didn't ask them to."

"Which makes it all the more incredible. We yelled at Paddy and Murphy for what they did, but by the end of the argument, Murphy had Mista and me signed up in your protection rotation."

"That valkyrie was always better than you deserved," said Loki.

"I always said the same about Sigyn," countered Heimdal.

Loki's laugh echoed with bitterness. "She was. A pity for her that it took her so long to realize it. A tragedy for me. No one to keep the acid away, at least until recently." Loki sighed. Even now he missed his wife, but he knew that not only was she better off without him, she was happy. With a mortal, no less. "So who else has Murphy signed up on my behalf?"

"The bartender even got Thor to consider it."

"Impressive, although my brother never hated me the same as the rest of you. If it hadn't been for Balder, we might have... I'm not surprised Murph tried to talk him into it. He may yet suceed. Murphy can be quite persuasive when he needs to be. Murph lead an entire army against a superior force and won," said Loki.

"He gave you most of the credit," said Heimdal.

"I deserve very little of it. Without him, I would never have tried to save the Karmans."

"Regardless of why, that you did impressed me," said Heimdal.

"Thank you," said Loki. "So did Murph try to convince One-eye to take a shift?"

"Nobody's that persuasive," Heimdal said. The pair bound by Fate to murder each other shared a soft chuckle. "And it would force this unspoken unsecret into the open."

Beyond them, the serpent started to stir. Heimdal notched his bow and let another poisoned arrow fly into the scaly hide. The acid-drooling monster returned to its slumber.

"So you are willingly spending an entire week with me?" asked Loki.

"Not sure I'll last the entire time. Let's just see how it goes, shall we?"

"Fair enough," agreed the trickster. "I'll take what I can get."

"Demeter sent some food with me. Would you like some?" asked the watchgod.

"Does Thor love karaoke?" asked Loki.

"Unfortunately," said Heimdal, opening a thermos. "Shall we start with some soup? Murph said it helps you regenerate flesh faster." The watchgod held the thermos up to the trickster's mouth.

"Easier to metabolize liquids," said Loki, gulping down the broth. He quickly downed the entire thermos and a second one. "Would you adjust the chain so I can lift my head up more?"

Heimdal did.

"These are much easier to bear than Narfi's intestines," said Loki, his mouth almost healed.

Heimdal cleared his throat. "I've always felt badly about what happened to your boy. Both boys. In truth, I much prefer the new chains Paddy arranged for."

Loki nodded his acknowledgement. "That wouldn't have been true at one time."

"No, it wouldn't," agreed Heimdal.

"Maybe I'm not the only one who's changed."

"Maybe not, trickster."

Loki struggled briefly against his chains. "These are no easier to get out of, though."

"That would somewhat ruin the purpose," said Heimdal.

"Only from your point of view," said Loki.

Heimdal's only reply was a nod. They sat in silence for some time, at least for the trickster. For the watchgod, it was only quieter than usual. When the serpent started to rouse again, Heimdal added another arrow to its pincushion of a hide. The watchgod stood and retrieved his arrows carefully, so they could be redipped and used again.

Heimdal returned and looked down at Loki's now-mended flesh, such a contrast from the burnt meat it had been before. For the first time, Heimdal tried to imagine what it must feel like while empathizing with Loki. He felt sympathy. "You really could have run?"

"To places and worlds even Old One Eye would never have found me," replied Loki.

"And you came back? You really aren't that bright, are you?" said Heimdal, but he was smiling.

"Maybe, but I'm smarter than the rest of you."

"Says you," replied the watchgod.

"Torture's bad, but it could be worse," said Loki.

"How? Replace the serpent with Thor doing his rendition of Hammer Time for all eternity?" asked Heimdal.

"Even Old One Eye isn't that heartless. No, I could be stuck standing watch on the top of a rainbow for centuries," said Loki.

"Trying to be funny now? I could always go if you like," said Heimdal.

"I can honestly say I prefer your company to the alternative," said Loki, staring out beyond Heimdal's shoulders.

"I know that look. What are you scheming about now?" said Heimdal.

"Not much," said Loki, contemplating what was happening here and adding in his mind, Only that there might yet be a way around the Norns. But that thought he kept in the silence of his mind, where not even Heimdal could hear.

SOUL FOR HIRE:
CUTE AS A BUTTON

"So you want me to take care of this?" asked Vince Argus, his eyes hidden behind shades as dark as night. His tone was as calm as it would be if he was ordering dinner.

"Not exactly," said Frank, the Rossa family consigliere.

"What then? I thought the business betweenVinnie and me over what happened with Jimmy was settled," said Argus.

"Mr. Rossa has no quarrel with you and wanted me to relate that you were more than generous when you protected his daughter Aniela for a week," said Frank.

"She's a good kid," said Argus, actually cracking a smile. Someone had been threatening Vinnie "The Rose" Rossa's family. Vinnie asked Argus to keep his five-year-old daughter safe. As Argus had lost his family when someone had made a move on his father, he would have taken the job even if it hadn't helped clear up the mess Argus had made with Vinnie's son Jimmy. Children and families should never pay for a man's crimes. A week with a five-year-old girl was something very different for the hitman, but he enjoyed it more than he would ever admit. The Soul for Hire had a soft spot for kids.

"Mr. Argus, Vinnie would like to ask you to do a job for him, just name your price," said Frank.

"What does he need?" asked Argus, far too gone from his long-lost innocence to agree without hearing the details.

"Someone has taken Aniela," said Frank, watching as Argus' face changed from its normal stony look to one of barely controlled fury. The last time Frank had seen that expression was years ago, when the hitman had been searching for his family's killers. After he delivered his vengeance, Argus evolved into the stone-cold taker of life he was today. "The kidnappers want five hundred thousand. We of course agreed. We dug up what we could; they are your basic wannnabe thugs and have done this twice before. Once, the child was returned. The other time, the parents gave all they had, but it wasn't as much as the kidnappers demanded. The child was found shot two weeks later, in a dumpster. We are not going to do anything to risk Aniela. The kidnappers insisted the ransom be delivered by a single man who was not a member of the family. Vinnie trusts you and would be deeply appreciative if you would handle this for him."

"Done. You want me to end this my way?" asked Argus.

"Personally, I would love nothing more, but part of the deal is that they walk out alive. The agreement must be followed. Vinnie and I gave the word that neither he nor I would not order their deaths. And you know that inclues any of our associates," said Frank. "This is contingent on them not hurting the girl. If they harm one hair on

Aniela's head..."

"The Devil himself won't be able to protect them from me," said Argus.

"Agreed," said Frank. His tone had more than a hint of approval in it.

"Where and when is the drop?" asked Argus.

The phone rang.

"Looks like we're about to find out," said Frank, pushing the speaker button on the phone. "Good afternoon."

"Hey Fink boy, I mean Frank. You have what we want?" said a voice trying to be manly and tough on the other end. The end result was close, but not quite there.

"We do. Now let me speak to Aniela," said Frank.

"She can't come to the phone right now," said the man.

"Why?" asked Frank, fighting to keep his tone even through gritted teeth.

"Chill, she's fine. She just kept singing this stupid song over and over and wouldn't shut up. We had to gag her to get her to be quiet."

"Ungag her now and bring her to the phone," ordered Frank.

"Relax. We'll get her."

"Hello," came the voice of a little girl whose tone indicated that she was handling things quite well.

"Aniela, this is Uncle Frank. Are you okay?"

"I guess, but these men are mean. They took me right out of the locker room at tap class and wouldn't even let me put my shoes on. I still have my tights on."

"Have they hurt you?" asked Frank.

"No, but they wouldn't let me bring my knapsack or my shoes or anything."

"What song were you singing?" asked Frank, trying to learn if the kidnappers were telling the truth..

"I wasn't cursing or anything," said the girl, worried she was about to get in trouble.

"I believe you. I'd just like to know what it was," said Frank. Aniela sang in Italian something that roughly translated as "Poophead, poophead, you're a stinkie poophead." Argus and Frank smiled at each other. The girl wasn't intimadated by the thugs; she was tormenting them.

"I'm going to send Mr. Argus to come get you, but I want you to be a good girl and stop teasing those men," said Frank.

"I like Mr. Argus. He's a lot of fun. He even let me braid his hair," said Aniela pretending not to hear Frank's request. Frank gave Argus a glance, but the revelation didn't break the Soul for Hire's legendary cool. "Would you please have him bring my shoes?"

"He'll have them. Put the man back on the phone, sweetheart," said Frank.

The man's voice returned. "Told you she's fine. We got a deal? Five hundred large, you get the girl, we walk away, and you don't send anybody after us. Ever."

"We have a deal, provided Aniela is unharmed. The slightest injury, and our arrangement will be over. That includes gagging her," said Frank.

"She'll be fine." The kidnapper gave the address of an old abandoned garage, and a time an hour and a half in the future, then hung up.

Frank pushed a briefcase across the table. "It's all in here. What fee—"

Argus lifted his hand. "Don't insult me by offering me money."

Frank nodded his head. "Thank you."

Argus nodded back, and handed Frank a bullet with his name engraved on it. Frank had done this enough before to not even blink an eye. "I swear on this bullet and my life that everything I have told you is true."

Frank handed Argus back the bullet that would kill him if he was lying. The hitman slipped it into his pocket.

"I'll have Vito and a couple of the guys drive you. You will go in alone; they will wait in the car for Aniela."

They got to the drop site early. Argus got out a block away to scout the area and make sure no trap was waiting for him.

There was nobody outside the building. Argus returned to the car to wait.

At the appointed time, he got out carrying the briefcase. The door was caked with grease and grime. He could see someone looking out through a rubbed away peephole. The door creaked open.

"C'mon in, tough guy," said a man in his early twenties, his arms covered with tattoos, his hands caked with oil and dirt. He closed the door behind him. "You got our money?"

"First the girl walks out," said Argus, opening the case so they could see the cash.

The man nervously motioned to his partner, who stood next to a back room door. The partner had a dozen piercings on his face and a bandanna tied around his head. He motioned and Aniela walked out.

Her face beamed when she saw the hitman. "Mr. Argus!"

The girl ran toward him and wrapped her arms around Argus. The Soul for Hire returned the little girl's hug. "Are you a-okay?" he said, knowing from their week together that that was one of her favorite terms.

"Yes. Did you bring my shoes?" she asked.

"Of course," he said, handing the footwear over.

The little girl put them on after taking off her tap shoes. "That's better."

"Your Uncle Vito is waiting for you outside to drive you home. Go now," said Argus.

"Okay," she said, motioning him to bend so she could whisper in his ear. "They didn't hurt me, but they were mean and not very smart." Argus opened the door, and she went out after saying, "Bye, bye meanies." And then she sang her little song.

The two men walked up to Argus and each nervously handed him a button that looked like it had been ripped from Aniela's sweater. "The girl said we had to give you these to get the money."

Argus was floored by the stupidity of the pair and the deviousness of the girl. He passed them the money. The kidnappers flipped through the bills quickly, getting very excited at their ill-gotten windfall. "You still here, tough guy?"

"We still have business, the two of you and I," said Argus.

"No we don't," said the one with piercings.

"Do you know what giving me that button meant?"

"No," said the one with the tattoos.

"Sometimes it is unwise to come out and say things when you want something illegal done. Symbols are used instead," said Argus.

The men realized something was going wrong and pulled their guns, but Argus drew and shot each of them in the hand first, making them drop the weapons. The Devil may have gotten the better end of the deal in their bargain, but what the Devil gave Argus made sure he never missed. Some people would consider that worth a soul. Vince Argus had never commented either way on the matter.

"When Aniela told you to give me the buttons, she was putting a hit out on you, and she got you to deliver it to me in person. What dumb bastards. You may be the stupidest people on Earth," said Argus.

"We had the consigliere's word he wouldn't have us killed!" screamed tattoo boy, clutching his bleeding hand to his chest.

"True, which meant you were going to get to walk unless someone higher up said otherwise," said Argus.

"The Rose never said nothing," said tattoo boy.

"No he didn't, but the argreement was that The Rose and his people wouldn't hurt you. If you had bothered to learn anything about your victim, you'd know that despite her age The Rose's daughter holds a higher rank than The Rose's consigliere. And she's not involed with any of his business dealings. Her orders aren't covered by the deal," said Argus, a gun in each hand pointed at each kidnapper's head.

"C'mon, have mercy," begged tattoo boy.

"Like you did on the second child you kidnapped?" asked Argus.

"We didn't want to kill him, but they didn't come up with all the ransom. It was just business," groveled tattoo boy.

"Pity. That little girl is a friend of mine, which makes this personal. Give the Devil my worst," said Argus.

Outside, the little girl in the car couldn't hear the twin pops of silencers as two bullets ended both kidnappers lives, but she smiled and waved as she watched the Soul For Hire walk out of the garage. Argus smiled and waved back.

THE KINDER:
HAIR TODAY, BALD TOMORROW

"Hey, chrome dome," mocked the boy in the white button-down shirt, navy pants, and matching tie. The neckwear was monogrammed with OLL, short for Our Lady of the Lake Catholic School.

George, who was the object of the nasty attentions, was ten years old and did indeed have a bald head, which he had been hiding under a baseball cap until Troy and his friends pulled it off and began teasing him.

"Give it back," said George, making an unsuccessful grab for the hat.

Troy was three years older and more than a head taller, which was amply demonstrated by the way he held the hat just out of the smaller boy's reach. "Make me."

George jumped unsuccessfully several times, but got nearer each time, which was apparently too close for Troy's comfort, because the older boy tossed the cap to one of his friends. A mean-spirited game of keep away ensued, with George trying to regain his headwear, becoming more exhausted with each effort, until he was breathing heavily and sweating.

George felt exhausted enough to lie down on the cement schoolyard, but he was a fighter. He wasn't about to give these jerks the satisfaction. Doubled over and gasping for air, George gathered energy for one last try.

The hat changed hands again, then was tossed high. George was debating whether this would be a good time to lunge when a girl in a plaid skirt and white blouse leapt in front of the hat's trajectory and snatched it from the air.

The girl handed it back to George.

"Thanks, Nellie," George said, putting on the hat.

"No problem," Nellie replied.

"If you know what's good for you, you'll mind your own business, Moran," said Troy. Laughing, he added, "Besides, what's a good black girl like you want to be hanging around with a skinhead like him anyway?"

"George had chemo, you idiot," said Nellie. "You bother him again and you'll deal with me."

Troy also towered over Nellie. His size and his side's superior numbers gave him courage. After all, there were five friends at his back, all bigger than these two. So Troy was stunned when he went to push the smaller girl and ended up on his back. He never even saw Nellie grab his hand and flip him.

Carefully getting up, Troy examined himself. The only thing really hurt was his pride, but he thought he knew a way to fix it.

"You just bought yourself a world of hurt," promised Troy.

Nellie wasn't intimidated. If anything, she was angry. "Touch me again, and I'll be the one hurting you."

Now it was Troy's turn to be intimidated by the fury in her eyes and voice. He had no way of knowing that, when she was younger, Nellie had lived on the streets and been victimized by those bigger and stronger. She had made herself a promise that it would never happen again, and with her adopted uncle—the legendary Hercules—training her, it probably never would.

Still, Troy couldn't accept the idea of losing face in front of his peers to a smaller girl, so he played the numbers card. "There are more of us than there are of you. You better apologize, or we'll kick your butt."

"Want to bet?" said Brian, Nellie's older adopted brother. He was in the same grade as Troy and the others, and just as big. "You mess with my sister, you mess with me."

Brian's early childhood had also been rough, with a stepfather who should have been shot for what he did to the boy and a mother who should have been horsewhipped for not protecting or believing her son. Brian ran away and also lived on the streets before he was adopted by Paddy Moran.

"And me," said Shellie, Nellie's other blood and adopted sister.

"All of us," said Waff, his twin sister Nal by his side. The werehuman siblings were only a few years old, but had grown and aged much faster as wolf cubs then they now did living as humans. Next to them, Corny, a human-fey shapeling, folded his arms across his chest and nodded his agreement.

"I've been through what George has been through," said Danny. He was human, but had been saved from his cancer by the angel Mathew and the god Hermes. "Ain't no way we're going to let you jerks pick on him."

"Now who outnumbers who?" said Nellie, grinning wickedly.

Troy realized he was outclassed, but still managed to fire a parting shot. "We'll let it slide this time, but this afternoon is the student of the month assembly. No hats allowed, and it's in front of the whole school. Have fun, baldy."

"Jerk," said Shellie. Her sister Nellie stuck her foot out and tripped Troy, but he recovered before hitting the ground. He only scowled as he left.

"George, Troy is an idiot. Don't let him get to you," said Nellie.

"Yeah, stress is the last thing you need," said Danny. "When I went through chemo, I lost my hair, too, and I wasn't strong enough to even go to school."

"Thanks, guys, but I don't know if it's even worth coming back to school. Sad part is my Mom said I didn't have to come back yesterday, but I wanted too. What was I thinking?" said George, his head sunk low. "I look ridiculous."

They said all the things you are supposed to say at a time like that, but they could tell George didn't believe a word of it as he walked off.

"It isn't fair," said Shellie.

"We have to do something," said Nal.

"But what?" said Waff.

"We could shave Troy's head," said Nellie, a glint in her eye.

"Dad wouldn't be happy with that," said Brian.

"I guess," sighed Nellie, thinking of the scolding Paddy would give them.

"When my hair fell out, I felt all alone, like I was the only kid this happened to. I was half convinced I was a freak. Someone like Troy would have crushed my spirit, too. I'm tempted to shave my head so George isn't the only kid who's bald," said Danny.

"That's brilliant," said Shellie, patting Danny's shoulder. "I'll shave my head, too."

"Are you serious?" said Nellie.

"Totally. And why not? It'll grow back, and I can always get extensions once a little grows in. Think about how it'll make George feel," said Shellie.

"I'd still rather shave Troy. Or I could sneak in his house and replace his shampoo with Nair," said Nellie.

"What about the rest of his family?" asked Corny. "They'd be bald, too."

"Fine. I guess I could shave my head, too. It'd show George that he has friends who care about him," said Nellie.

In short order, Brian, Corny, Waff, and Nal also agreed to shave their heads.

Corny actually looked around and closed his eyes. The rest watched as his hair receded into his head, leaving the skin smooth. "What do you think?"

"You look as goofy as ever," said Nellie, smiling and rubbing his bare head.

"Me? I guess you pretty much avoid looking in the mirror, huh?" teased Corny.

"The rest of us aren't shapelings. We're going to need a razor or something," said Shellie.

"The store across the street has battery operated ones," said Brian.

"I've got money," said Waff.

"Let's go," said Nellie.

"But we're not supposed to leave school grounds," said Nal.

"And Troy would squeal if he saw us go," said Shellie.

"Leave it to me," said Nellie who, despite living with a leprechaun as a father and four uncles and an aunt out of Greek myth, was obsessed with ninjas. Hermes had been teaching her the art of stealth, and she was an excellent student.

Walking casually to a corner, she was up and over the school yard iron fence with nobody being the wiser, and made it back into the schoolyard with the mechanical razor.

A ringing sounded.

"That's the warning bell. We've got less than ten minutes until the assembly," said Shellie.

They rushed back inside. Shellie, Nellie, and Nal headed to the girls' room.

"We can't go in there," said Corny.

Nellie rubbed the shapeling's bare head again. "You don't need to, the other boys do. Go to our lockers and get our baseball hats." The lot of them played in the

Bulfinche's softball league, as it was unfair for the staff and customers to play against regular teams. The hats had different colors, but all had the shot o' gold logo. "I'll keep watch. Go."

Brian, Waff, and Danny reluctantly went into the no-man's land that was the girls' bathroom. Shellie couldn't get the plastic packaging apart.

Nal concentrated, and changed from girl to weregirl, halfway from human to wolf. Putting the packaging in her mouth, she made a hole in the plastic with her teeth, then ripped it open with her hands. The plastic tore like tissue paper. "Here you go." The weregirl was grinning as she transformed back to human.

"Thanks," said Shellie, putting the batteries in. She put the waste basket in the sink and leaned her head over it. Flipping the on switch, she started at her scalp and took a deep breath. It took only a few passes to shear the hair mostly off.

"You missed a spot," said Nal, who took it and cleaned it up, then turned the razor on her own scalp, then her brother's.

Next went Brian, Danny, and finally Nellie, who came in and did her own. Looking in the mirror, she turned right and left. "Even bald, I look good."

"And they say you don't need glasses," said Shellie. Nellie stuck her tongue out at her sister.

Corny knocked on the door as the late bell rang. Everyone grabbed their hats, put them on their heads, and ran to the auditorium. The werekids got there first, with Nellie and Corny close behind. They waited until the rest had arrived and walked in together. George had picked a seat in the middle and off to the side by himself. The kids all moved toward him, some in the row in front or behind, then climbing over the seats so George was surrounded.

"What's with the hats?" George said, looking at them with interest.

"You'll see," said Nellie.

The assembly started with Dr. Applestone, the principal, walking onto the stage. When she looked out onto the sea of students, she saw one hand raised and waving for her attention.

"Yes Troy?" she said.

"Isn't there a rule about no hats in school? George is wearing a baseball cap," said Troy.

The principal frowned. "I think in George's case we can make an exception. And I think you better see me in my office after this assembly."

Troy's face darkened. He looked over at George and saw the other kids' headgear. "What about the rest of them?"

Dr. Applestone looked, saw seven extra hats, and sighed. "I appreciate what you are all trying to do, but you will have to remove your baseball caps."

Nellie stood up. "No problem." And she removed her hat. The ripple that went through the assembly was almost a living thing, alive with ohs of shock and giggles of laughter. The most mocking sounds came from Troy.

"Happy to," chimed in Brian, rising to his feet and taking his hat off.

One by one, Corny, Waff, Nal, Shellie, and Danny all stepped up and followed suit.

Shock was running unfettered around the auditorium, but people soon recovered. Father Mike Ryann, who was on the stage, grinned from ear to ear.

"It seems like there are a lot of people I'll be seeing after this assembly," said the principal.

Three hours later, the parents of all the hairless children were called into the principal's office without explanation. Most of them assumed they were there because their children had done something wrong.

"Anyone have any idea what's going on?" asked Ted Brand, werewolf and father of the werekids.

"No, I don't," said Paddy. "Do any of ye?"

"No," said Caylee, Corny's mother.

"Neither do we," said Mira and Carlo, George's parents.

"I'm sure they didn't do anything wrong," said Shan Brand. Most considered her naive because she had spent most of her life as a wolf and was still new to being a woman. The truth was that she was just unburdened with the usual cynicism most adults picked up over a lifetime.

Dr. Applestone and Father Mike walked in.

"I think we're about to find out," said Nancy, Danny's mother.

"Mike, why are ye here?" asked Paddy.

"Mr. Moran, Father Mike is here at my request. I am aware of his special relationship with you and your children, and felt he should be present. I asked all of you parents here today because we had a very ugly incident earlier: some students were making fun of George." His parents let out a gasp, assuming the worst about the other kids. "Father, would you show the children in?"

Father Mike opened the door. First through was George, proudly holding his head high without a cap.

The parents who didn't know George frowned, until Danny walked in next, bald as a cue ball. Close on his heels came the rest of them.

When they saw all the bald children, Mira and Carlos wept and hugged each other close. Beneath the tears, their smiles were unmistakable.

"What's going on?" asked Ted, but knowing grins had begun on several of the other parental faces.

"George has Hodgkin's Lymphoma and he's been going through chemotherapy. He just finished, and we're waiting to see if it worked. George asked if he could go back to school, and his doctors said it might boost his spirits. We weren't sure he was ready, but we couldn't talk him out of it. His first day back was yesterday. Last night he came home crying because some kids were teasing him about losing his hair," said Mira.

"We weren't sure what to do, but we discussed it, and George was going to try one more time today. I know kids can be cruel, but I figured it had to be a fluke—to pick on a sick kid," said Carlos, his hands balled into fists. "Apparently, if it happened again today, it wasn't."

"And for your kids to do this for our son, to shave their own heads…" It was like floodgates had opened behind Mira's eyes. "It means so much to us, especially since with all the medical bills and me being out of work to take care of George, we've had to scrape together the tuition. Thank you all so very much." Mira embraced and kissed each of the children.

"You must all be very proud of your kids," said Carlos.

Paddy looked at all of the kids when he answered for all the parents. "Almost always, but never prouder than right now." There was a tear rolling down his cheek as he spoke. He opened his arms, and all three of his kids were enveloped in a hug. There was a lot of that going around the room. "Ye all certainly prove the old saying 'Bald is beautiful.'"

Nellie ran her fingers down her scalp. "I know. It's scary how good I look."

Paddy kissed her shiny head. "It certainly is."

The leprechaun pulled aside Father Mike and whispered in his ear. Mike nodded and smiled.

"Mira, Carlos, I also wanted to let you know you'll be getting a full refund of your tuition for the remainder of this year," said Mike.

"Father, we don't take charity," said Carlos, slightly offended.

"Actually, Our Lady of the Lake has several scholarships which are given to children who show unusual courage. Your son has earned one," said Mike.

"Does the church pay this?" asked Carlos.

"No, it's a private donor who prefers to remain anonymous," said Mike. Dr. Applestone tried to hide a smile. She knew Paddy's financial generosity was the only reason her school remained open after the diocese had closed so many Catholic schools in the city because of decreasing enrollment.

"Father, please tell the donor thank you for us," said Mira.

"I will," said Mike.

"Children, I would like to invite all of you to our apartment for lunch on Saturday. I'd make it dinner, but sometimes at night George is very tired," said Mira.

"I own Bulfinche's Pub. We are having an early dinner tonight, and we'd be honored if ye'd join us," said Paddy. "I really have to get a picture of all the kids for the wall of Bulfinche's."

The faces of the kids who had been to Bulfinche's lit up at that. The walls were decorated with mayors, presidents, popes, and other great and famous people. There was also a special section for people who had done great things. To make the wall was a great honor.

Mira and Carlos exchanged hesitant glances, but George looked up at them. "Please, can we go?"

"If you're up for it," said Mira.

"I am," promised George.

"I won't take no for an answer. Coincidentally, one of the world's foremost physicians—" actually Hermes, the god of physicians "—will be joining us for dinner.

I'm sure he'd be happy to talk to ye about your son's case." He added to Mike in a whisper, "And for once he won't be the baldest man in the room." The priest hid a chuckle. Hermes always wore a hat because of his pattern baldness.

"That would be wonderful," said Carlos.

"You all have some fantastic children. Now, if you will all excuse me, I have another group of students and parents to talk with," said Dr. Applestone. "And this group won't be so pleased with the meeting."

Everyone filed out the door. In the outer office waited Troy, his friends, and all their parents, who watched the bald children with interest. Dr. Applestone had planned the meetings so the second group would see the first leaving, making what those children did more real and horrible.

Troy scowled at the lot of them. Corny stuck his tongue out. Shellie ignored him. Brian chuckled. Nellie ran her fingers across her scalp and made a gun finger at Troy as she winked at him.

"How'd she find out it was them?" asked Nal.

"Yeah, none of us told," said Danny.

"Troy broke when Dr. Applestone was questioning him," said Nellie.

"How do you know?" asked Waff.

Nellie shrugged and smiled. "I may have been listening outside her office." Shellie rolled her eyes.

"At least they'll get theirs," said Corny.

"I could still shave Troy's head," said Nellie.

George spoke up, putting his arm around Nellie's shoulder. "Don't bother. I was thinking we could make fun of him tomorrow for still having hair."

"Works for me," said Nellie. "But if you change your mind, just say the word. I'd like to see if I could do it while he's asleep without waking him up."

THE INFINITE JESTER:
THOSE WHO LIVE BY THE HORN

"**I** want to see the unicorns," said Mark.

"Me too," I replied.

"How are we going to do that from back here?"

"An excellent question," I said. Several rows of spectators were blocking our view of the upcoming parade, almost all of them more vertically endowed than we were. In short, vertical envy had reared its ugly head and was making faces at us.

At twelve, Mark was nearly as tall as I was, and the kid hadn't even hit his major growth spurt. They say good things come in small packages, and I often like to think I was the inspiration for that cliché. Of course, I've also been told that I once spent a weekend thinking I was a peacock; my own fault for shaving half of Merlin's beard. A timeless piece of advice: never get into a practical joke war with a wizard. The peacock thing was one of his tamer pranks.

Compared with dodging lightning bolts, getting past a small crowd should be a breeze. My plan was ill conceived, against convention, and, above all, silly. I loved it the moment I thought of it.

"And I may have an excellent answer. Follow me—with your mother's permission of course," I said.

"Mom, can I go with Dagonet?"

Cheryl, the mother in question, contemplated her answer. She and her son had only made the dubious pleasure of my acquaintance the day before, when I had checked into their bed and breakfast, the Camelot. The moment I saw their homepage, I knew I wanted to stay there. Maybe I was waxing nostalgic, but that was certainly better than waxing my legs. I don't know how women do that—the legs, not the nostalgic part.

Cheryl had been slightly put off when I threatened to leave. I felt I had no choice; they had tried to stick me in the Lancelot suite. I tried to tell her the real deal that the legends tend to leave out, but she didn't want to hear it. The woman was too hero-struck to believe the truth about the knight who let his loins help extinguish the greatest light the world has ever seen. It's been centuries, but some grudges even time won't heal. Fortunately, the couple slated for the Tristan and Isolde suite hadn't arrived, and Cheryl was able to switch me. Sadly, there was no Dagonet suite. When I asked, Cheryl told me nobody really knew who King Arthur's jester was, let alone requested a room named after him. She had the nerve to tell me the only reason I had probably even heard of me was that I was named after me.

Rather than argue the point of who I was and still am, I thanked her for the new suite and considered, not for the first time, getting a publicist. I decided against it. The legacy of the Round Table takes precedence over personal fame.

The short end of it, no offense to myself, was that she didn't know me long and was debating if she should let her son go off with me. A sensible attitude, even in a small town like Mares, where most people still don't lock their doors and cars still have the keys tucked above the sun visor. However, we wouldn't be more than fifteen feet from her, and one shout from Mark would bring all the locals in the town down on me.

"Okay, but don't wander off."

"We won't," said Mark to his mother. To me, a smile on his face, he asked, "What's the plan?"

"Since the high road is denied to us, we take the low road. Much more appropriate for those of us who are closer to the ground." I got down onto all fours, then began crawling through the rows of legs between us and a better view of the parade.

For some odd reason, some people didn't appreciate our route. There's usually at least one in every crowd, and for some reason he tends to take a dislike to me.

"What are you doing down there?" demanded a middle-aged man with a beer belly which, from the angle I was seeing it, looked like it should topple the guy forward. Hopefully, his out-of-shape body would continue the fight against gravity long enough for us to safely pass by.

"Just doing my job," I replied.

"What job would have you crawling around by people's feet?"

"Shoe inspector, sir."

"There's no such thing."

"Hold your tongue. We're a division of the Texas Rangers. Usually we just sneaker around looking for heels."

"Do you then take them to headquarters and pump them for information?" asked Mark.

"Yes, but that's because headquarters is so much closer than hindquarters, although up until the recent budget cuts, we had headdollars," I said, then added with a whisper, "Trying to shoehorn in on my act, huh?"

The kid smiled. "Anyone ever give you the slipper?"

"One or two, but in the end we are rarely defeeted," I said. The man blocking our way was wearing sandals on bare feet. "I'm afraid I do have to warn you, sir, that you should be wearing something under your footwear."

"Why?"

"You're not practicing safe socks. It looks like you may have the start of some athlete's foot, although in your case that is obviously a misnomer. Fortunately, it's not my job to enforce laws for truth in advertising."

"I have athlete's foot?" asked the man, looking down at his feet. The rest of my commentary sailed merrily over his head.

"That's what it looks like, sir. I recommend a good antifungal cream and wearing socks to prevent it from spreading. We don't want an epidemic on our hands, or feet, for that matter. Like that foot in mouth disease a few years back."

Still clueless, the man said, "The one that killed all that cattle?"

"Yes, sir."

The man became quiet. Cattle were practically sacred in most parts of Texas, although not as much as in India. Indians, sadly, aren't considered sacred in either place.

"I'm sorry sir, but it's my job to make sure you toe the line. In the end, we're not just about policing shoes. We're in the business of saving soles. Can I get a hallelujah?" Two women, from different parts of the crowd, were so ingrained in church life that they obliged without thought or complaint.

"Can I at least watch the parade?" he asked.

"I suppose, but if you don't take care of this problem, I'm going to have to give you the boot, although I'd much rather spur you on to greatness. Now, if you'd be so kind as to step aside and let us finish our inspections."

The man obliged, and we moved past, almost making it to the front of the crowd. One man wouldn't let us pass, going so far as to tell us to "Git lost." We ended up standing up behind him.

"I still can't see," said Mark.

I put my finger to my lips in the universal conspirators' sign for "quiet" as I picked the man's pocket. I flipped open the wallet and looked at the name on the driver's license before I tossed it to the back of the crowd. Both he and his picture were wearing a big, black cowboy hat.

"Excuse me, are you Bart Whitter?"

"I answer to Bubba."

"And I'm sure the two of you are tremendously happy with that arrangement."

"Huh?" asked Bubba. "What ya want? I done got here early to git this spot and I ain't a moving."

"I was trying to let you know that I think your wallet is back on the sidewalk," I said.

"Nice try, shrimp, but I already tole you, this here's my spot."

I've been enduring short cracks since back when England was still a Catholic country, and they don't bother me. Much. However, the people usually making them are another story. They tend to get my dander up, and dander is so hard to get back down, especially in my case. My first instinct was to attack back. The name of this guy alone would give me plenty of ammunition. Don't get me wrong. I don't think everyone with the name Bubba is an ignorant hayseed. As a matter of fact, a good friend of mine is named Bubba and she's a lovely woman, although she too would take offense at this guy. She's even closer to the ground than I am.

I toned things down a notch. "And to think you found it without marking it with a chalk 'X'. Very impressive tracking skills. And an early riser, too." I almost went with a performance-related put-down, but decided against it since Mark was standing next to me. I know he's heard worse on TV and the movies, but I learned long ago the importance of setting a good example for others, especially kids. "Must be nice not to need money."

"Huh?" he said again. I was guessing it was his favorite word.

"Anyone who doesn't even blink at losing his billfold must be rich."

"Billfold?"

"Wallet."

"Oh, it's not my wallet. Couldn't be. My wallet's right here." Bubba reached for his right rear jeans pocket, then his left, and both his front pockets. Finally, he took off his black cowboy hat and searched the inner brim.

"My wallet's gone!" he exclaimed.

"Really? What a shocker. Did I mention I saw a wallet with your driver's license in it back there on the sidewalk?"

There was no thank you, not even a grunt as Bubba pushed his way back through the crowd. Of course I did throw it back there, but he didn't know that.

I turned to Mark. "Ta da. Front row, and it looks like we made it just in time."

The parade was starting. In front was a banner held by four teenagers that read UNICORNFEST and below that MARES, TEXAS. The leader of the local high school marching band lifted up his baton, and the music started. Appropriately enough, they were playing the "Unicorn Song".

They weren't bad as high school bands go. Right behind them were the color guard, who seemed to be having a genuinely good time which, as far as I'm concerned, is the point of such things and life in general.

My quiet enjoyment was shattered by the return of Bubba.

"Hey, midget, you and the kid git outta my spot."

"And here I thought we midgets usually stuck together," I said.

"I ain't no midget."

"Of course you are, only one of the mental variety."

"Huh?"

"You really love that word, don't you?"

"You saying I'm mental as in crazy?" asked Bubba, balling his hands into fists in preparation for my answer.

"I said nothing of the sort. I was just commenting on exactly how smart you are."

Bubba's fists relaxed back into open palms, but the palms were still swaying. "Okay, now git outta my spot."

"I'm sorry, but you left. It's our spot now." Mark was tugging on my arm to leave, but I turned and winked at him.

"I got here early this morning to git this spot."

"Bubba, you got here twenty minutes ago," said one of the men standing nearby.

"Shaddup!" yelled Bubba. "That spot is mine, and I want it back now."

"Well, do you know what I'd like? A pony. Get me one and we'll discuss a swap," I said.

"I lost my spot and you're in it!"

"Lost your Spot? Oh, you're missing your dog. Did you say I'm in it?" I said, lifting up my shoes and looking on the bottom. "They're clean, but thanks for the heads up. I haven't seen any dogs, but I'll keep my eyes open. If I spot one, I'll let you know." As each moment passed, Bubba was getting more upset by the fact that I didn't seem to understand how he thought the universe worked. If he demanded something of someone smaller, they should jump to get out of his way. The fact that I seemed to be both ignoring and failing to understand his demands simply infuriated him more. The fact that the people around us were laughing wasn't helping his temper.

"Listen you..." Bubba started, emphasizing his point by jabbing me in the chest with his index finger. I grabbed hold of it and bent it back fast. Bubba went down to his knees. I let go so quickly he wasn't sure exactly what happened. He got back up to his feet.

"Wait, Bubba, I think I solved your problem. I think I see your Spot from here," I said.

"Of course you do! You're standing in it!"

I nodded my head and raised my eyebrows. "Nice try, but you already got me once with that one. There's nothing on my shoes, but I think I see your dog."

"Huh?"

"Still going with the 'huh'. Have you ever considered the 'wha' or 'what'? Perhaps 'I don't understand' or 'please explain'. There are so many options, but I guess you have to go with what you're most comfortable with," I said. "What I'm trying to tell you is I may have located your dog. I see a dalmatian up on the fire truck. Spot's probably looking for you, too. Go to him."

"I ain't looking for a damn dog. Now move or I'm gonna move you."

"That would be a mistake, but I'm sure you're used to making those. In a town this size, you'd never live down the embarrassment of having someone my size clean your clock. Besides, you don't seem the kind of fellow that keeps his timepieces unsoiled. Luckily, that wind is going to save you from all that."

"What wind?"

"Excellent. You didn't use 'huh' as a question. And the wind is the one that's going to make something of yours fly away," I said.

"There ain't no wind."

"How do you know? Did you break the wind?"

"Huh?"

"Oh, and you were doing so well. Better get a running start so you can catch it."

"Catch what?"

"Your hat."

And before Bubba could even mutter his catchphrase, his black cowboy hat was lifted off his head and into the air. It wasn't due to any atmospheric disturbance. There was barely a breeze to cool off the hot summer afternoon. There was, however, Hayden, my sword: a mystic weapon with several unique properties. First, it's invisible, which meant Bubba never even saw the second property coming. Hayden's blade can telescope many yards: an excellent tactical advantage for someone of my stature and limited reach. It also allows me to be somewhat creative in how I deal with lunkheads like Bubba.

In this case, I used it to help his western bowler appear to defy gravity. Bubba leapt into the air in an attempt to grab hold of his headgear a fraction of a second too late. The hat soared across the street, and Bubba casually strolled after it in a vain attempt to look cool. As soon as he got close, I flicked my wrist, and it flew ten feet to the side. We went on like that for a while, with me occasionally having it flutter back and forth across the street. Bubba had given up any pretense of looking cool; he was racing after the cowboy hat in a vain attempt to catch it.

I decided to put him out of his misery. As an open convertible carrying Miss Unicornfest was passing by, I retracted the blade. I'm proud to say my skills were in good form; the hat landed on the beauty queen's head like a ten-gallon UFO, not even jarring her tiara. Its jeweled horn jutted proudly out from under the front brim. I used the opportunity to tuck Hayden back in my special belt sheath.

The teenage beauty queen was shocked at first, but reacted with grace, lifting the hat up and waving to the crowd with it.

The crowd, which had been enjoying Bubba's antics, were amused by the gesture, and some of them even clapped. Bubba wasn't, and ran alongside the slow-moving car.

"Give me my..." Bubba used several terms that I feel should never be uttered in the presence of ladies or children. The teenaged beauty queen qualified as a little of both. "... hat."

Miss Unicornfest's eyes narrowed. "This is your hat?"

"Yeah. I already tole you that." Bubba accented the word as if he were speaking to an idiot.

The girl didn't appreciate his tone. "You want it back?"

"Duh," said Bubba.

Miss Unicornfest smiled. She was under the false assumption that Bubba had thrown the hat, trying to use her head as the pole in a game of horseshoes, so she tossed the headgear to a group of adolescent boys, who proceeded to play a game of "keep away" with it and Bubba.

"How'd you do that?" whispered Mark.

"Do what? I asked.

"With the hat."

"It was the wind," I answered.

"There's no wind, so you must have—"

"Look, here come the unicorns," I said, pointing to the perfect distraction, and it worked.

I had to admit the town had done a good job with their faux unicorns—good enough that some people might be momentarily fooled into believing the six horses with face masks and horns were real. Sadly, I couldn't be. A unicorn doesn't look any more like a horse than a horse does a mule. Sure, there are many similarities, but anyone familiar with both species is not going to mistake one for the other. Unicorns are taller, thinner, with longer legs and ears. Their manes go further down the nape than a horse's. I will admit that the fabricated horns were impressive, made by local artists for a contest. The best twenty were used by these horses. One of the artists even got the horn right—impressive for someone who, in all likelihood, had never seen a real unicorn. Then again, I had no way of knowing that for sure.

The horses and their handlers walked past us. The next marchers were a group of women from a senior citizens group who had dressed up like the characters in the fifth tapestry of The Unicorn Hunt. It's the most famous of the bunch, the one with the virgin being used for bait while the hunters lie in wait for the unicorn. The lady playing the rear end of the unicorn was having trouble keeping up with the front end, and went off on her own a number of times, which entertained the crowd. Behind them was the fire truck with the dalmatian. Bubba had apparently regained his hat and left.

"I'm hungry. Want to get something to eat?" asked Mark.

"Sure. Let's check to see if your Mom wants anything," I said.

Mark made his way through the crowd, this time upright. I did likewise.

"Mom, we're going to get hot dogs. You want anything?"

"Sure, get me a Texas hot with sauce and onions, and a root beer." Cheryl reached into her purse and pulled out some bills to give Mark.

"Don't worry. It's on me," I said.

"I can't let you do that," said Cheryl. She was a sweet woman who worked hard and paid her own way.

"Sure you can. It would be my pleasure."

"Are you positive?"

"Absolutely.

"Thank you. I guess chivalry isn't dead after all."

"Nope, it just likes to take extended vacations. I'd better catch up to your son."

Along the way, I passed vendors selling a horde of unicorn-related merchandise. There were balloons, stuffed animals, ice pops, and lollipops shaped like horns. Mark was already in line at the hot dog vendor by the time I caught up to him. The vendor's sign was advertising 'Unicorn dogs'.

"Hi, Mr. Dwayne."

"Hi, Mark. How are you feeling today?"

Mark seemed almost embarrassed by the question. His mother had told me he had cystic fibrosis and had been much better of late. It was one of the reasons she started the Camelot. Cheryl needed a job that would let her take care of her son when he was sick, which was often. "Pretty good. Can I have a hot dog with mustard please?"

"You mean unicorn dog, don't you?"

"Yeah, right." Mark smiled the smile kids get when they are trying to humor well-intentioned adults.

Mr. Dwayne reached into a middle drawer, pulled out a link, and put it in a bun. The other dogs he had been serving had been on the top shelf. "I made this one special for you. I think you might feel better after you eat it."

"If a hot dog could do that, I should have been perfect after our barbeque last week. I ate so many my stomach hurt." Turning to me he said, "Mr. Dwayne has the best hot dogs. He makes them himself."

"I should hope so. I am a butcher, after all, and that one has real unicorn meat in it."

"Sure it does," said Mark, handing over his money before I could offer to treat him.

It was waved away. "Your money's no good here. Now go eat that; it'll cure what ails you. What can I get for your friend?"

"Dagonet." I extended my hand, and we shook.

"Nice to meet you. I'm John."

It took me a second. "John Dwayne?"

John smiled and rolled his eyes. "I know. My mother was a huge fan."

"I guess she had True Grit," I said.

"Wow, I've never heard that one before," said John.

"Your voice is dripping with sarcasm. Careful you don't get any on the food," I said with a smile.

"I'll try."

"You should respect your elders," I said, trying again with a more obscure film reference.

"Only if your mother's name is Katie. Besides, I'm older than you are."

"No, you're not. I'm just well preserved."

"If you say so. What can I get for you, Gramps?"

I gave him Cheryl's order, and added two more dogs with ketchup for me. John gave me the total and I paid him. I guess my money was good here.

"Before you go, take one bite and tell me what you think," John said.

I obliged. "Excellent," I said around a mouthful of food, and it was.

"Thanks."

"No unicorn in this one, huh?" I said before I could stop myself from using Bubba's favorite word.

John's face suddenly had a very nervous expression. "No, just beef."

"That's good. Unicorn meat doesn't really cure, anyway. Not anything major at least," I said.

Now John's face shifted to a mode strongly resembling smugness. "Really? And how would you know?"

"You wouldn't believe me if I told you. Bye," I said, moving on to deliver Cheryl's snack.

She thanked me, and promised me an extra large portion at breakfast in the morning. We watched some Shriners go by on little go-karts, fez tassels flying in the wind. They did some formations and fancy driving as they moved along the parade route. We watched the rest of the procession, which consisted mainly of scout troops, local politicians, and some locally made floats.

When the parade was over, the street fair began. The rest of the weekend featured such highlights as a bake off, barbeque cook off, demolition derby, and a dance at the fire hall with a live band.

The spectators moved into the closed-off street to check out the vendors who were already there and those who were just setting up when honking and shouting began disturbing the peace. A trio of Shriners were speeding along the now-filled roadway. At first I thought they were drunk, then I realized they were yelling for everyone to get off the street. People stood still and looked around until they shouted one word that Texans respect, even those who have never had anything to do with cattle.

"Stampede!"

It was pandemonium as hoof beats clomped in the distance. People rushed to get off the street as the twenty faux unicorns turned the corner galloping. The Shriners had done a good job of clearing the streets, but one person had slipped through, and only her mother and I noticed. A little girl had gotten separated from her mother in the commotion, and was right smack in the middle of the blacktop. The lead faux unicorn was well on his way toward trampling her.

Her mother rushed toward her, but she would be too late. I, too, was moving toward the girl. I was fast for a guy with legs my size, but there was no way I was going to reach her in time just by running.

Instead of stopping, I picked up speed, sprinting all out as if I was a linebacker intent on tackling the horse. I could hear gasps from the crowd, but I ignored them to concentrate on solving the problem at hand. I had one chance, but it was a long shot. I pulled out Hayden and braced the hilt under my left shoulder. With my right arm, I grabbed the girl. At the same time, I extended Hayden's blade into the asphalt as I leapt into the air. I had to time each action so the blade would lengthen as I was into the latter half of my arc and propel me up, not back or forward.

When we were high enough, I waited an instant, then retracted the blade just as the lead horse passed beneath us. If I was off, we'd end up back on the street, stomped by one of the other horses.

I got it right. We landed on the back of the horse, facing the wrong way. I tucked Hayden away and put my left hand on the horse's back, using it as a fulcrum to spin around to face front.

Bracing myself with my legs on the horse's flanks, I leaned forward and managed to get hold of the end of the reins. I snapped them back over the horse's head. An especially good trick, considering that I was riding bareback.

I had to convince the horse I was in charge, but if I pulled too hard on the reins, the horse would rear up. I had no illusions about being able to stay on a bucking horse bareback while carrying a child; we'd go down hard.

There was a better way. "Clear me a path to the park!" I yelled to the nearest Shriner. He nodded and sped ahead on his go-kart with his two companions, honking and screaming.

Horses tend to follow the horse in front of them, even when stampeding. I guided the leader toward the park at the end of town. The Shriners did an excellent job of getting everyone out of the way. The park had a large round fountain with a circular cement path around it. I made sure the leader started around the fountain. The others followed. With each lap, I pulled back on the reins to slow him. By the fifth lap, I was able to get him to stop, and the others followed suit.

I thought about getting off the horse, but decided against it for the moment. I wasn't sure my legs would take my weight yet, and my heart was pounding like it wanted out of my chest. Besides, I had something more important to do.

Turning to the little girl, I asked, "Did you have fun?" Kids are resilient; they can handle a lot more than most people give them credit for. Sometimes they get upset because they sense the adult talking to them expects it, and they hate to disappoint grown-ups. If I had asked if she was okay, that would imply there was a reason she might not be. My question instead suggested that she might have had fun.

The girl's brown eyes looked at me as she contemplated her answer. Meekly, she offered a "Yes."

"Me too. Do you like unicorns?" Again, a safe question with safe implications.
"Yes."

"Weren't these unicorns acting silly, running around like that?"
She nodded her head.

"It's a good thing we were here to stop them, wasn't it?"

"I guess."

"No guessing. You were great. I couldn't have done it without you. Thank you."
Now she was smiling. "You're welcome."

One of the handlers had arrived, standing on the back of a Shriner's cart, and took the reins from me. My legs felt strong enough to try to bear weight again, so I climbed down. Once on solid ground, I reached up and helped the girl down. I was barely able to reach her on my tip toes.

Another Shriner cart pulled up with a passenger—the girl's mother. She leapt off and ran to her daughter.

"Nina!" She squeezed her daughter, showering her with kisses. Her cheeks glistened with tears. "You're okay."

"I'm fine. I helped stop those silly unicorns."

The mother looked confused, so I chimed in to help out. "Nina was a big help."

Her mother picked up Nina in one arm and wrapped the other around me. Then she bent down and kissed me on the lips. "Thank you." Next she began kissing my face all over in between teary thank yous.

"My pleasure."

A large hand grabbed my shoulder and spun me around. I was face to chest with a man who was easily 6'4" and two-twenty. His stony face looked enough like Nina's that I knew it was her father. He did not look happy that his wife had just been kissing me.

I concluded what seemed to be the logical thing. "Don't get the wrong idea—" Before I could say anymore, the man had wrapped his bear-like arms around me and lifted me off the ground. At first I thought he was attacking me until he started kissing me too, thankfully not on the lips.

"Thank you for saving my Nina," he said.

"As I said, it was my pleasure."

"If there is anything I could ever do for you..."

"For starters, you could put me down," I said.

He obliged, and introduced himself and his wife, Miguel and Selina, respectively. I returned the favor.

"Dagonet, I don't know how we'll ever be able to repay you," said Selina, as she started the kissing thing again.

Nina pulled on my pant leg. "My parents really like you. I've never seen them hug and kiss somebody so much."

Selina laughed and started crying again as she picked up her daughter and gave her more of the hug and kiss treatment.

"You don't have to give me anything. To see Nina's smiling face is all the thanks

I'll ever need." Maybe I sounded cornball, but it was the truth. I've got enough money to squeak by; I have a good life, good friends, and periodically get to help someone. I don't really need anything else, except the chance to make other people laugh.

"Well, you have to come by for dinner. I insist. I won't take no for an answer," said Selina.

"Dagonet, you might as well agree. When she's like this, there's no arguing with her," said Miguel.

"I'd be honored," I said. We agreed on two days later. Apparently, the dinner was going to be a family affair. They had a large extended family, and needed that much time to put things together.

"Excuse me for interrupting, folks, but I'd like to talk to the hero of the hour," drawled a man with a paunch, a tan uniform, mirrored sunglasses, and a star badge.

"Certainly, Frank—I mean, Sheriff Martin," said Selina, handling me her business card. "You better show up or I'll hunt you down, understand?"

"Yes, ma'am." Selina kissed my cheek one last time, Nina gave me a hug, and this time Miguel shook my hand.

The sheriff put a hand on my shoulder and steered me away. "What you did back there was amazing and brave."

"Ah shucks, Sheriff, 'tweren't nothing," I said, thankful to be able to use the word shucks for the first time in years.

"Call me Frank. That was the damnedest thing I've ever seen, especially for someone so..." the sheriff caught himself before he finished the thought.

"Handsome? Charming? Funny?" I offered.

"Frankly, I was going to say short, but I sure as hell don't want to offend you."

"No offense taken."

"You must know a lot about horses to have pulled that off."

"I was raised around horses." As long as you counted the stint I did as a stable boy when my parents abandoned me to die. "And I spent a few years as a rodeo clown."

"And an acrobat, I'd wager."

"No bet."

"This town owes you a tremendous debt, not just for saving the girl, but for saving the Unicornfest. Mares doesn't have a lot going for it, but ever since we started having those sightings, we've become the unicorn Graceland. We get tens of thousands of tourists each year, and we depend on the business. During Unicornfest week you visitors practically outnumber us locals. An accident like that could have crippled us."

"I'm glad I could help."

"I'd like to offer you the position of Unicornfest Grand Marshal, as a small token of our appreciation."

"Well, I wouldn't want to offend the current Marshal."

"Hell, boy, don't worry 'bout that. They gave it to me this year, and it won't hurt my pride none. Besides, it's not an election year," he said with a grin. "What do you say?"

"Sure, why not."

The sheriff slapped me on the back hard enough to rock me forward, but it was from enthusiasm, not malice. "Glad to hear it, but that means you have duties. The judging for the pie bake-off is in ten minutes."

"Never let it be said I turned away free homemade pie. Let's go."

The contest was on the other end of the main street, near a gazebo. Sheriff Martin offered me a ride in the front seat of his squad car. As we circled around the closed street, the radio squawked, followed by a man's voice. "Sheriff, there's a problem. We think we found what spooked the horses."

"One of my deputies," said Sheriff Martin before picking up the radio handset. "Well, Sandy, what was it? Skunk, firecrackers?"

"It's better not to say over the radio. Just get over here to the parking lot behind the diner, pronto."

"On my way. Martin out." The sheriff put down the handset. "Sorry, Dagonet, we're going to have to make a detour."

"Hopefully, there'll be some pie left when we get there."

The sheriff grinned. "Don't worry, they'll wait. I'm still one of the judges. I may be generous, but I ain't stupid."

When we got to the parking lot, three deputies were trying to keep a dozen or so people back. One of the deputies, a skinny guy with a baby face and crew cut, moved to meet us.

"Sandy, what's going on? What's so bad you couldn't tell me over the radio?"

"Gracie Logan is dead. Murdered."

The sheriff cussed, but it was understandable.

Sandy led the way to the body. I tagged along, and nobody stopped me. It was Miss Unicornfest. She was lying on her side.

"Looks like someone stabbed her in the chest."

"Damn." The sheriff took off his hat and yelled at his deputies. "Show some respect!" The three of them took off their hats. A couple of men in the crowd pulled off their baseball caps. "Damn," repeated the sheriff. "Excepting a couple of DWI's and home accidents, nobody's been killed in this town as long as I can remember."

"Do you have an ME?" I asked.

"Jas Sayer from the Sayer Funeral Home fills in when we need a medical examiner. Sandy, have Joe get Jas here pronto, then get the camera. Anybody touch her?"

"I checked her for a pulse. She didn't have one. Then I called you."

"Good. Anybody see anything?"

While the sheriff questioned his deputies, I wandered around the lot and examined the convertible. There was blood on the door and traces of blood splattered on the asphalt between the car and her body.

I went back over by the sheriff. "No witnesses yet," he said.

"I think she was attacked near the car and ended up over here," I said.

"That's over fifty feet. What makes you think that? And who are you?" asked Sandy.

"This is Dagonet. He saved the little girl."

"He's not a cop," Sandy pointed out.

"What? You haven't heard about the show they named after me?"

"That's Dragnet."

"That explains why I never got any royalties."

"Sheriff, he shouldn't be at a crime scene."

"I used to be in law enforcement," I said. Being a Knight of the Round Table certainly counted. Not to mention a few stints as a consultant for the Department of Mystic Affairs.

"That's nice, but—"

"Sandy, shut up. He might have more experience at this than we do. I want to catch the sonna bitch who did this before he does it again. Dagonet, tell me what you think."

"Judging by the size of her chest wound, it wasn't a knife; it was something bigger. Judging by the blood spatter, I'd say she was lifted off her feet and shook by whatever was in her chest." I pointed to the pavement. "Between here and the body, there's almost no blood on the ground. I'd have to say she was thrown."

"That has to be twenty feet," said Sandy. "Who could throw her that far?"

"I'm not thinking who, I'm thinking what."

"That's ridiculous. It was probably some nut with a spear."

"No. If a spear was used to lift her off the ground, her own body weight would have pushed it out the other side of her chest, or dislocated all of the ribs on that side. The ribs are in place, and there's only a tiny exit wound in her back. A spear would have left a larger wound."

"Maybe it was some sort of lance."

"No, the wound would look different," I said.

"How the hell would you know?" demanded the deputy.

I walked up to Sandy and stared him in the eyes. He broke off first. "Deputy, I'm trying to help, so stow whatever problem you have with me and deal. I have a lot more experience with this type of thing than you do. Let's just leave it at 'I know'."

"What department were you with? I want to check you out."

"Sandy, shut up," barked Sheriff Martin. "Look at the scene. What he's saying makes sense. Dagonet, what are you thinking it is?"

I hoped I was wrong, because if it was what I thought, this town wasn't prepared to deal with it. I didn't even know if I was.

"First, I suggest you check the unicorn horns on the horses for blood residue.

The horns came back clean. That meant my hunch was probably right, but it wasn't something I could tell the sheriff. Mares, Texas, had real unicorns, and one of them had just become a killer. The sheriff's department did more interviews. Nobody saw her killed, but people heard her screams. Her driver had run into the diner to use the bathroom. He hadn't been gone ten minutes. Someone who heard the screams swore they saw her body hit the pavement, but couldn't see what threw her. The horses were on the opposite side of the lot, and the scent of a unicorn on a rampage would be enough to set them stampeding.

The problem was, I couldn't figure out why. I looked for answers as I wandered the streets of Mares for hours, hoping to catch a glimpse of the rogue unicorn. I had no luck. When I checked back in with Sheriff Martin, his department had gotten video from an ATM which had shown part of the crime: the end.

"Looks like you were right," the sheriff said before showing me the footage. Gracie's killer had hurled her through the air, and she could be seen landing on the ground. She bounced once before she ended up on her side. The camera's angle wasn't wide enough to show what had done the throwing.

I watched in silence. When it was done, the sheriff turned to me. "Nothing human could have thrown her that far. Jas Sayer says the wound is consistent with a goring. None of the parade horses did it, and there were no bulls anywhere near the scene of the crime. I have a theory. Around here, we have a lot of cars and pick-ups sporting bull horns. I think it was a hit and run. A horn impaled poor Gracie, and when the vehicle stopped short, she was thrown free. What do you think?"

"It's a good theory."

"But it's not the right one, is it?"

The sheriff was looking at me, his face overwhelmed by sadness. I didn't say a word.

"Don't get me wrong. I could easily sell that version to the town papers. It explains everything. Might even make me seem like a great detective. Wouldn't hurt me next year come reelection time either."

"But?"

"But my gut tells me it's wrong. There're no skid marks, and a car braking hard enough to throw a girl that far would have burnt a lot of rubber. I'm afraid that whatever happened to Gracie is going to happen again."

"Your gut again?" I asked.

"Yep." The sheriff patted his ample belly. "It may be big, but it's not often wrong."

"So why ask me?"

"Because my gut tells me you know something you ain't telling me. In order to do my job, I need to know. Tell me. Please."

I thought about his plea. "You seem like a good man, and you have a good gut, whatever its size. The problem is, I don't think you'll believe me."

"Why?"

I said nothing.

"You think it's a unicorn don't you? A real one."

To say I was shocked wouldn't begin to cover my mental status, but I told the truth. "Yes."

"I was afraid of that."

"You don't seem shocked," I said.

"The town tourist board claims that we've had unicorn sightings that haven't been reported. They're right."

"You've seen them," I said.

"Only one, just once. It saved my life. I had pulled over a sedan for a routine traffic stop and taken the driver's license to run a check. Once my back was turned, the man got out of his car and pulled out a gun. I spun in time to see it pointed at my chest. My life flashed before my eyes, and then I saw something that I thought must be a hallucination. Out of nowhere, a unicorn appeared and broadsided the gunman. Smashed him against the side of the car and knocked him out. The unicorn turned toward me. My head told me I should have been afraid, but I wasn't. He was beautiful, noble even. I whispered 'thank you' and he nodded, his horn saluting like a swordsman. Then he ran off and disappeared before my eyes. I handcuffed the guy and arrested him. Turns out he was wanted for killing two cops in Austin. Everyone thought I was a hero. That arrest helped me win my first election. That unicorn could have slain that killer—it would have been easier to run him through—but he didn't. My gut tells me that unicorn couldn't kill in cold blood."

"Unicorns can and have killed, but usually it's in self-defense. Their horns are deadly weapons when they need to be," I said.

"Gracie wasn't self-defense."

"No."

"Then why?"

"I once saw a hunter who had tried to hunt a unicorn to impress his lord. Things didn't go well. He got a wound very similar to Gracie's."

"I thought unicorn horns healed? Wouldn't they heal the same wound they made?"

"No. The unicorn decides who it wants to heal. A horn without the unicorn can undo poisons, but that's about it."

"How do you know this? And how long ago did you see this hunter trying to impress his 'lord', Sir Dagonet?"

"Sir?" I said.

"Sandy can be a real butthead, but he's not always wrong. I checked you out. You checked into the Camelot B&B as Dagonet White. I couldn't find any record of a cop with that name, although I can hardly claim to have checked every department in the country."

"Call the DMA. They'll vouch for me."

"Good to know. Next I used a search engine. Did you know the most famous Dagonet was King Arthur's jester? Became a knight. According to one urban legend site, he's still alive. They call him the Infinite Jester."

"Interesting. My favorite is the one about albino alligators in the New York sewers." Of course they're really earth dragons.

"I found another Dagonet who chased Jack the Ripper and wrote about it. Yet another, Dagonet Black, who was big back in Vaudeville days. Apparently he had movie offers for lots of money, but turned them down. Supposed to have been very acrobatic."

"It's an unusual name."

"Yes, and so many of them seem to have colors as a last name. But it's Dagonet Black who interests me the most. I found a site that had a black and white picture of him. Here," said the sheriff, handing me a printout. "What do you think of it?"

"Not my best side. Or my best act, for that matter."

"You're not denying it? Not going to try to say it's your grandfather or some such."

"Not much point, is there?"

"Nope, I guess I'm just used to people lying during interrogations."

"Is that what this is?"

"No. I need your help, but you have to be honest with me."

"I haven't lied."

"No, I guess you haven't. According to that site, you have something in common with unicorns: you both have healing powers."

"True."

"Why didn't you heal Gracie?"

"She was dead. I don't have that kind of power. I'm much more limited than a unicorn. I was the first knight to encounter the Holy Grail. I almost died defending it from a mad goddess. The Grail healed my wounds. It also made me relatively immortal. I age very slowly. I can heal some things, but only under certain circumstances. The wounded person must be found worthy, or have gotten hurt in a noble cause. I don't get to choose what's noble and what's not. I tried to heal the unicorn hunter, but couldn't. It took him three days to die from that gut wound. Not a pleasant way to go."

"I'm sorry."

"Me too. The difference between then and now is that that unicorn acted in self-defense, but this one seems to have killed with malice and forethought."

The sheriff put words to my biggest fear and unanswered question. "Could we be dealing with a serial killer?"

"I don't know."

"How do we catch it?"

"It'll be tough. Unicorns have something Merlin used to call a shroud."

"A what?"

"It's a kind of glamour, a magic which prevents them from being seen unless they want to be seen. Merlin could always see them."

"What about you?"

"I've often been able to see them after my encounter with the Grail. Most people might sense something out of the corner of their eye, but can't see them straight on. They have a scent, but are stealthy in their movements. I've seen them wandering the streets of New York City, happy and safe as can be."

"How do we lay a trap? Virgins?"

"They are attracted to purity, either mind, soul, or body. Especially a combination." Then it hit me like a cream pie. "Did your ME check her for signs of sexual assault?"

"It's standard procedure. You don't think the unicorn—"

"No. What did he find?" I said.

"There was none. In fact, Gracie was a virgin. You think someone was laying a trap in the parking lot?"

"No, not then. Before, and maybe Gracie was the bait. Maybe the unicorn got away and is looking for some payback."

"Which means anyone involved would be at risk. We better find out if there were others, fast."

I accompanied the sheriff when he went to question Gracie's parents. They were devastated, but willing to talk. Without us explaining too much, they told us she had gone hunting last week with her uncle, who turned out to be none other than John Dwayne.

We returned to the squad car. "John was claiming he made a special hot dog made of unicorn meat for Mark."

"The idiot must have been trying to make the boy better. But that means he must have caught one, so what killed Gracie?"

"A child or mate maybe, looking for revenge."

We didn't need to speak as he hit the siren and we sped toward John's place.

The radio squawk momentarily rose above the wail of the siren. "Sheriff, we have a medical emergency. Please respond."

"What is it, Sandy?"

"Cheryl Beman's kid is having a breathing attack. It's pretty bad. The last volunteer fire department's ambulance crew just took Mrs. McCoy to the county hospital with angina and the other two haven't come back from their runs. You're the only one on duty with EMS training."

"I'm on my way to the Camelot," said the sheriff, hitting his brakes and swinging into a sharp U-turn.

We got to the B&B, and the sheriff beat me inside. He quickly went over the specifics with Mark's mother. It didn't look good.

"Hey there, Mark. I'm going to take you to County General in my car. You ready?" Mark was wheezing too much to answer; he just nodded. Frank lifted him up and rushed back out to the car. "Cheryl, you can ride with us."

Frank put him in the back seat.

"How far is the hospital?" I asked.

"Too far. Do you think the kid's worthy?" asked the Sheriff.

"I never know until I try." Part of me selfishly hoped it wouldn't come to that.

I climbed in the back with mother and son. The car took off.

I had stared death in the face too many times in the past not to recognize the Grim Reaper coming for Mark. "Mark, I'm going to try something to help you. Will you let me?"

Mark nodded.

"I'm his mother. Shouldn't you be asking me?"

"I'm sorry, Cheryl, but it's not your decision to make. At this point, it's up to a higher power."

"What are you, some kind of faith healer?" asked Cheryl. I didn't answer. I needed all my concentration for the task at hand.

"Cheryl, he's one of them Knights of the Round Table you're always going on about."

"He's Sir Dagonet? That's impossible! Even if he was, Dagonet was a jester. He never had any healing powers in any of the books I've read."

"You've been reading the wrong books. You even think Lancelot was a hero."

"Listen—"

"Shut up!" I shouted, louder and harsher than I meant to. "I really need to concentrate."

"But—"

"Cheryl, let the man do his job."

Luckily, she decided to listen. Mark didn't have much time. I made the sign of the cross and bowed my head in prayer. Out of the corner of my eye, I saw the sheriff do the same. Cheryl followed suit. Next, I lifted up Mark's shirt, and laid my hands on the skin over his lungs. Mark closed his eyes and his head dropped back.

"He stopped breathing!" screamed Cheryl, each word racked with sobs.

I prayed harder. I couldn't see why a child wouldn't be worthy, but I'd been wrong before. Finally, I felt the energy flow from my hands into Mark's body. We were both enveloped in a golden glow, and I felt a mix of rapture and pain as my gift did its work.

Done, the glow faded, leaving us back in the darkness.

Mark gasped. He was breathing again.

"Oh my God!" Cheryl exclaimed.

"Exactly," I said. I looked heavenward, as I did each time it was successful, and whispered, "Thank you." Then I winked out the window at the night sky, sharing the secret with the only other who knew what healing others cost me. I don't know how long I have to live; only now it would be significantly shorter. Even though I've lived many lifetimes, I still find that I don't want to die, but not trying to help an innocent because I'm afraid of dying is unacceptable behavior for a Knight of the Round Table. Although much has happened since Camelot ruled, I will never sully its memory by my own cowardice.

"Mark, are you okay?" asked Cheryl, undecided if she was still frantic or not.

"I'm fine, Mom. I feel fantastic! I can breathe and it doesn't hurt. Thanks, Mr. Dagonet."

Cheryl grabbed my hand and squeezed. "Yes, thank you."

I could see Frank's grin in the rear view mirror, as well as the thumbs up sign he flashed me.

"What will happen the next time he has an attack?" asked Cheryl.

"There won't be a next time. Mark's cured."

Cheryl's eyes went wide, and she grabbed me by the back of the head, pulling my lips to hers. This kiss was more involved than the one I had gotten earlier from Selina. It also went on far longer. When our mouths finally parted ways, I was breathless, but managed to whisper "You're very welcome."

"Mom!" yelled Mark, but it was with a happy tone. Cheryl blushed and brushed her hair away from her face with her fingers.

"Dagonet, I figured out why you save people. It helps you get women," said Frank.

"That, and my sense of humor and good looks." Frank laughed. "Plus, haven't you heard? Short is sexy."

"Yes, it is," said Cheryl, who then covered her mouth when she realized she had spoken aloud.

"You like Dagonet?" asked Mark. "Mom and Dagonet, sitting in a tree—"

"As much as I'm enjoying this, Dagonet and I had some business we were attending to earlier and we—"

The squawk of Sandy on the radio interrupted again. "All units respond. Wild animal attack at 273 Break Road. At least three people injured."

Frank picked up the radio mike. "Sandy, the Beman kid's fine. I'm on my way. Bring the tranquilizer gun, and have everyone wear their kevlar."

"For an animal, Sheriff?"

"Don't argue with me, Sandy, just do it." He put the mike down. "Looks like you were right again. That's the Dwayne place. We don't have time to take you two home. When we get there, the pair of you are staying in the car, understood?"

"Sure, Sheriff, but what's going on?" asked Cheryl.

Frank sighed before he could utter the words, "Unicorn attack."

"For real?" asked Cheryl.

"I'm afraid so," said the sheriff.

"Cool," said Mark.

"Not cool. The same unicorn probably killed Gracie," I said.

"Oh," said Mark, getting very quiet.

We were the first unit on the scene. Frank pulled his own Kevlar vest out of the trunk and put it on. Dwayne's property was outside of town. There was a crowd running and scattering across the front and back lawns. Several of them were bleeding from arm and leg wounds.

One hysterical woman ran up to the sheriff. "It's trying to kill us!"

Frank was still a cop, and our theory could have been wrong. "What is?"

"The unicorn. She smashed the door in and attacked us." The gender of unicorn males, like that of ungelded stallions, is unmistakable.

"Why would a unicorn be trying to kill all of you?" asked the sheriff.

"I don't know."

Frank grabbed her by both shoulders. "Either you tell me or..."

"Or what?" she asked.

Frank was a good cop, and was stumped. I stepped in and helped out. "If we don't know what we're dealing with, we'll have to go back out to the squad car and wait there for backup. You'll be on your own until then. Good luck if it comes this way."

That managed to push her over the line from hysterical to freaked. She got real talkative, real fast. "We killed her mate! His head is hanging on John's mantle."

"Why the hell would you do that?" asked Frank, genuinely shocked.

"Because of the magic."

"Explain it to me."

"Unicorns heal, so do their body parts. John butchered it and tanned its hide. We used the leather to get rid of our aches and pain. Martha made wrist bands to get rid of her carpel tunnel. John made a truss for his back. Jan made a headband for her migraines."

"What'd you get?" demanded the sheriff.

The woman bowed her head, unable to look us in the eyes. "A face mask to wear at night, to get rid of wrinkles."

"So all of you were involved, and used Gracie as bait?" asked Frank, disgusted.

"Yes, yes. Just save us."

"Why were you all here?" asked Frank.

"John was having a barbeque. Eating the meat is supposed to make us immortal."

The sheriff looked at me. I shook my head no. He told her, "It doesn't work that way."

"The horn didn't work right, either. Greg doesn't have a new leg because of it."

"Greg doesn't have a leg because he was drunk when he was haying and tripped in the bailer. And the horn has to be used by a unicorn to work," said Frank, unable to hide his disgust.

A new set of screams brought our attention to a couple running around the house, the man dragging the woman. Behind them was a female unicorn with death riding on the end of her horn.

The couple barely got behind a tree as the horn embedded itself in the soft wood. The couple fled. The unicorn was only trapped momentarily. It surveyed the scene. Everyone had frozen, not wanting to attract her attention. Then John Dwayne came racing around the house, a huge shotgun in one hand, a mounted unicorn head in the other. I felt for the unicorn; if someone had mounted the head of a person I loved, I'd probably try to kill them, too.

"I killed one unicorn with this, and I'll kill me another!" John fired half of his double barrel. The unicorn moved and vanished, the buckshot taking chunks out of the tree trunk. Even I couldn't see her at this point.

The sheriff moved to one side of him and I went to the other. Each of us had drawn our weapons: Frank, his pistol and I, Hayden.

"John, put down the gun," said Frank.

"What, and let that thing get me? No way!"

I moved in, planning to disarm him with my invisible blade, when I saw the unicorn reappear, seconds before anyone else could. "John, look out!" I shouted, too late to save him.

The charging unicorn impaled his chest upon her horn and lifted him off the ground. The shotgun fell as both his hands grasped the horn impotently, trying to push his body free. The unicorn shook her head violently, and he was thrown across the lawn. Frank ran to the fallen man, removed his bulletproof vest and then his shirt and held it to John's abdomen in a futile attempt to stem the bleeding.

The unicorn didn't bother to shroud herself as she looked around for her next victim. She sniffed the air and turned her attention toward the squad car where, Mark was leaning out the window, staring at the proceedings. Something about him seemed to infuriate her even more than the others. She charged the car.

I placed Hayden at the base of a nearby tree and started running, extending the blade as I went. When I had enough speed I leapt into the air and made the blade shoot out faster. I flew forward through the air with slightly less than the greatest of ease, but too late to stop the unicorn's charge.

The sheriff's car flipped on its side, with Cheryl and Mark still inside. The unicorn was preparing for another pass. Mark had climbed out the open window and was standing on top of the side of the car that was pointed skyward, trying to help his mother out.

I got between him and the unicorn. "Don't do this, please," I begged.

The unicorn spoke. Well, not speaking as humans do, but close enough that I could understand. Another gift of the Grail.

"No, the boy means you no harm."

"He was meant to be the bait in my trap."

"No, he wasn't."

"He helped kill my love. For devouring his flesh, he must pay."

"The boy didn't help kill your mate. What happened wasn't right, but neither is what you've done. And the boy didn't eat..." I stopped, remembering the special hot dog. She could smell it through Mark's pores. That's how she found the rest of them, by scent. John was cooking in an open pit. All of the people with wounds were wearing something made with unicorn hide. She could smell that, too. Gracie had probably had a piece of hide on her. The unicorn's belief even made a twisted kind of sense: a male virgin would attract a female virgin. Mark was not a man, but had started puberty. It was enough for the unicorn to justify thoughts of a conspiracy against her. "The man you attacked fed him the food in an attempt to heal him. The boy didn't know."

"The boy doesn't smell ill."

"That's because I healed him."

"Enough lies. You were not part of this. Stand aside, or join him in death."

"I don't want to hurt you, but I won't let you harm the boy."

The unicorn snorted and brought her head down. "So be it."

"Mark, whatever you do, don't move."

Mark was shaking, but trusted me. "Okay."

The unicorn charged. I shot out Hayden's blade, bracing the hilt against the car. In the infinite second I waited for that exquisite creature to gore herself on my sword, I openly wept. There are few things—first love, the sun rising on a day you knew you should be dead, a sword rising out of a stone—that can rival the beauty of a unicorn, a beauty I was willing to destroy. Sometimes even doing the right thing can rip your heart out. The lesser of two evils is still an evil. Don't let anyone ever convince you otherwise, at least not if you want to keep your soul.

The impact of her impalement rocked me back and spun the car around twenty degrees. She fell to her front knees and tumbled to the ground. Blood ran down the unseen blade, pooling at my feet. The unicorn's screams were a sound I'll carry to my grave. I had to fight so as not to allow the force of her weight to rip Hayden from my hands.

Her round eyes stared at me, and as much as I wished to avert my gaze, I would not take the coward's way. She deserved at least that much. "I'm sorry."

She seemed to ignore my hollow, yet heartfelt words. "I beg of you, save my children."

"Children? Where are they?"

"In me, waiting to be born. They were to enter this world the next full moon. If I die before..."

The due date was only four days away. "I'll do what I can, Mother, but the only safe way means I will have to hurt you even more than I already have, unless... Can you heal yourself?"

"Not after this, using my horn for death. In revenge, my power is forfeit. Do what you must to me. I no longer matter."

Frank had gotten someone else to try to staunch the blood flow from the human victim's wound. "Dagonet, can you help John?"

"No. He got hurt in violence without a just cause. He's beyond my help."

"I called for an ambulance. All three are on the way, but it'll be twenty minutes before they get here from County General. Can you help her?"

"No. The unicorn was wounded in the course of vengeance, but we have other problems."

"What?"

"Let me put it this way," I said. "How are you at delivering babies?"

"I used to deliver pizzas in high school. Why?" asked Frank as his mind answered his question. "The unicorn's pregnant?"

"Yes."

"How do you know?"

"She told me. I'm going to have to do a C-section."

"What should I do?"

"Think you can graduate from veterinary school in the next two minutes, or find me someone who has?" I asked.

"I doubt it," said Frank.

"Then stand by and do what I say," I said.

I shortened Hayden to the length of a dagger. I palpated around the abdomen to locate where the foals were before I cut in. I sliced gently, until I had an incision big enough to get the babies out. Since the mother was going to die anyway, I didn't have to worry about cutting something I shouldn't. "Get ready to pull."

Frank watched the flesh seemingly part at my touch. "How are you doing that?"

"No comment," I answered. Explaining about Hayden cripples my tactical advantage, so I'm very picky about who I tell. Otherwise, it'd wind up on one of those web sites. I pulled away the stomach flap I had made, then moved fatty tissue aside, and saw a head with a tiny horn. I grabbed hold of the foal's front quarters and pulled. I needed help. "Frank, grab hold where my hands are and pull."

He did, and I reached further inside to guide the rear quarters out. With a squishy sound, the foal slid out. "It's a boy!" I said so the mother could hear. She nodded, and I said to Frank, "Clean out his mouth. I'm going in for his twin. You wouldn't happen to have a wet suit on you, would you Frank?"

"Nope. Never took up scuba diving, seeing as though there's no ocean nearby and all."

I shrugged, and went in up past my elbows. From there it was easy, and number two came out even quicker than the first.

"It's a girl." I cleaned her mouth out. Both were breathing fine. The umbilical cords detached without help. The twins stood for the first time and shook themselves, splattering us with, for lack of a less gross term, unicorn juice.

"They're beautiful, Mother."

"Thank you. Please protect them until they can protect themselves."

It was a huge responsibility, but I had taken her life. It was a debt I owed. "I will."

The daughter walked over to the mother and placed her horn to her mother's. A silver glow flowed out, enveloping the elder unicorn. Her flesh began to knit back together as we watched.

The son had gone to where John lay dying, and touched horn to belly. Silver light covered him, and his wound began to mend.

Healed, the former enemies stood and faced each other. They moved closer, until nose almost touched muzzle. The healing had affected mind, body, and spirit of both, making them the best they could be.

John hung his head. "I'm sorry. I didn't realize."

To me, the unicorn said, "Tell him I am also sorry. The evil he did by killing my love drove me mad, but was no excuse to do the evil I did to that girl or to him."

"The hormones from being pregnant probably didn't help," I whispered in her ear. I relayed her message.

"So what do we do now? I can't exactly arrest either one," said Frank.

"There's no way to make things right at this point. Everyone needs to go on the best that they can. You've both been given a second chance. Don't waste it," I said. They both nodded.

"My love's remains..."

"Will be taken care of," I promised.

With the help of the sheriff and John Dwayne, we tracked down all the body parts, but we had trouble prying some of the leather pieces from people. Apparently, they really worked. The sheriff convinced the reluctant ones to cooperate by mentioning he would not be providing protection when Mama Unicorn came looking.

Frank and I put the parts in canvas duffle bags in the back of his pickup, and drove out to the woods, where I built a funeral pyre. We placed the bags atop it, and poured gasoline on the bags and wood.

"What are we waiting for?" Frank asked.

As if on cue, the three unicorns took off their shrouds and appeared at our side. I took a prepared torch, lit it, and held it out. The mother took it in her mouth, and set the pyre ablaze.

The five of us stood and watched in silence for a long time, until flesh was made ash. The three unicorns turned to leave.

"Wait!" said Frank. "Your mate once saved my life. I owe him, and my debt now falls to you. If ever there is something you need, let me know and I will do anything in my power to solve it."

The mother bowed her head in acknowledgment. The foals came up and nuzzled my hands. The mother watched, then joined them, and bent her head forward to touch mine. I brought my hand up to touch the side of her face. She whispered in my ear, and I smiled. Then they left for real.

"You even get the unicorn women," said Frank with a grin.

"Short is sexy to any species."

"What did she say?"

"She understood, and will remember your offer."

"Anything else?"

"Yeah," I said. "She forgave me for almost killing her, and gave me a unicorn name."

"Does it mean anything?"

"Yes. Uncle."

That's pretty much the end of the story. Frank explained Gracie's death as a freak animal attack. Neither she nor the dead unicorn were coming back, and the world would be that much poorer for their loss.

On a personal note, as a way of showing her gratitude, Cheryl got rid of the room bearing Lancelot's name.

Now guests can stay in the Sir Dagonet Suite, complete with cans of nuts with springy snakes and whoopee cushions on all the seats. It's not the same as my own publicist would have done, but it's a start.

PATRICK THOMAS – With over a million words in print, PATRICK THOMAS keeps busy writing the popular fantasy humor series Murphy's Lore (which includes Tales From Bulfinche's Pub, Fools' Day, Through The Drinking Glass, Shadow Of The Wolf, Redemption Road, Bartender Of The Gods, Nightcaps, Empty Graves and Startenders) as well as the After Hours spin-offs Fairy With A Gun, Dead To Rites and Lore & Dysorder. His Mystic Investigators series has grown to include the books Bullets & Brimstone and From The Shadows both with John L. French and Once More Upon A Time and the upcoming Partners In Crime both with Diane Raetz. He and John French also wrote The Assassins' Ball, the first book the Jack Gardner Mysteries. He has co-edited two anthologies - Hear Them Roar and the vampire themed New Blood. Patrick's syndicated humorous advice column Dear Cthulhu has been collected in Have A Dark Day and Good Advice For Bad People. A number of his books are part of the set and props department at the CSI television show. Laurence Fishburne's production company Cinema Gypsy Productions has taken a film and television option on Patrick Thomas' urban fantasy Fairy With A Gun. As an artist his work has graced covers for Dark Quest, Padwolf and Marietta, interiors and a cover for Space & Time magazine and comic covers for Ghostman. A mockumentary about him has recently surfaced on Youtube. To learn more, drop by his website at www.patthomas.net.